ACCLAIM FOR ROBIN LEE HATCHER

"In *Cross My Heart,* book two of her Legacy of Faith series, author Robin Lee Hatcher continues to delve into the powerful influence of a spiritual family heritage. She weaves together two touching stories that examine life choices and their consequences. Utilizing a dual-time plot set against World War II and present day, Hatcher writes with realism and compassion about how hope and healing can grow from our deepest wounds."

—Beth K. Vogt, Christy Award–winning author

"Hatcher *(Who I Am with You)* continues her chronicle of the Henning family in the powerful second installment of her Legacy of Faith series . . . This touching story of forgiveness and redemption will appeal to fans of Colleen Coble."

—*Publishers Weekly* on *Cross My Heart*

"Robin Lee Hatcher tells the story of two people dealing with addiction in their lives in *Cross My Heart* . . . This is a good romance that deals with some very tough issues that happen all the time now."

—*Parkersburg News & Sentinel*

"As usual, Hatcher is an auto-buy for all library collections."

—*Library Journal* on *Cross My Heart*

"In this seamless time-slip novel, Hatcher provides inspiration in each character's growing relationship with the Lord and prompts readers to reflect on their own journey. This story of loss and redemption is sure to win the hearts of contemporary and historic romance fans alike."

—*Hope by the Book* on *Who I Am with You*

"This [is] a lovely story of love and loss and forgiveness."

—*The Parkersburg News & Sentinel* on *Who I Am with You*

"Bestselling inspirational romance star Hatcher weaves a story of love and identity lost and found . . . The characters are authentic, the butterflies of anticipation are persistent, and the protagonists' deferred attraction is thrillingly palpable; you cannot help but hold your breath until they realize it too."

—*Booklist* review on *Who I Am with You*

"Hatcher's moving novel is rich in healing and hope and realistically portrays the tough introspection that sometimes comes with being hurt."

—*Publishers Weekly* on *Who I Am with You*

"Tender and heartwarming, Robin Lee Hatcher's *Who I Am with You* is a faith-filled story about the power of forgiveness, second chances, and unconditional love. A true delight for lovers of romantic inspirational fiction, this story will not only make you swoon, it will remind you of God's goodness and grace."

—Courtney Walsh, *New York Times* and *USA TODAY* bestselling author

"Whenever I want to fall in love again, I pick up a Robin Lee Hatcher novel."

—Francine Rivers, *New York Times* bestselling author

"Hatcher's richly layered novels pull me in like a warm embrace, and I never want to leave. I own and love every one of this master storyteller's novels. Highly recommended!"

—Colleen Coble, *USA TODAY* bestselling author

"Engaging and humorous, Hatcher's storytelling will warm readers' hearts . . . A wonderfully delightful read."

—*RT Book Reviews*, 4 stars, on *You're Gonna Love Me*

"Hatcher has written a contemporary romance novel that is a heartwarming story about love, faith, regret, and second chances."

—*CBA Market* on *You're Gonna Love Me*

"Hatcher (*Another Chance to Love You*) creates a joyous, faith-infused tale of recovery and reconciliation."

—*Publishers Weekly* on *You're Gonna Love Me*

"*You're Gonna Love Me* nourished my spirit as I read about a hero and heroine with realistic struggles, human responses, and honest growth. Robin Lee Hatcher makes me truly want to drive to Idaho and mingle with the locals."

—Hannah Alexander, author of *The Wedding Kiss*

"I didn't think *You'll Think of Me,* the first book in Robin Lee Hatcher's Thunder Creek, Idaho, series, could be beat. But she did it again . . . This second chance story will melt your heart and serve as a parable for finding redemption through life's lessons and God's grace. Thunder Creek will always hold a special place in my heart."

—Lenora Worth, author of *Her Lakeside Family,* on *You're Gonna Love Me*

"With two strong, genuine characters that readers will feel compassion for and a heartwarming modern-day plot that inspires, Hatcher's romance is a wonderfully satisfying read."

—*RT Book Reviews,* 4 stars, on *You'll Think of Me*

"A heart-warming story of love, acceptance, and challenge. Highly recommended."

—*CBA Market* on *You'll Think of Me*

"*You'll Think of Me* is like a vacation to a small town in Idaho where the present collides with the past and it's not clear which will win. The shadows of the past threaten to trap Brooklyn in the past. Can she break free into the freedom to love and find love? The story kept me coming back for just one more page. A perfect read for those who love a romance that is much more as it explores important themes."

—Cara Putman, award-winning author of *Shadowed by Grace* and *Beyond Justice*

"Hatcher is able to unravel emotions within her characters so brilliantly that we sense the transformation taking place within ourselves . . . Readers will relish the warmth of . . . the ranchland."

—*RT Book Reviews* on *Keeper of the Stars*

"Hatcher fans will be left smiling and eagerly awaiting her next novel."

—*CBA Retailers + Resources* on *Keeper of the Stars*

"True to the contemporary romance genre, Robin Lee Hatcher's *Keeper of the Stars* will satisfy romance fans and give them a joy ride as they travel the road of pain and forgiveness to reach the happily-ever-after."

—*BookTalk at Fiction 411*

"Robin Lee Hatcher weaves a romance with heart that grabs readers and won't let go. *Whenever You Come Around* pulled me in from the get-go. Charity Anderson, a beautiful, successful author with a deadline and a painful secret, runs into Buck Malone, a handsome, confirmed-bachelor cowboy from her past, and he needs her help. I was captivated, and I guarantee you'll be rooting for them too."

—Sunni Jeffers, award-winning author of *Heaven's Strain*

"A heartwarming and engaging romance, *Whenever You Come Around* is a splendid read from start to finish!"

—Tamera Alexander, *USA TODAY* bestselling author of *To Whisper Her Name* and *From a Distance*

"A handsome cowboy, horses, and a hurting heroine make for a winning combination in this newest poignant story by Robin Lee Hatcher. A gently paced but delightful ride, *Whenever You Come Around* will take readers on a journey of healing right along with the characters. Readers will feel at home in Kings Meadow and won't want to leave."

—Jody Hedlund, bestselling author of *Love Unexpected*

"First loves find sweet second chances in Kings Meadow. Heartwarming, romantic, and filled with hope and faith, this is Hatcher at her best!"

—Lisa Wingate, *New York Times* bestselling author of *Before We Were Yours*, on *Whenever You Come Around*

"In *Whenever You Come Around,* Hatcher takes a look at the pain of secrets that kill the heart. But love indeed conquers all. Robin Lee Hatcher is the go-to classic romance author."

—Rachel Hauck, award-winning, *New York Times* bestselling author of *The Wedding Dress*

"Robin Lee Hatcher has created an emotionally engaging romance, a story of healing and self-forgiveness wrapped up in a package about small-town life and a cowboy who lives a life honoring God. I want to live in Kings Meadow."

—Sharon Dunn, author of *Cold Case Justice* and *Wilderness Target,* on *Whenever You Come Around*

"*Whenever You Come Around* is one of Robin Lee Hatcher's pure-romance best, with a heroine waiting for total redemption and a strong hero of great worth. I find myself still smiling long after the final page has been read."

—Hannah Alexander, author of the Hallowed Halls series

"In *Love Without End,* Robin Lee Hatcher once again takes us to Kings Meadow, Idaho, in a sweeping love story that captures the heart and soul of romance between two people who have every reason not to fall in love. With an interesting backstory interspersed among the contemporary chapters, and well-drawn, relatable secondary characters, Hatcher hits the mark with her warm and inviting love story."

—Martha Rogers, author of the series Winds Across the Prairie and The Homeward Journey

"*Love Without End,* the first book in the new Kings Meadow Romance series, again intertwines two beautiful and heartfelt romances. One in the past and one in the future together make this a special read. I'm so glad Robin wrote a love story for Chet who suffered so much in *A Promise Kept* (January 2014). Kimberly, so wrong for him, becomes so right. Not your run-of-the-mill cowboy romance—enriched with deft writing and deep emotion."

—Lyn Cote, author of *Honor*, Quaker Brides, Book One

"No one writes about the joys and challenges of family life better than Robin Lee Hatcher, and she's at the top of her game with *Love Without End*. This beautiful and deeply moving story will capture your heart as it captured mine."

—Margaret Brownley, *New York Times* bestselling author

"*Love Without End,* Book One in Robin Lee Hatcher's new Kings Meadow series, is a delight from start to finish. The author's skill at depicting the love and challenges of family has never been more evident as she deftly combines two love stories—past and present—to capture readers' hearts and lift their spirits."

—Marta Perry, author of *The Forgiven*,
Keepers of the Promise, Book One

"I always expect excellence when I open a Robin Lee Hatcher novel. She never disappoints. The story here reminds me of a circle without end as Robin takes us through a modern-day romance while looping one character through a WWII tale of love and loss and the resurrection of hope and purpose. *Love Without End* touched my heart and guided me to some wonderful truths of how God's love is a gift and a treasure."

—Donita K. Paul, bestselling author

"A beautiful, heart-touching story of God's amazing grace and how He can restore and make new that which was lost."

—Francine Rivers, *New York Times*
bestselling author, on *A Promise Kept*

How Sweet It Is

ALSO BY ROBIN LEE HATCHER

You're Gonna Love Me

You'll Think of Me

The Heart's Pursuit

A Promise Kept

A Bride for All Seasons

Heart of Gold

Loving Libby

Return to Me

The Perfect Life

Wagered Heart

Whispers from Yesterday

The Forgiving Hour

The Shepherd's Voice

LEGACY OF FAITH SERIES

Who I Am with You

Cross My Heart

How Sweet It Is

KINGS MEADOW ROMANCE SERIES

Love Without End

Whenever You Come Around

Keeper of the Stars

WHERE THE HEART LIVES SERIES

Belonging

Betrayal

Beloved

THE SISTERS OF BETHLEHEM SPRINGS SERIES

A Vote of Confidence

Fit to Be Tied

A Matter of Character

COMING TO AMERICA SERIES

Dear Lady

Patterns of Love

In His Arms

Promised to Me

STORIES

I Hope You Dance, included in *Kiss the Bride* and *How to Make a Wedding*

Autumn's Angel, included in *A Bride for All Seasons*

A Love Letter to the Editor, included in *Four Weddings and a Kiss*

How Sweet It Is

A LEGACY OF FAITH NOVEL

ROBIN LEE HATCHER

How Sweet It Is

Published in Nashville, Tennessee, by Thomas Nelson. Thomas Nelson is a registered trademark of HarperCollins Christian Publishing, Inc.

Thomas Nelson titles may be purchased in bulk for educational, business, fund-raising, or sales promotional use. For information, please email SpecialMarkets@ThomasNelson.com.

ISBN 978-0-7852-1935-4 (trade paper)
ISBN 978-0-7852-1936-1 (e-book)
ISBN 978-0-7852-1937-8 (downloadable audio)

Library of Congress Cataloging-in-Publication Data

CIP data is available upon request.

Printed in the United States of America

20 21 22 23 24 LSC 10 9 8 7 6 5 4 3 2 1

In memory of my beloved grandmother and my beloved mother, who each had a part in leaving me a legacy of faith.

Prologue

March

TACOMA, WASHINGTON

Jed Henning strode down the hallway toward his father's office. Thomas Henning's assistant had made the message crystal clear. There would be no delaying the meeting this time. No rescheduling. Not for any reason, no matter how urgent it might seem. Jed was fairly certain he knew what the meeting was about: Jed's screwup brother, Christopher. With any luck, their dad was as fed up with Chris as Jed was.

His steps slowed, and he looked down at his hands. They were balled into fists, a common reaction whenever he thought about his kid brother. Especially lately. The two of them had almost come to blows the last time they'd been together. Shaking out his hands, Jed hurried on toward the end of the corridor.

Thomas Henning, a successful businessman who'd also practiced law for a few years in the early nineties, ran a commercial construction firm and sat on the boards of several corporations, including Jed's. In a family or social setting, his dad was friendly, affable, sometimes even funny. But in his impressive office, with floor-to-ceiling windows that offered a stunning view of Mount Rainier, he was all business. And with each step Jed took, that latter fact about his dad began to bother him. Why had Jed been summoned here? Why hadn't his dad come to the much more low-key Laffriot offices instead?

Brittany Wales looked up from her desk when Jed entered the outer office. "Good morning," she greeted him with a smile. But there seemed to be a warning in her eyes.

That didn't bode well.

"I'll tell Mr. Henning you're here." She reached for the telephone on her desk.

Jed didn't bother to sit down. It was one minute before the hour. His father was nothing if not punctual—something Jed had inherited from him.

Brittany returned the handset to its cradle and looked at Jed. "You can go in now."

In most every setting, Jed was a man who exuded confidence, but he wasn't feeling that way at the moment. Something felt off to him. Again, he suspected it had to do with Chris. But Chris was the problem. Not Jed. So why was he worried?

"Hi, Dad."

His father rose from behind his massive desk. "Jed."

Although they spoke frequently by telephone, Jed hadn't seen his father in person since Christmas. Not since right after his parents had separated. It seemed to him now that his father had noticeably aged. There were deeper lines etched around his eyes and the corners of his mouth, and his hair seemed more peppered with gray. He still looked distinguished and powerful, yet he had changed too.

"You wanted to see me?" Jed said.

"Yes." His father motioned to one of the two leather chairs on the opposite side of the desk. "Sit."

Jed was thirty-one years old. He had his MBA from the University of Washington. He'd proven himself in a top-notch high-tech firm right out of college, and then he'd successfully launched his own company. Yet right now he felt like a ten-year-old called to the principal's office.

He sat.

After regaining his own seat, his dad steepled his hands in front of his mouth while tapping his index fingers together. His gaze was intense but inscrutable.

Jed resisted the urge to squirm.

After a lengthy and uncomfortable silence, his dad asked, "Have you talked to Chris?"

"No, sir. Not recently. Not since we fought about his work on the new project."

"Did you try to call him like I asked you to?"

Jed drew a quick breath. "No. Not yet."

"Why not?"

"You know why not. Because it won't get us anywhere. Because he'll tell me I'm wrong and he's right and he wants to do things his own way and in his own time. But he has no concept of time or the demands of the market, and he doesn't care either. All he wants to do is sit in a dark room swigging Red Bulls one after the other while he stares at a screen, playing games or thinking up code."

If Jed could go back four years, he wouldn't make Chris a part of Laffriot, Inc. He would find somebody else to do the creating. Only . . . even he knew there wouldn't be a Laffriot without Chris.

Jed could start a different kind of company without his brother. Any other kind of company. But he couldn't found Laffriot.

"Son." His dad leaned forward, forearms now resting on the desk. "I'm proud of you. You know I am. But it's time you got things right with your brother."

Jed bristled. "Did you tell him the same thing?"

"No."

"So why am I the one who's supposed to fix things? I'm not the one who took off and isn't doing the work and isn't answering calls. I've been right where I'm supposed to be. I've been living and breathing Laffriot for four years. I'm the one whose hard work put our very first game onto the bestseller list. *Caliban* is going strong, but we've got to follow it up with something even better, and we've got to do it soon. I didn't start Laffriot to be a one-hit wonder. If Chris won't do the work he's supposed to do, then we'll hire somebody else. We've got the rep now to attract the right people. Chris isn't the only creative person in the country."

His dad sighed. "I don't think you're hearing me." He rose and walked to the window, staring off toward Mount Rainier.

The silence dragged on so long Jed started to wonder if he'd been forgotten.

"Son." His dad faced him again. "I'm going to say this as plainly as I know how. You and your brother will work things out, or I will shut down Laffriot for good and sell its assets to a competitor. *Caliban* would turn a tidy profit."

Jed was on his feet. "You're not serious."

"Oh, but I am."

"Dad, we can't—"

"Maybe *we* can't, but *I* can. I own the controlling share of the company, and I am authorized to make this decision by the agreement you and I made when you founded Laffriot."

"Exactly. *I* founded it."

"Then do what you have to do to save it. Get things right with your brother. And I don't mean simply getting him back to work. I mean what's wrong between you two personally. Do it fast, because I'm not watching this drag out forever."

Chapter 1

April
KUNA, IDAHO

"I wish I could tell you something," Ben Henning said, his brow creased with a frown. "But I haven't heard from Chris. I didn't even know he was in Boise."

Jed sat opposite his favorite cousin at the table in the kitchen of the old farmhouse, a large mug of coffee in his right hand. He and Ben had been born the same year, and as boys they'd spent a lot of time together before Jed's family relocated to Washington from Idaho. That had been more than twenty years ago. Trips back to Idaho some summers had kept the two of them close. Much closer than Jed was with his own brother.

Jed took a gulp of coffee before saying, "Chris left Washington at the end of February. He told Mom he had something personal to take care of. Then he was gone. No idea what that personal matter is, and it's only recently I found out he's in Boise." Guilt sluiced through him. He wasn't being entirely honest with his cousin. Still, he wasn't ready to tell anyone, not even Ben, about the mess his brother had left behind him. That his absence could put an end to Laffriot.

"He hasn't contacted me, and Grandpa would have told me if he'd been in touch with him."

"I'm not surprised, but I was hoping."

Ben leaned back in his chair, his gaze searching.

For a moment Jed considered opening up, getting everything off his chest. He just might find a sympathetic ear in Ben. Despite all the dumb stuff Chris had done, their dad always seemed to forgive him, seemed willing to give him another chance and then another and another, always making excuses for him. Dad never did the same for Jed. But then he'd never needed to make excuses for Jed. Chris had dropped out of high school at eighteen. Jed got his MBA at twenty-three, graduating at the top of his class. Chris hadn't stuck with any job for long. Jed had succeeded in employment and then out on his own. If Chris knew how to read a clock, his tardiness belied it. Chris couldn't care less about the accolades that had been heaped on Laffriot after the debut of *Caliban*. He had no ambition whatsoever. It seemed to Jed that his brother would be just as content if he was penniless and living on the streets. He'd never even tried to live up to their dad's expectations.

So why was Jed, who'd excelled in school and business, the one who had to fix things with his brother? The question left a bitter taste in his mouth.

"How long are you going to stay in Boise?"

"Not sure. As long as it takes for Chris to take my calls and meet with me. I'm not going back to Washington until I do."

"Would you like to stay here at the farm? Nothing fancy, but I've got a spare room you're welcome to."

"No, thanks. I appreciate the offer, but I think it'll be better if I stick closer to Boise. Besides, I don't want to be a bother to anybody, especially if I end up working until all hours." That wasn't likely to happen. His dad had shut operations down for the time being and given the employees a month's leave with pay. Jed had to hope they wouldn't all spend that time looking for new jobs. If they did, there might not be much to save when he got back.

"Sometimes being your own boss means you work 24/7," Ben said, intruding on Jed's darker thoughts. "I've learned that the hard way."

"Yeah. It can mean that."

Silence stretched between them a second time, Ben's gaze once again searching. Jed was good at hiding his thoughts and feelings. A man didn't succeed in business negotiations if his face gave away too much. But he had the uncomfortable feeling his cousin could see through him despite his efforts.

"You know, Jed, I have something I want to give you." Ben got up from the table and left the kitchen, returning a short while later with something in his hands. When he placed it on the table, Jed saw it was a time-worn Bible. "This belonged to Andrew Henning."

"No kidding? Great-Grandpa Andrew's Bible. How'd you come by it?"

"In a roundabout way. He left it as a legacy to his descendants. It comes to one of us, and then when we feel like God says it's time, it's supposed to be given to somebody else. I think that time is now. God wants you to have it."

"Me? But why—"

"It's hard for me to explain why. Just a nudge in my spirit. That old Bible meant a great deal to me as I was getting the equine therapy program off the ground. Sometimes it seemed I could feel Grandpa Andrew's prayers for all of us as I sat holding it, reading it. It was as if he'd prayed for me and what I would one day do on this farm." A fleeting smile curved the corners of Ben's mouth. "I imagine he did pray for us. All his descendants. Those who'd been born, by name. Those who hadn't been born yet, in a more general way."

"Did he know my name?"

"Sure. He died the year after you and I were born, and from what my grandpa told me, Andrew Henning was as sharp as a tack right up to the last week or two of his life."

Jed looked down at the Bible again, this time opening its cover. It fell open to the title page, and he paused long enough to read the words scrawled there.

To our beloved son,
Andrew Michael Henning,
on the occasion of his graduation
from the university.
Follow God and you will never lose your way.
Papa and Mama
Kuna, Idaho
1929

"'Follow God and you will never lose your way.'" Jed looked up. "Good advice, I've found."

Have I lost my way? It wasn't a question Jed had asked himself before. He wasn't the kind of man who spent time on doubts or even much in the way of self-examination. He determined something to do, then did it. He decided what he wanted to be, then became it.

Have I followed God? That question caused a bit more discomfort. He knew the answer: not in a long time. Who had time to go to church or get involved with small groups or even pray when getting ready to launch a new business or while working to make a success of it?

He closed the Bible and held it as he rose from the chair. "I'd better get going. I've got some phone calls to make this afternoon."

"Are you sure you don't want to stay here at the farm?" Ben stood too.

"I'm sure. But thanks for the offer."

"Okay. You've got my number. Call if you need me. For anything."

"I will."

Holly Stanford groaned as she reached to turn off the alarm on her phone. Here she was, napping in the afternoon when she had a million things to do. But all she wanted was to stay there and sleep straight through the rest of the day and the night as well. She was so blooming tired. It seemed she was always tired.

"No rest for the wicked," she whispered, quoting her grandmother.

She allowed herself about thirty seconds to lie back with her eyes closed before she shoved aside the sheet and blanket and sat up on the side of the bed. Hopefully a quick shower would help open her eyes all the way.

Within a few minutes, she stood beneath a fine spray of warm water, still wishing she could go back to bed. It seemed she hadn't had two minutes to herself in ages. She was either working on repairs to the house or working at the restaurant. Working but never accomplishing enough. There was always something more that needed repaired or replaced. There was always a need for more money than what she had available. There were always decisions to be made. She was so incredibly tired of making decisions. Especially since she'd made more than a few poor ones.

"God." Eyes closed, she pressed her forehead against the tile. "I hate my life. I thought Nathan was Your plan, but he wasn't. I thought the restaurant was Your plan too. Now I don't know anything. Nothing's going the way I want, the way I imagined. I don't see a way through. I don't see a way out. I've already lost so much. Am I going to lose everything that's left? Can You help me, please?"

It was a pathetic, complaining, self-pitying kind of prayer, one she'd prayed more than once over the past year, the kind that left her feeling guilty for even voicing the words aloud. Yet her younger sister, Trixie, would tell her it was honest and raw, and that God could handle it. She hoped Trixie was right, because it seemed to be the only kind of prayer she uttered.

Move forward, Holly. Just keep moving forward. You're tired and discouraged, but you aren't beaten yet. Don't give up.

With a sigh, she turned off the water and reached for a towel.

Half an hour later, she was outside, readying her flower beds for spring planting, when she saw a man on the sidewalk, staring at her. He didn't move at all. Simply stared. Flustered, she pushed loose strands of hair off her forehead with the back of her wrist. Then she realized he wasn't looking at her but at the *Furnished Apartment for Rent* sign behind and above her.

Oh, please, she thought as she stood. *Let him want it. I need that extra income.*

At last he seemed to notice her. After a moment more he moved toward her, climbing the two concrete steps midway up the sidewalk. "Hi," he said as he approached. "Is this your house?"

"Yes." Her pulse quickened with hope. He looked both normal and respectable. "Are you here to see the apartment?" She removed her gardening gloves and dropped them on the lawn. "I can show it to you if you'd like."

His gaze flicked to the *For Rent* sign again, then to the entrance of the basement apartment. "If you've got time, I'd like that."

"Of course." *Oh, please, God. Let him want to rent it.* She turned and led the way to the steps on the east side of the house.

For much of the past eight months, she'd used the apartment as a vacation rental. But the demands of the restaurant made it difficult to have people coming and going all the time. With rotating guests, sheets always needed changing and the apartment needed cleaning. And too often there were vacancies when she wanted it—needed it—occupied. She'd finally decided that renting in a more conventional manner would work better for her. Let the renters take care of their own bedding and cleaning.

But it hadn't been as easy as she'd hoped to find the right renter, even in this market. Perhaps she was asking too much for a one-bedroom basement apartment in an older section of town. Perhaps she was too particular about the type of renter she'd allow to live below her. At least this guy looked like he could be gainfully employed.

She stopped at the top of the stairs and faced him again. "I'm sorry. I didn't introduce myself. I'm Holly Stanford."

"Jed Henning." He put out his right hand. "Nice to meet you."

She guessed him to be about her own age. Thirty or so. Dressed in Levi's and a blue shirt, he was tall with longish brown hair and a close-trimmed beard—the kind that was just a bit more than a five o'clock shadow. It was a good look on him, she thought as she shook his hand. Not that she cared. Her interest was only in his ability to pay rent. "Nice to meet you too." She started down the eight steps to the door. "Are you from around here?"

"No. Not really."

She glanced over her shoulder. "Not really?"

He smiled. "I was born in Boise but grew up in a town in Washington, outside of Seattle. I've been back to Idaho for family reunions over the years. I've got plenty of cousins and an aunt and uncle who live around here."

"Ah." She opened the door and led the way inside.

Built to bring in extra income for the owners—as had been common back in the forties and fifties—the one-bedroom apartment took up half of the basement. It had a living room, a small kitchen, a postage-stamp-size bathroom with shower stall, and one bedroom. It didn't take long for Holly to show her potential renter around. He asked a few questions, including how much the rent would be, and he didn't seem concerned about the amount when she answered. She took that as a good sign.

While staring into the bedroom closet, he asked, "Are you willing to rent on a month-to-month basis?"

Her heart fell. "I wanted a year's lease." *I want to know I've got money coming in every month.*

"What if I doubled the rent you're asking?"

"'Doubled'?"

He faced her. "And I'll give you first and last month's rent up front, of course."

"I'm not sure . . . I don't know. I—"

"Ms. Stanford, I'm—"

"Call me Holly. Please."

He nodded as he cleared his throat, then continued, "To tell you the truth, I didn't come here to rent an apartment. I was just having a look around Boise. But now that I've seen your little place, I really would prefer it to staying in a hotel. Even paying twice your asking price, it'll still cost me less than where I'm staying. Not to mention being able to cook for myself when I'm in the mood. I'd consider it a bargain."

Double the rent was tempting. But month-to-month?

As if he'd read her mind, he said, "How about a three-month guarantee?"

Three months at double the rent. Half a year's worth. Better than nothing. And far less trouble than the vacation rentals had been. "All right. It's a deal."

He grinned, and her heart did a little flip in her chest. Not a welcome sensation. She wanted a quiet renter who added no complications to her life.

He closed the closet door. "I'll be happy to provide references, of course."

"Of course." She couldn't believe she'd forgotten the application. Desperation had made her foolish. She knew nothing about this man, and she'd committed to renting to him without checking a single fact. Well, if she found something wrong, she would be within her rights to cancel the arrangement. At least she believed that would be her right.

"Have you got a form you need me to fill out?"

That was the second time he'd guessed her thoughts, and she didn't like it. "Yes. I'll get it for you."

"I'll wait here," he said as she hurried away.

After Holly Stanford left the apartment, Jed returned to the living room and sat on the sofa. It wasn't the most comfortable piece of furniture in the world, but then he didn't plan to spend a lot of time sitting on it.

Am I crazy?

He had no idea how much longer he would be in Boise. Now he'd committed himself to three months of rent. Funny thing was, he'd only come here to see where Andrew and Helen Henning had lived back in 1929. He'd needed to stretch his legs, and he'd been curious. That was all. But for some reason, once he'd stepped inside the apartment, he'd felt an irresistible urge to stay awhile.

He looked around the living room again. Besides the sofa, there was a coffee table, an easy chair, two end tables, and a small entertainment center complete with a television. The tops of the long, narrow windows were at ground level and had window wells to let in the light. Enough light that the apartment wasn't grim. The flooring was tile with a couple of large area rugs breaking up the space. The place would suit him for the time it took him to find and talk sense into his brother.

He heard the sound of Holly's footsteps on the concrete steps and rose from the sofa before she came through the open doorway. She looked a little flushed, and he suspected she'd rushed to return before he could change his mind. The color in her cheeks matched the pale pink of her shirt. Nice. Very nice.

She smiled as she held out a pen with her left hand and a clipboard with a form on top with her right one. "Here you go, Mr. Henning."

"If I'm supposed to call you Holly, you'd better call me Jed."

She nodded as he took the items from her and settled onto the sofa a second time. The form was basic. He wrote his name, Tacoma address, and mobile phone number quickly. For credit references he put his mortgage company and a credit card. For employment he wrote "Self-employed" instead of entering the name of his company, not stopping to analyze why. Finally, for personal references he entered the information for two of his local cousins: Ben Henning in Kuna and Jessica Chesterfield in Hope Springs, assuming that Idaho references would be preferred. For the third name he chose his friend Mike Hanover, who worked for him at Laffriot. At least he hoped that was still the case.

Finished with the rental application, Jed stood and handed the clipboard and pen to Holly. "My mobile number's on there. Once you're satisfied that you want to rent to me, call and I'll bring you a cashier's check. I'll bring it today if I know early enough to get to the bank."

"You sound as if you're in a hurry to move in."

"Not so much in a hurry to move in as I am eager to leave the hotel." He smiled, hoping it might help convince her.

"I'll call you and let you know as soon as I can." She glanced at the form on the clipboard. "It will depend on if I can reach your references right away."

"Of course." He took a few steps toward the open door. "I look forward to hearing from you. Thanks for your time."

Friday, May 30, 1969

In southwest Idaho, a person never knew if Memorial Day would be cold, a scorcher, or somewhere in between. This year the weather was pleasant as Andrew and Helen walked across the small cemetery toward the grave of their middle son, Oscar. This was the twenty-third time the couple had made this walk on a Decoration Day, as it used to be called, and although the sense of loss was different after more than two decades, the grief never completely went away.

Andrew held his wife's arm close to his side, offering silent comfort. When they reached Oscar's grave site, Helen handed the jar of flowers to Andrew before kneeling on the ground and sweeping the white headstone—and the grass surrounding it—clean. When she was finished, she held out her hand for the jar of flowers. First she poured the water from the jar into the receptacle in the ground, and then she placed the red-and-white peonies from her garden into the water, arranging them carefully. When she was done, Andrew leaned over to place a small American flag into the ground beside the flowers before helping his wife to her feet.

"He would have turned forty-two in March," Helen said softly.

Andrew nodded, his thoughts shifting to their grandson, Ted Valentine, now serving in Vietnam. Ted was twenty-one, already older than his uncle Oscar had been when he died during the battle for Okinawa. But still young. Too young. The soldiers and sailors and marines were always too young. And this current war, more than any other he'd witnessed in his lifetime, was controversial. The country was ablaze with angry protests, sit-ins, and draft-card burnings. Sometimes it seemed to Andrew that the way of life his oldest sons had fought to preserve in the Second World War had been lost already.

Helen patted his arm. He assumed she'd guessed the direction of his thoughts, as she so often did.

"Let's go home," she said.

"Yes." He offered his arm again, and she hooked her hand in his elbow.

At least they could be thankful that no new graves had been added to this small cemetery because of Vietnam. Not yet. He hoped it would remain that way, just as he continued to pray the war would soon come to an end.

He glanced one more time at the grave of their son before he and Helen walked back to the car. After helping her into the Jeep—the vehicle she called his late-in-life crisis—he went around to the driver's side and settled behind the wheel. Pain jabbed his lower back as he reached to insert the key, and a gasp escaped him.

"Are you all right?"

"I'm fine. Just a twinge in my back."

"Again? You should see the doctor."

He grunted as he turned the key, starting the engine. He wasn't about to waste good money on a few aches and pains. He was in his midsixties. Aches and pains were a part of aging. He'd accepted that. He'd have thought the same was true for Helen. He'd seen her rubbing her hands and fingers at the end of the day, as if to loosen her joints.

"We should have planned a dinner or a picnic with the family," she said as Andrew steered the Jeep onto the road.

"Everybody had plans already."

"I should have tried sooner, before they made other plans. It's good that you and I like each other."

He glanced over at her. "What does that mean?"

"Because we spend so much time together, just the two of us. Our kids and grandkids are always so busy."

"I hope you're not complaining about being stuck with me."

"No." She laughed. "Remember when I used to complain because some days I didn't have two minutes to myself? Back when all the kids were at home. Glory. That seems so long ago."

Without taking his eyes off the road, he reached over and covered her hand with his. "It *was* a long time ago, my girl."

"Funny. As I get older, those times from long ago feel more real to me than what I did yesterday. Am I getting senile?"

"Not hardly."

She turned her hand over and squeezed his.

Chapter 2

Holly hated making phone calls to inquire about individuals. She hated it when hiring personnel for the restaurant. She hated it now while trying to discover if she should rent her basement apartment to Jed Henning. It felt intrusive somehow. On one level, she knew it made sense. It was for safety and security reasons. She was protecting her finances and her property. But on another, it seemed a waste of time. After all, would anybody list a reference who would say something negative?

Nonetheless, she began with a cursory search on Facebook. The name Jed Henning brought up a number of prospects, none of them with profiles that matched her renter. A true investigator could probably find his footprint somewhere, but she wasn't an investigator. She simply wanted a reliable renter. She reached for the application and dialed the first number, a man who shared the same last name as Jed.

Well before the end of her phone calls—all of them brief and all of them highly positive—she'd made up her mind. She would rent the apartment to Jed. Why wouldn't she? His references confirmed his character and his financial stability. Plus he'd guaranteed her double the rent she'd requested for three months. He'd promised to pay two months of it up front. Her brain was already listing what she could do with that money.

Then again, was she making the right choice? What if he wasn't at all who he appeared to be, who his references said he was? He seemed nice. But appearances could be deceiving. She knew that all too well.

Only, what choice did she have? She needed to rent the apartment, and he was the first applicant who met her requirements.

Jed answered her call on the second ring. "Hello?"

"Mr. Henning? Jed. This is Holly Stanford."

"Yes. Hello."

"The apartment is yours, if you still want to rent it on the terms we discussed." Actually, they hadn't truly discussed the terms. He'd made an offer and she hadn't refused. But that seemed to be splitting hairs.

"Great. I'll head over to the bank right now. Will you be at your place in about an hour or so?"

"Yes, I'll be here."

"Should I have the check made out to you?"

"Yes."

"Great," he repeated. "See you soon. And thanks. I'm grateful."

It was nice of him to say so, Holly thought, but he couldn't be more grateful than she was.

With the call ended, she set her phone on the kitchen counter and turned to look at the ancient stove. Replacing it was high on her list of priorities, right after paying her most pressing bills. And if she had a modern range, she would be able to do more baking at home. She missed those times of experimenting with a new idea for a special creation. The restaurant required management skills from her—management skills and money—when what she really wanted was to be wearing an apron and making sweet confections.

She sank onto a nearby kitchen stool, fighting a sudden urge to cry. Her world had been out of control for so very long. The broken engagement. The death of her dreams. And the debt. The crushing, smothering debt. Sometimes she wanted to throw up her hands and cry, "Forget it!" Sometimes she wanted to run away from everything, to hide from the whole world.

But she wouldn't. She wouldn't run away. It wasn't in her nature to cut and run—sometimes to her detriment. She'd held on to Nathan Estes, her ex-fiancé, long after she'd known, deep down, that he didn't really love her. Long after she'd known he wasn't the man she'd believed him to be. But she'd already said yes to the dress, and the invitations had been mailed, and so many friends had said how happy the two of them would be, how perfect they were together. So she'd held on, hoping for something that would never be. In the end, Nathan had left her. Not quite jilted her at the altar but close enough for the label to feel accurate.

Drawing a ragged breath, she looked around the kitchen and living room. She'd bought the house thinking it was where she and Nathan would make a home and eventually start a family. Thinking it would be where she would start her cake-baking business while Nathan ran Sweet Caroline's, the restaurant once owned by her aunt and uncle. Looking back, she'd realized Nathan had already decided not to go through with the wedding even while he continued to encourage her to buy the house and update the restaurant. Otherwise, his name would have been on the home mortgage alongside hers. His name would have been next to hers on the bank loan for the restaurant remodel. Funny how his reasoning had made sense to her at the time.

"I'm an idiot. I was so swept away with the idea of romance that I was blind to what was right in front of me." She covered her face with her hands, repeating words she'd said often over the past year. "I'll never do that again. I'll never put myself at risk that way again. So help me, I won't. I won't."

She released a sigh. It wasn't memories of Nathan that had her fighting tears. She'd come to terms with what she'd once felt for him. No, it was the fallout from their doomed relationship that continued to plague her, continued to make her feel stupid and foolish and afraid to trust. She understood it was the weight of responsibilities and debt that kept her emotions on edge. But understanding was different from controlling. It certainly didn't make the problems all go away. She wished it could. Oh, how she wished it could.

Jed drove toward the apartment, his suitcases and a number of boxes in the back of the vehicle. The two suitcases had come with him from Tacoma. The boxes he'd picked up from one of his Idaho cousins. They contained Henning family photos and letters that had been left to his dad.

"Feel free to go through them while you're in Boise," his dad had said on the phone last night. "Maybe they'll serve as a kind of reminder about what it means to be a family."

The comment had angered Jed. Who was his dad to talk?

Jed loved his parents. He loved his great-aunts and uncles and all the cousins. He loved his brother, too, despite everything. He knew what it meant to be a family. Sure, maybe he hadn't spent much time with those closest to him in the past few years. Getting Laffriot off the ground had made for long days, long weeks, long months. He'd declined more than one invitation from his mom to come to dinner. He'd missed the last few Henning family reunions. But that didn't mean he didn't understand about family.

Maybe if he wasn't always trying to clean up after his brother, he would have more time to spend with family. Had his dad thought of that?

He drew a deep breath, remembering the last time he'd been with his brother.

"When're you going to grow up, Chris?"

"When are you going to stop riding me?"

"We've got obligations."

"You've got obligations. Not me. I just work for you. Remember?"

"There's no way you become a partner until you've earned it."

"I've earned it. You just aren't able to admit it."

That had been the moment when Jed nearly threw a punch. That was also the moment he might have saved himself a world of trouble by admitting Chris was right. At least partially right. His younger brother didn't know anything about running a successful company, and he didn't have a lick of business sense. But creativity oozed out of his pores. He was a genius in many ways. He was also irresponsible, undependable, and a gambler.

If he would just . . .

An unexpected sense of shame washed over Jed. Sure, he could blame their argument that day on losing his temper, on being fed up with his brother's careless actions. But there was more to it than one argument, one loss of temper. The anger and resentment had been welling up between them for years.

Holly Stanford's house came into view, allowing Jed to push back the unpleasant thoughts for now. A few moments later, Jed pulled his rental car to the curb. For a short while he stared at the small stucco residence. He'd only come there that morning because of a letter at the top of one of those boxes behind him. It was a letter from Jed's great-grandfather, Andrew Henning, to Jed's grandfather, Andy Jr. In it Andrew had written about the apartment where he'd lived with Great-Grandmother Helen for a short while after their wedding in 1929. Andrew had included the apartment address in his story. Between that letter and the old family Bible now in Jed's possession, curiosity had forced him to look up the residence on the internet. Seeing it still existed—a minor miracle considering how much Boise had grown over the past one hundred years—and discovering it wasn't all that far from the hotel, he'd headed off to see it. Just from the outside. It hadn't occurred to him he might have an opportunity to actually see the apartment itself. Let alone that it would be for rent—and that he would end up renting it. What on earth had possessed him to do it? He didn't hate living in a hotel as much as he'd made it sound. And with any luck at all, he wouldn't be in Boise more than a couple of weeks, let alone for three months.

Drawing a deep breath, he got out of the car and followed the walk to the front door. After ringing the doorbell, he took a step back. He didn't have to wait long before the door opened. Holly's eyes filled with a look of relief when she saw him, and he wondered if she'd thought he might not come after all.

"Ms. Stanford. Your tenant has arrived."

"Come in. Please." She pulled the door all the way open.

Jed stepped into the house. He glanced into the living room on his left. There was a sofa with matching easy chair and ottoman plus end tables. The upholstery was white with pink flowers, and for some reason, he thought it suited his new landlady. To his right was a kitchen and eating nook, neither of them what he would consider large. At home, his kitchen and dining room were enormous—unnecessary since he made little use of either one. A short hallway led to what he assumed were the bathroom and a couple of bedrooms.

"This is nice," he said.

"Thanks." She swept the adjoining room with her gaze. "I love it here."

Jed saw a flicker of sadness in her eyes. Not contradicting her words, exactly, but there was pain connected to this house too. He wondered what was behind it.

He thought again of his own house. He felt no sentimental attachment to it, that was certain. Not like what Holly obviously felt for her home. He pushed away that thought while clearing his throat, then said, "I've got your cashier's check." He pulled it from his pocket and held it out to her. He saw relief fill her eyes a second time. His gut told him she hadn't just wanted a renter. She'd *needed* one.

After drawing a breath, she set the check on the kitchen counter. "Here's the key to the apartment, and this one is to the detached garage in back. Use the parking stall on the right for your car." She dropped the key ring into his open hand.

"Thanks. Appreciate it."

Holly gave a nod and took a step backward.

Jed took that as a cue to leave. "I'll move my car around to the garage and get myself settled in." He turned toward the door, then stopped and looked back. "Where's the nearest grocery store?"

"About five blocks from here. Two blocks west and three blocks north." She pointed as she spoke, indicating the two directions.

"Thanks."

He whistled softly as he walked to the car, feeling better than he'd felt in months, although he wasn't sure why.

Monday, June 16, 1969

Fingers of early-morning light crept around the window curtains as Andrew got out of bed. It wasn't yet six o'clock, but a lifetime of farming made it impossible for him to sleep in whether or not there were chores awaiting him. Milking the cows used to be his first priority. No longer. They'd sold their last milk cow a couple of years after Andy Jr. graduated from college. That had been the summer before John and Jackie Kennedy moved into the White House.

Milking was one chore Andrew hadn't been sorry to do away with. Although there was something soothing about it—the warmth of the animal as he leaned close, the rhythmic sound of milk hitting the bucket—a man was also tied to the chore, morning and evening, rain or shine, good health or bad. No, he didn't miss it.

In the bathroom, he leaned over the sink and splashed his face with water. While straightening, he felt a stab of pain in his back so sharp he nearly cried out. He staggered back against the wall, trying to catch his breath, and waited. Waited for the pain to subside. Waited for it to let him stand at his full height. But unlike the previous occasions when his back had bothered him, the pain didn't pass, and each time he tried to straighten, he made it worse.

Swallowing a groan, he turned toward the bathroom door and shuffled his way back to the bedroom. Helen's side of the bed was empty. She was up making coffee, as she did every morning not long after he rose, her habits as ingrained as his own. He didn't bother to swallow the next groan as he sank onto the edge of the bed. Thank God he'd made it there. He wasn't sure how much farther he could have gone before the pain would have dropped him to the floor. Shutting his eyes and holding his breath, he managed to lie down.

"Andrew? Andrew, for heaven's sake. You're in bed again. What is it?"

Through gritted teeth, he answered, "My back."

"I'll warm up some salt to put in a sock."

He grunted.

"And I'll call the doctor as soon as it's time for him to be in the office."

For a change he didn't argue with her.

"Oh dear. Weren't you to start cutting today?"

"It'll have to wait until I'm better." Even as the words came out of his mouth, he knew it wasn't a real option. Some things on a farm could wait. Harvesting a crop when it was ready—like milking a cow when she was ready—wasn't one of them.

"I'll go get that salt pack. You lie still and don't worry yourself."

"Lie still and don't worry." Staying still wouldn't be a problem. It hurt too much to move. Even hurt to breathe. But not worrying? That was more difficult.

"Lord, You'd think after all these years that I'd have mastered Your instructions about not worrying. I don't mean to borrow trouble from tomorrow. But sometimes it's hard not to."

It was more than the hay cutting that worried him. He'd never been one to take to his bed. The whole household could have had colds or the flu or whatever, and Andrew had kept on keeping on. He'd been hurt before—who worked on a farm without getting banged up now and then?—but nothing so serious it laid him up. Feeling like he couldn't get out of bed and go back to work troubled him. No, more than troubled. It scared him a little.

Chapter 3

Holly stood in the showroom of the appliance store, looking at her dream range. Well, at least it was the dream for her kitchen at home. She'd already invested in a top-of-the-line commercial stove for the restaurant. This one was so she could spoil herself in her free time.

"As if any of that exists," she said softly.

"May I help you, miss?"

She glanced toward the eager-looking clerk. He was young, with cheeks that looked like he didn't need a razor. She swallowed a grin and said, "Yes. I'm interested in this range." She touched the price tag. "Does this include delivery and installation?"

The clerk, his smile doubled, rattled off more information than she'd asked for. Had he ever used a stovetop, let alone done any baking or broiling? Doubtful, but she didn't care. She'd already done her research. This was the one she wanted. With this, she could bake beautiful cakes and pastries. With this, she could see her dreams come true.

That thought stole some of her joy about the purchase. Because when would she have the time or the money for such a thing?

In truth, she probably shouldn't buy it. The smart thing would be to tuck the money away to cover the next crisis. And there was sure to be another crisis.

She clenched her jaw against the rising dread and guilt and worries. No, she would buy this stove, and after it was delivered, she would make something wonderful in it. Just for herself. Just for the pure fun of baking.

Within another thirty minutes, she'd paid for her purchase and arranged for the stove's delivery. She left the store with a smile on her face, refusing to feel guilty. Yes, there were needs at the restaurant, but this once she was going to do something for herself, for her own happiness. But as she drove away from the appliance store, her determination not to feel guilty began to falter. The closer she got to the restaurant, the heavier the weight felt upon her shoulders.

Decades before, Sweet Caroline's had been a popular eatery on State Street, a gathering place for friends and families, especially those who lived in nearby neighborhoods. It had been a place to enjoy comfort-style food along with good company. A spreading city and growing restaurant competition had taken their toll as the twentieth century waned, but it had been cancer that finally closed the doors of the restaurant. Holly's great-aunt had battled the disease for six years before God took her home to heaven. After Caroline Duthie's passing, her husband, Ray, had closed Sweet Caroline's, boarding over the windows and doors, and left it to sit empty, gathering dust while harboring small creatures bent on destruction. He could have sold the building at any time, but he never had.

Holly remembered the day she'd learned the former restaurant had been left to her in Uncle Ray's will. Her first thought:

How crazy is that? She knew nothing about running a restaurant. But her fiancé had thought it a great opportunity. Nathan had convinced her not to sell the building. He'd persuaded her instead to borrow money—enough to update and reopen the restaurant. He'd written a business plan with all kinds of charts and graphs to prove that, within two years, Sweet Caroline's could compete with other restaurants in the area.

"It succeeded for years. No reason it can't do that again."

Nathan had convinced Holly and then convinced the bank. And then he'd abandoned her—along with a boatload of debt.

Sweet Caroline's came into view, and Holly flipped on her blinker before turning into the parking lot. Only a few cars dotted the spaces at this time in the afternoon. But in another couple of hours, they would be busy.

Busy. Her heart sank. *Busy* was a generous term. They were doing better than when they'd first reopened. But not enough better. Not nearly enough.

When she entered the restaurant kitchen from the rear, she was greeted with a "Hey, boss."

"Hey, Zach." She forced a smile she didn't quite feel, the thrill over the new range completely faded by this time.

Zachary Holmes—tall, handsome, and happily married with two precious daughters—was her chief cook, and a harder worker she'd never known. If it weren't for him, Holly didn't know how she would have managed. The restaurant probably would have closed in its first month.

"Get your shopping done?" he asked.

"I sure did." She moved toward the entrance to her small office. "A shiny new range will be delivered to my house tomorrow."

"Good for you."

Good for me. Ignoring another wave of guilt, she opened a desk drawer and dropped her purse into it. "Maybe I'll come up with an idea for a new dessert for the restaurant."

"I'll bet you think them up in your sleep."

She used to. But not for a long while.

"Well, when you whip up that future award-winning concoction, you'd better share it with your tenant. After all, his rent check paid for the stove."

"True." She removed an apron from the hook in her office, slipped the loop over her head, and tied it around her waist.

Zachary frowned at her as she stepped out of her office. "You aren't planning to work the tables again tonight."

"We're still short a server." She shrugged. "But I hope that will be fixed by tomorrow. I have an interview in the morning, and I'm really hopeful about this one."

Finding good wait staff had been harder than expected. Holly had interviewed plenty of qualified servers, but the salary she could offer wasn't enough for most of them. She tried to make up for it in other ways. Still . . .

She gave her head a shake, chasing away negative thoughts. Positive. She was determined to be positive. About her life. About the restaurant. About it all. She would smile and face the world with a good attitude. She would think on good things. She would run the good race.

Zachary gave her a wave as she headed toward the swinging doors. She paused on the other side and glanced around. The restaurant was L-shaped, but from this vantage point, she could see all of the tables and booths in addition to the counter area. Lindsay was pouring coffee for a customer at the counter while Bobbi took orders from three people in one of the booths.

The entrance door swung open, drawing her gaze. She pasted on the smile she'd promised herself and moved forward. Surprise caused the smile to falter for a moment when she recognized the new arrival—her tenant. Her surprise was mirrored in Jed's expression when he recognized her too.

"Holly."

"Hi, Jed. Welcome to Sweet Caroline's." She stopped before him. "One for dinner?"

"Yes. It's just me."

She grabbed a menu from the nearby slot. "Is a booth all right?"

"Sure."

"If you'll follow me, please." She knew she must sound less than welcoming, but for some reason, having her renter walk through those doors unsettled her. Was she embarrassed to be found waiting tables? No, that wasn't it.

She turned and moved toward one of the booths in her area.

"I didn't know you worked here," he said.

"Only until I can hire another server." She stopped and set the menu on the table.

He gave her a questioning look as he slid onto the bench.

"I own the restaurant."

"Ah." He grinned. "Then you can probably recommend what I should order."

"Everything here is good."

"Says the unbiased proprietor."

"Completely unbiased and completely true. But I highly recommend the ribeye." She opened the menu before him and pointed. "Or if you like lighter fare, the lemon-pepper rainbow trout is amazing." She touched a second spot on the menu.

"'Amazing,'" Jed said softly. Then louder, "Sounds good."

"Everything here is good," she repeated. "I'll give you a minute. Be right back with your water."

It had been a discouraging day for Jed. He'd left three messages for Chris, all but begging him to return or take his calls. Hoping to meet with him face-to-face, he hadn't told his brother that he was in Boise. What if Chris took off and didn't tell anyone where he was going next? That would be a complete disaster for Jed and for Laffriot. As if things weren't bad enough as they were.

In an attempt to burn off some of his anger and frustration, he'd decided not to cook for himself in the little apartment. He'd seen Sweet Caroline's two days earlier when he'd gone to the grocery store. So he'd decided to walk there for dinner. He'd never expected to find his landlady present, let alone find her waiting tables.

Funny how his mood improved upon seeing her.

In addition, there was something warm and friendly about the restaurant. It almost felt as if he'd walked into Ben's farmhouse kitchen—except, of course, this was larger. There were three servers, including Holly. More than enough for the number of customers at the moment, but he imagined they must be kept hopping when all of the restaurant was full.

Holly returned to the booth with a glass of ice water and a straw. "Did you decide what you want?"

"I think I'll go with the rainbow trout."

"Good choice. And what about your sides? You get two."

He glanced at the menu again. "I'll take the mac and cheese and the green beans."

A tiny smile tugged at the corners of her mouth as she wrote on the menu pad.

"What?"

"Nothing, really. Those were my uncle's favorite sides with the trout." She waved around the room with her pencil. "This was his restaurant. His and my aunt Caroline's."

"*Sweet* Caroline?"

"One and the same." She nodded. "Anything besides water to drink?"

"No, thanks. The water's fine."

She slipped the order pad into the pocket of her apron. "I'll have your dinner right out to you."

After she walked away, Jed turned his gaze toward the window. It wasn't much of a view. Mostly he saw the heavy traffic of rush hour on State Street, a main thoroughfare leading out of downtown Boise. A few ancient trees separated the restaurant parking lot from a neighboring business.

Without anything interesting to distract his thoughts, they returned to his brother. He and Chris had been close when they were younger. Four years separated them in age, and for a long time, Chris had looked up to his big brother, idolized him in lots of ways. But when Chris became a teenager, the fights had started. Not only between the two of them. Chris had picked fights with nearly everyone. Their parents. School friends. Teachers. Anybody who seemed to look at him the wrong way or who disagreed with something he said or did. He'd let his schoolwork slide. He'd lied to his parents, and he'd lied to his teachers. He'd quit school during his senior year, the instant he'd turned eighteen. Quit school and shut himself away with video games, forgetting to eat, forgetting to shower. No doubt Chris would still be living in the house they'd grown up in if their dad hadn't finally had enough.

Several years later, Jed had brought Chris to work for him at Laffriot. He'd thought the work would help his brother. It had made sense in lots of ways. Chris knew computers and programming upward, forward, backward, and upside down, and he could come up with ideas for games in the blink of an eye. For a while, it had looked like he would settle into Laffriot and become an integral part of the company. But he'd chafed under his older brother's leadership. A heavy-handed leadership, if Jed was completely honest.

Clenching his jaw, he forced thoughts of Chris into the back of his mind before slipping the mobile phone from his pocket and checking for messages. No calls, but he did have a few texts. He answered each of them before opening his mail app. Nothing there that required his attention. Why would there be with Laffriot on hold? He drew a breath as he dropped the phone back into his pocket.

"Here you go."

He glanced up as Holly stopped nearby.

She smiled as she set the large plate in front of him. "Anything else you need?"

He spared a quick glance at the food before shaking his head. "I think I'm set. Looks great." He wasn't lying. The fish did look amazing, as promised.

"Well, then. Enjoy."

"I'm sure I will."

More customers entered the restaurant. Holly gave Jed a nod, then strode toward the new arrivals while he turned his attention to his dinner.

Thursday, June 19, 1969

From the bedroom where Andrew lay flat on his back for the third day in a row, he heard his grandson, Grant Henning, talking to Helen, but he couldn't make out their words. It frustrated him that he couldn't simply rise and walk out to join the conversation. He felt like a condemned prisoner, stuck there in his bed.

The same day that Andrew's back had gone out on him, Grant had arrived to mow the hay, eliminating any worry that it would fall victim to late spring rains. No surprise there. Grant loved this farm the same way Andrew did. The young man had studied agriculture in college—primarily horticulture and animal husbandry—and according to him, his current employment was only a stopgap. His goal was to own a farm of his own.

Andrew closed his eyes. *At least one of them turned out to be like me.*

As much as his children talked fondly about growing up on the farm, none of them had wanted to be farmers. They'd all chosen other paths as young adults. And of his and Helen's eight grandchildren, only Grant—Ben's oldest boy—wanted to be a farmer. The others were all living out their own dreams and aspirations. As it should be, Andrew knew. But he was glad that Grant loved the land and the animals like his grandfather.

It hadn't always been that way. Andrew's goal had been to become a successful businessman after graduating from the university. He'd wanted to live in the city and own a fancy car and buy his wife a large house. But then had come the crash, followed by the decade known as the Great Depression. Those years had changed everything. If he was honest, they'd probably saved him from himself. They'd put his feet firmly on God's path, and he was thankful for it.

"Hey, Grandpa."

Opening his eyes, Andrew turned his head on the pillow and looked toward the doorway.

Grant smiled at him. "How're you feeling?"

"A little better, I think." Not true, but it seemed the right thing to say.

"Well, don't try to rush anything. Grandma's worried you'll get up too soon and make your back even worse."

"I wouldn't dare incur her wrath." He chuckled, but stopped when the small action caused pain to shoot through him.

Grant crossed to the side of the bed and sat on the nearby chair. "I've rounded up help for the baling on Saturday. The weather's supposed to stay dry into next week, so we'll be good. Nothing for you to worry about."

"Can't tell you how much I appreciate the help, my boy."

"I'd rather be doing this than anything else."

"I know."

Grant glanced toward the doorway and back again. "I was thinking, maybe I should come stay with you and Grandma for the summer. She says the doctor wants you to take it easy for quite a while. If I was here, I could do lots more than take care of this one cutting."

"That's a lot for you to add on top of your job. Not to mention getting ready for your wedding in the fall."

"My work's no big deal. Just a bit of extra driving each day there and back." His grandson grinned. "As for the wedding, my mom and Charlotte's mom have everything under control. My only job is to turn up when they tell me to."

"Come to think of it, that's the role of most grooms." Andrew kept from laughing again, but only just.

"Then it's settled. When I come on Saturday for the baling, I'll bring all my stuff with me."

Chapter 4

Photographs were spread across the coffee table on that Sunday afternoon, filling every square inch of the surface. Most of them were black and white but there were colored photos as well, beginning in about the 1960s, he guessed. One by one, Jed picked them up, studying the subjects, turning the photos over to see if any names or years or locations had been written on the back. When he discovered identities, he placed them in associated piles. Photographs still in question went in other piles.

Jed hadn't expected the boxes of letters, journals, and photographs to be of any interest to him, but once he'd started poking through them—more out of boredom and the need for something to fill time—he'd found himself intrigued to know more about the family members he'd never met or had barely known. Of course, he had his own memories of his grandparents and host of cousins from his early childhood and other memories from the times his dad had brought them back for family reunions. Still, there was so much he didn't know, and the glimpses he was getting from the past intrigued him.

He picked up a photo of Andrew and Helen Henning. Their wedding photograph. The paper had cracked over time, but their faces were clear. Young faces. Still in their early twenties, their lives stretching out before them, filled with hope. Andrew had been a recent college graduate at the time they'd married, and they'd moved into this basement apartment soon after the photograph had been taken.

Jed glanced up, trying to imagine the newlyweds in this small living room. Hard to believe that had been over ninety years ago. Imagine that. Ninety years ago, members of his own family had sat in this room. Perhaps in one of the nearby boxes he would find a photo or two taken here.

His gaze moved to a small end table where Andrew's Bible rested. It contained a treasure-trove of underlined passages, brief thoughts, names, dates, even some prayers. Jed had only flipped through the book quickly, but he intended to return to it for a more thorough study. He suspected that between the photos and letters found in these boxes, plus that Bible, he would uncover a great deal about his extended family.

He looked at the wedding photo again. Chris bore a rather strong resemblance to their great-grandfather. The same dark hair, a bit scruffy around the collar. The same thick eyebrows. The same prominent nose. In the photo, Andrew had attempted a serious look, but the corners of his mouth had tipped up enough to reveal his happiness.

Jed tried to picture Chris looking happy. He couldn't remember such a look in recent years. Not since childhood. In his mind he heard a particular squeal of joy that had been uniquely his kid brother's. It could have pierced an eardrum. Then he remembered the years when Chris had tried to tag along with Jed and his friends. What a pest, but more often than not Jed had let him come.

What had changed that happy-go-lucky, fun-natured kid into a surly teenager and then a man with no ambition? He wished he knew. He wished he understood.

With a shake of his head, he returned to sorting photos and had been at it for about ten minutes when he heard a loud crash from overhead. He looked at the ceiling, wondering what his landlady had dropped. Had to be big and heavy, whatever it was. He lowered his gaze, but the silence from above seemed louder than the noise had been. What if Holly had fallen? Or what if something had fallen on her? Still hearing no movement, he couldn't take it. He rose and headed out of the apartment.

The steps to the back door of the main house were a short distance from the apartment stairwell. He climbed them and knocked. The seconds seemed to drag by while he waited. He was about ready to try the knob and go in without invitation when the door opened before him. He felt relief, seeing Holly was unharmed.

"Jed?"

"Sorry to bother you. I heard something crash, and I got worried when I didn't hear you moving around afterward." The words made him feel foolish, maybe even intrusive. He'd never been one to get involved with his neighbors. He wasn't sure what had compelled him to do so now.

"I've got a bit of a mess, I'm afraid." Leaving the door open, she turned and disappeared.

Jed hesitated a few moments, then followed her into the kitchen.

There was, indeed, a mess. Batter of some kind was splattered on the countertop and the cupboard doors beneath it. There was a thick pool of the mixture on the floor, an overturned stainless-steel bowl in the middle of it.

Holly walked to the counter to inspect a red mixer, also covered in batter. "It better not be broken." Then, glancing over her shoulder at Jed, she said, "It got knocked onto the floor with everything else."

He was about to say something—he didn't know what—but a loud *meow* beat him to it. He turned his head in time to see a long-haired orange tabby cat serpentine its way through the legs of a bar stool.

"You are *not* my favorite at the moment." Holly cast a glare in the feline's direction.

Jed took a step into the room. "Can I help?"

She faced him. "Oh, I couldn't ask you to—"

"No problem." He pointed toward the paper towels at the far end of the counter. "Shall I start with those?" He didn't wait for her answer. "What happened? The cat didn't push the mixer off the counter, did he?"

"She. And no, Pumpkin didn't push it off. She's big but not that big."

Paper towels in hand, he squatted opposite Holly and began wiping up the gooey mess before him.

"The fault was mine," she continued, ending with, "But she started it."

"Sorry. I'm a little confused."

Holly stood and ran water over a cloth. After wringing it out, she knelt again, washing the floor with it. "Pumpkin isn't allowed on the kitchen counters. I'd turned off the mixer when up she came, right where she knows she shouldn't be. I reached to shoo her off, and somehow my arm got tangled with the cord, and when I pulled back, down the mixer and bowl went. It was so stupid of me." She pushed hair from her face with the back of her wrist, looking as if she might cry.

"Why don't you see if the mixer's all right, and I'll finish wiping things up."

"You don't have to—"

"No problem," he answered a second time. "Besides, I'm already doing it." He smiled, hoping it would make her do the same. It didn't work.

Jed returned to wiping up the last of the batter with the paper towels, but he stopped again when he heard the sound of the mixer running, first low, then medium, then high. He looked up. Holly was smiling at last.

She must love that mixer.

"What was this going to be?" He stood and tossed the paper towels into the trash.

"A cake."

"Somebody's birthday?"

She shook her head. "No. Just trying out a new recipe."

"At least the mixer's okay."

"A good thing. That one cost me a pretty penny. I bought it when I had plans to . . . do more baking."

He ran water over his hands, washing them. After shutting off the water, he said, "You must enjoy it if you do it on your day off from the restaurant."

"Oh, I don't do the baking at Sweet Caroline's. No time for it." A shadow passed over her face as she handed him a towel.

Holly could have told Jed that she'd once fantasized about inventing some marvelous concoction that would become a perennial on restaurant menus everywhere. Later, she'd focused on creating wedding cakes that were works of art. She'd even envisioned herself on the cover of magazines. *Chef Holly,* the headlines of her imagination had proclaimed, and the whole world would have known who she was. She swallowed a sigh, determined to drive away such thoughts. They had no place in reality.

"Well . . ." Jed folded the hand towel and laid it on the counter. "I guess my work here is done."

"I'm really sorry you got sucked into helping with the cleanup."

"Hey. Stop apologizing. I heard a noise and came to make sure you were all right."

Holly wasn't too keen on the idea of this man—*any* man—rushing to her rescue. Better that she look out for herself. Jed seemed nice enough, but she didn't know him. Couldn't know him. A man's true nature could be disguised well and for a long time. Nathan had taught her that. Better to be wary. Casual friendships might be okay, but she wasn't about to let anyone get too close.

Jed tipped his head to one side. "If it'll make you feel better, I'll take a slice or two of that cake when you get it made." He grinned. "Well, not *that* cake. I'd prefer one that hasn't been mopped off your floor."

Despite herself, she had to smile at his joke. "Deal."

"Okay. I'll hold you to it." He moved toward the back door but came to an abrupt halt when Pumpkin jumped into his path. The feline promptly rubbed against his legs, her purr reverberating in the room.

The sound surprised Holly. Pumpkin didn't warm to strangers. Especially not men. The cat had never liked Nathan. That should have been Holly's first clue. "She likes you."

"You think?" He glanced over his shoulder as the cat continued to rub back and forth against him.

Going to his rescue, she picked up Pumpkin, cradling the cat close to her chest.

"I didn't want to step on her," he said, as if an explanation was needed.

"Or trip over her."

"Yes, that too."

"You're safe now."

"Appreciate it." He touched his forehead, as if tipping a hat. "See you later."

Holly waited to set the cat on the floor until the back door had swung closed behind Jed. "Stay out of trouble, you."

Pumpkin meowed, then strolled toward the living room with obvious superiority.

Laughing softly, Holly turned toward the sink again. She took another dishcloth from a drawer and washed away the last remains of her mixing disaster from the cabinets and floor. When she was done with that, she cleaned the mixer, bowl, and countertop. Once everything was back in order, she considered a second attempt at cake making, but the desire had left her. Perhaps she would spend the rest of her Sunday afternoon on the sofa with something cool to drink and a good book. Reading was a favorite pastime, but usually the only free time she had to pursue it was bedtime. And then she was so tired that she had to turn out the light after only a few minutes, no matter how great the book was.

Her phone rang, intruding on her thoughts. When she picked it up, she smiled, seeing her younger sister's photo on the screen. "Hi, Trix," she answered.

"Hey, Holly. What are you up to?"

"Nothing much. How about you?"

"Same."

Holly settled onto the sofa, preparing for a nice long visit. She'd always been close to her younger sister. More like best friends than relatives.

Her sister cleared her throat. "Well, that isn't entirely true. I have been up to something. Something I need to tell you."

"What?"

"I'm afraid it might upset you."

"Why would it upset me?" What-ifs sprang to mind, and her gut tightened.

Silence followed for what seemed a long while before Trixie answered, "Brett proposed last night."

Holly sucked in a breath of air. She didn't want the news to make her feel sorry for herself, and yet that was the first emotion to shoot through her. She pushed it away as fast as she could. "Proposed. That's wonderful. Brett's a great guy. When do you plan to get married?"

"In June."

"In June?" Holly straightened away from the back of the sofa. "*This* June? Two months is hardly enough time to plan a wedding."

Trixie laughed airily. "You know I always wanted a June wedding. And I'm not waiting another whole year."

Holly and Trixie's older sister, Beth, had been married twelve years and had made the two of them aunts three times over. Now Trixie, not even two years out of college, was getting married too. As for Holly . . .

She closed her eyes against the memories. She'd fought through the rejection. The depression. The feelings of being lost and alone. The feelings of hopelessness. And yet they still tried to claw their way back at times.

"Holly, I want you to make our wedding cake. Is that too much to ask?"

"Me?"

"Who else? You are the absolute best pastry chef in the world. Your cakes are gorgeous."

"I'm a little out of practice."

"No, you aren't. I mean, if you don't want to, I'll understand. Really I will. But if you could . . ."

How could she refuse? Her specialty had always been wedding cakes, and she loved her sister. How could she not want to do this, even if it was a reminder of her own disappointment?

"Before you answer," Trixie continued, "you should know that I also want you to be my maid of honor. Can you do both? Please tell me you can do both."

She swallowed hard and answered, "Of course I can do both."

"Perfect! Absolutely perfect!" After drawing a breath, Trixie launched into a quick rundown of everything she hoped to have happen. First on her list was to find the perfect venue for the wedding. Their mom wanted it to be in their church in the Stanford family's hometown of Thunder Creek. But Trixie had her heart set on an outdoor ceremony, preferably with mountains as a backdrop. "We've thought about McCall or Garden Valley, but that's asking guests to drive a long way and probably have to rent rooms to spend the night before they could go home again. I'm hoping we can find something in Boise or Eagle maybe."

They talked for another fifteen or twenty minutes before Trixie announced that her fiancé had arrived at the house. "Gotta go. We'll talk again soon. Love you."

"Love you back, Trix. Later."

Holly punched End and set the phone on the coffee table.

A wedding. In about eight weeks' time. Maid of honor and cake baker. Good grief! How would she manage those duties while running the restaurant? She should have said she could do one or the other but not both. Then again, when had she ever been able to deny her little sister anything? She shook her head as she rose and went to a bookshelf that held some of her favorite wedding cake cookbooks.

Tuesday, July 1, 1969

Andrew sat on the front porch and watched as a hot breeze swirled dust down the driveway. His dog, Chester, slumbered beneath the porch swing, and the horses stood in the pasture with heads drooping. The afternoon heat had made every living thing lethargic, including Andrew, who had a hard time keeping his eyes open.

But he was determined not to fall asleep in this blasted chair. For one thing, he might end up at some odd angle that would aggravate his back. If he did that, Helen would consign him to the bed again, and that he couldn't abide. He also didn't want to give his doctor a reason to mention the possibility of surgery again. He wasn't about to let anyone take a knife to his back, no matter how renowned they might be. He would get through this with prayer and an extra measure of care.

Besides, they didn't have the money for surgery. He wasn't yet sixty-five—that was still a good ten months down the road—so he wasn't covered by Medicare. There'd been quite the brouhaha when President Johnson signed that insurance for seniors into law four summers ago, but Andrew hadn't given it a lot of thought at the time. Although he'd known the time was fast approaching, he'd refused to think of himself as retirement age or as a senior citizen. He'd always been healthy as a horse. He'd intended to go on that way. So what did he need with government insurance?

Only look at him now. Ordered to sit still in this porch chair and to lift nothing heavier than a glass of lemonade. It made him feel old, like it or not. He undoubtedly looked old, especially with his careful, shuffling gait.

He closed his eyes, his thoughts drifting. Youth, as the saying went, was wasted on the young. There was no appreciation for ease of movement or quick minds or new experiences. Not for most, at least.

Even in times as tumultuous as these, even with inflation and civil unrest and foreign wars, the young felt invincible. Age and experience made a man more pragmatic.

"Care for some company?" Helen asked.

He looked toward the front door, watching her approach, a pitcher of lemonade in her hand.

"I thought you might need a refill." She poured some of the pale-yellow liquid into his glass on the table beside his chair. "How are you feeling?"

"Bored."

"Need me to bring you a book?"

"I'm tired of reading."

"You? Tired of reading?" She smiled as she settled onto the chair opposite him. "Maybe you need a hobby."

"A hobby?"

"People do have hobbies, Andrew."

"I know that." He sounded bad tempered, even in his own ears. Terrific. He was getting old *and* crotchety. He tried to soften his words. "What would you suggest?"

"I don't know. Something you can do while relaxing, while sitting down."

"Besides reading."

She gave him another small smile. "Yes. I was thinking something along the lines of painting. You know. Watercolors or oils. Something like that."

"Me? An artist?"

"You actually have a very artistic soul, my love."

What was she talking about? An artistic soul? No one had ever described him that way. Nobody else ever would. Everyone knew Andrew Henning was practical, sensible, and down-to-earth.

"It isn't too late to try something new." Helen pushed gray wisps of hair off her forehead. "Grandma Moses didn't start painting until she was in her late seventies, and Winston Churchill wasn't a child when he started either. He was forty, I think. Later Mr. Churchill wrote that painting came to his rescue in a most trying time."

Now *that* was sneaky, he thought. His wife knew full well how much he admired the former prime minister of England. Reminding him of Churchill's hobby had been a master stroke on her part.

"Won't you think about it, Andrew? It might keep you from feeling so restless. It might help you in your recovery." She leaned forward and took hold of his hand. "Think about it." It sounded more like an order than a request, but it was laced with love.

"I will." He nodded. "I promise."

Chapter 5

Jed walked along the Boise Greenbelt, the branches of tall cottonwoods casting shadows across the path before him. It being a Friday, he saw few others at this time of day, mostly young moms with babies and toddlers in strollers.

With a sigh, he sank onto a bench and stared at the river, running high on its banks in mid-April. Taking his phone from his pocket, he touched his brother's photo and waited, fully expecting to need to leave another message.

"What do you want, Jed?"

Chris's voice surprised him so much he couldn't answer at first.

"You there?"

"I'm here. I didn't think you'd answer."

"I almost didn't."

Jed drew a deep breath and let it out. "I need to see you, Chris."

"About what? I think we pretty much said everything the last time we were together."

Words rushed into his head. Sharp words. Words meant to slap some sense into his brother. As if that method had worked in the past.

"I shouldn't've said what I said." The words tasted bitter as they crossed Jed's tongue. "I'd like to try again. Will you tell me where you are?"

"Why? You planning a trip? Because I don't have plans to come back to Washington."

Jed took another breath to steady himself. "I'm already in Boise."

"You're what?"

"In Boise. I came to find you. To talk to you."

Chris released a curse, then ended the call.

Jed lowered the phone from his ear and stared at the blank screen. He considered calling his brother back, but he knew without trying that Chris wouldn't answer again. Not this soon. He supposed it was better to let it go for now.

He lifted his gaze to the water flowing past. Some of the trees that lined the river showed the beginnings of new leaves. Others were still bare and wintery in appearance, belying the warmth of the sun upon his back.

If Chris wasn't staying with their family, why even come to Boise? It didn't make much sense to Jed. His brother didn't have many memories of living in Idaho. He hadn't been in school yet when the family moved to Washington. So why Boise? Because it was a name he knew? Because it was just a day's drive from Tacoma?

And how much money could he have? Chris had never been responsible when it came to his finances. Laffriot had paid him a good wage, but from the looks of his apartment, Chris had spent it on every electronic gadget known to man. A lot of good that was doing him here.

"I'll never understand him," Jed whispered to himself.

He closed his eyes and tried to release the growing anger inside of him. After a few moments the words he'd read in the front of Andrew Henning's Bible drifted into his thoughts. The part about following God so that he wouldn't lose his way.

I've lost my way, haven't I? Dad wants me to make things right with Chris, but maybe being here is about more than the trouble between brothers. Help me find my way back to You, God.

The prayer surprised him. He hadn't felt lost. Only angry at Chris. But Ben giving him Andrew Henning's Bible meant something. It had stirred emotions inside of him. He wasn't sure what those were or what they meant, but they were there all the same.

"Excuse me."

Jed looked in the direction of the voice. A man stood about ten feet away. He was tall and thin, what Jed's grandma would have called a beanpole. He guessed him to be around his own age, although it was hard to be certain due to his unkempt appearance.

"Could you make a call for me?" The stranger pointed at the phone in Jed's hand.

Glad for something else to acquire his attention, Jed stood. "Sure."

"I was supposed to work this afternoon, but somebody stole my bike. I'm walking, but there's no way I'm going to get there for the start of my shift."

"You live around here?"

The man shook his head, his gaze suddenly on the ground.

Sensing he'd made the man uncomfortable with his question, he said, "My name's Jed." He waited to see if the man would respond with his own name. When he didn't, Jed added, "Would a ride be of more help to you than a phone call?"

The man's eyes widened as he met Jed's gaze again.

"I could drive you to your job."

"You'd do that?"

"Sure."

Now the eyes narrowed. "Why?"

The strange thing was Jed didn't know why he'd made the offer. Maybe it was because he'd just asked God to help him find his way. Maybe it was because he had nothing else to do. "Come on. I've got no ulterior motives. I'm just offering you a ride to work. My car's parked over this way." He took a couple of steps, then waited to see if the other man would join him.

He did.

Exhausted, Holly dropped onto the sofa in her living room, wanting nothing more than to sit there until it was time to go to bed. It had been one of those days at the restaurant. One of their suppliers had failed to deliver some promised items, and the server Holly had hoped to hire hadn't shown up for her interview, meaning they still didn't have a full wait staff. At least Zachary had found a part-time cook to fill in for him on his one day off a week. That was a godsend.

"How soon before Zach's burned out?" Holly asked Pumpkin when the cat jumped onto the sofa, demanding attention. "He might up and quit, and then where would I be?"

She knew the answer to that question. She would be stuck on a sinking ship, a ship that had been taking on water from the start.

"I hate it," she whispered. Then, louder, "I hate it. I hate it. I hate it."

Her doorbell rang. She considered not answering it. Then came a knock and a familiar voice. "Holly, it's me. Are you there?"

She groaned as she pushed up from the sofa. A moment later she pulled open the door for her sister.

"Oh, good." Trixie grinned as she entered. "You're home."

"Barely."

Trixie looked into the kitchen. "Did you already eat? I'm starved."

"I had a sandwich at the restaurant."

"Any good leftovers in the fridge?"

Holly laughed softly. Her sister ate like she had one of those proverbial hollow legs and then had the nerve to remain reed thin. "I'll see what I've got." She walked into the kitchen.

"I wanted to show you some pictures of the dresses I'm considering. Mine and the bridesmaids. We'll have to make a decision pretty fast about your dress. We've got our date. It's Saturday the twentieth of June."

"You found a venue already?" She looked over her shoulder.

Trixie's face glowed with happiness. "Yes. It's a barn with a stage and a small kitchen for the catering. It's perfect."

"A barn?" Holly turned all the way around.

"I know. I know. It doesn't sound like much. But it is. Wait until you see it. They've remodeled it for weddings and other special events. Brett loves it too."

Holly opened her mouth to say something but was stopped by another knock, this time from the back door. "Hold that thought." She went to answer the sound.

Jed waited on the stoop. "Sorry to bother you, Holly."

"It's all right."

"I don't have power in the apartment. I looked for an electrical panel, but there isn't one in my unit. I assume it's on the other side of the basement or upstairs."

Electrical problems. Just what she needed. "I'm sorry. I didn't know the power was off. I've got it up here."

Jed's gaze moved beyond Holly's shoulder, and she guessed that Trixie had stepped into view. She looked, confirming her suspicion.

Her sister spoke before she could. "You must be the new renter. I'm Trixie, Holly's younger sister."

"Nice to meet you. I'm Jed."

Trixie moved forward and held out a hand, which he shook.

"Let me get a flashlight," Holly said once her sister had backed away. "Hopefully it's nothing serious." She headed for the drawer in the utility room where she kept a flashlight.

Right behind her, Trixie whispered, "He's cute."

"Shhh."

"Well, he is. Is he single?"

Ignoring the question, Holly said, "Fix yourself something to eat, Trix. I'll be back as soon as I can."

She hurried to the back door, hoping Jed hadn't heard her sister. "The electrical panel is down here." She took the stairway to the basement, keenly aware of the sound of Jed's footsteps as he followed her. Using the flashlight, she located the electrical panel, and Jed flicked a couple of the switches. The power for the basement came back at once.

"Thank God," Holly said beneath her breath. The mere possibility of serious electrical problems made her heart race.

"You okay?"

Feeling her cheeks grow warm, she faced him. "Yes. Just glad it was an easy fix."

"Me too." He smiled.

Trixie was right. Jed Henning *was* cute.

The warmth in her cheeks turned to a fire. She looked away, hoping he hadn't seen and unhappy with herself for entertaining even a brief thought about his appearance. She didn't care about his looks, only about his rent.

"How about I order pizza as a way of saying thanks?"

"That's not necessary." She started toward the stairs.

"I'd like to do it. I'd still be sitting in the dark if you hadn't come home when you did."

"I didn't do anything but provide a flashlight and show you to the panel. You're the one who flipped the switches. Besides, you have a right to expect power in your apartment."

He laughed as he followed her up the stairs. "Agreed. Now, what kind of pizza do you and your sister like?"

Still out of sight, Trixie called out, "Did I hear pizza?"

Holly would have happily strangled her sister. The same sister who was still talking.

"I'm good with anything except anchovies." Trixie stepped into the kitchen doorway where she could be seen. "Oh, and I like thin crust the best."

Holly swallowed a groan. She could see what Trixie was up to. Her sister was as subtle as a steamroller. Because Trixie was in love and happy with the whole world, she wanted the same for Holly. Well, she could forget it. And as soon as Jed returned to his apartment, she would tell Trixie just that.

Dinner with the Stanford sisters proved to be a lively one, an evening that Jed enjoyed far more than expected. His offer to buy the pizza had been more selfish than it sounded. He hadn't wanted to return to the empty apartment right away. He'd already spent too much time that day lost in his thoughts about Chris and his worries about Laffriot's future. He'd needed a distraction, if only for an hour or two.

Trixie Stanford was certainly a distraction. Vivacious and good humored, she seemed to fill the room with her personality. As for Holly, her affection for her younger sister was obvious in her eyes.

"Selfishly," Trixie said, "I'm glad Holly didn't leave Boise to go off to some pastry-chef school. I'd miss her something awful if she moved too far away."

Holly's smile this time was a little strained.

"Did she tell you she's making the cake for my wedding?"

Jed shook his head. He hadn't seen his landlady since Sunday when he'd helped her clean up the cake batter. Occasionally he'd heard her moving about the house above him, but their paths hadn't crossed in the past five days.

Jed wasn't used to being idle. Since starting Laffriot, he'd worked twelve- and fourteen-hour days. He paced his office while talking on the phone. Except when he was working on his computer, his desk chair rarely got used. He was a man of action. To keep himself from going stir-crazy while he tried to find his brother, he'd kept himself busy, driving around Boise, becoming reacquainted with the city, checking out places he thought Chris might be. Out of curiosity, he'd investigated the tech companies headquartered locally. When in the apartment, he'd kept current on Laffriot email, studied company spreadsheets, and stayed in touch with a number of key employees. And in the evenings, he'd continued to look through the photographs and letters found in the boxes meant for his dad. Between those and the notes in his great-grandfather's old Bible, he'd started to feel as if he knew Andrew Henning.

"Holly's amazing in the kitchen," Trixie continued, unaware of his wandering thoughts. "Her cakes are masterpieces, but she can make any dessert you might want. They're all so good. You should—"

"Trix," Holly interrupted softly but firmly.

"Sorry." Trixie waved a hand in the air. "Enough about us. Tell me about you. Where are you from?"

"Here, originally. But I did most of my growing up in the Seattle area. It's where I still live."

"Do you go to church? Because if you do, you should check out Holly's. Brett and I attend services in Thunder Creek, our hometown, but Holly says great things about Covenant Fellowship."

"Covenant Fellowship?" He looked at Holly. "That's where my cousin and his grandfather go. Maybe you know them. Grant Henning. Ben Henning."

She shook her head. "Sorry. It's a big place, and I've only been going there for a year."

Just yesterday, Ben had called Jed and suggested he join them on Sunday. He hadn't made any promises, but maybe he should go with them. It had been far too long since he'd been faithful in church attendance.

"And what do you do?" Trixie asked, intruding on his thoughts.

"I have my own company. We develop computer—"

"You're a nerd?" Trixie's eyes widened. "You don't look like one."

He laughed. "Thanks. I think."

"You should at least wear glasses."

"Trix. Really." Holly blushed. "What a thing to say."

This wasn't the first time Jed had seen the pink rise in her cheeks. He thought it made her blue eyes look even bluer.

Trixie wasn't about to be diverted. "Are you thinking of relocating your company to Boise?"

"Well, no. That isn't why I—"

"I just thought, since you rented the apartment for three months, maybe you're scoping out the business scene. It's strong, you know. Boise's among the fastest-growing cities in the US. Great for the workforce." The younger sister's eyes widened. "You should talk to my fiancé. Brett's an attorney, and he knows so many people here in the Treasure Valley. I'll bet he could help you make up your mind."

Strange, how the idea seemed to strike a chord with him. Maybe he wouldn't mind coming back to Idaho. Laffriot's success didn't depend upon its physical location. Assuming that he got Chris to come around and their dad didn't shut down the company for good.

Saturday, July 12, 1969

Using the cane forced upon him by the doctor and family members, Andrew made his way slowly beyond the chicken coop to the edge of the alfalfa fields. Three weeks had passed since the first cutting of hay was baled, stacked, and most of it trucked away. Now the field was deep green with new growth, on its way toward the second cutting of the season. The morning air smelled sweet with it.

During the war years, Andrew had grown mostly corn on these forty acres. And in the years since, he'd tried other crops off and on, rotating fields, letting some ground rest now and again. But there was something about the alfalfa fields that called to him. He couldn't say for sure what it was. Perhaps he simply liked looking at them. Perhaps it was nostalgia.

"Grandpa?"

He turned to watch Grant's approach. Except for the brown hair, his grandson bore a striking resemblance to his dad—tall, blue-eyed, and handsome.

"Does Grandma know you're out here?"

"No."

"You know she worries when you walk on uneven ground."

"She'll have to get used to it. God didn't pave the world."

Grant chuckled. "No, He didn't."

"What are you up to this morning?"

"I'm making some repairs on the shed next to the hay barn."

"Need a hand?"

"Grandma would tan us both."

"Then I'll simply observe." Andrew moved forward with slow, careful steps.

Grant turned on his heel to walk beside his grandfather.

"Are we going to see Charlotte this weekend?"

"Yes, she's coming tonight for dinner, and Grandma invited her to use the spare room and stay the night, then go to church with us in the morning."

"That'll be nice. I don't imagine the two of you are getting much alone time since you've been staying on the farm."

"Not as much as we'd like, but she's cool with it. She knows I'm happiest here, so she hasn't complained."

Andrew glanced over at Grant. "She's a sweet girl, your Charlotte."

"I know. I think I knew the moment I met her that she was the one for me. Was it like that between you and Grandma?"

"In some ways. We fell in love young, but I was determined to do something different with my life rather than farming. So I went off to the university with that in mind."

"I can't imagine you doing anything else."

"I guess God couldn't either, because He sure got me back to it soon enough." Andrew drew in a deep breath. "I must've been crazy to think I'd want to live in the city, away from all this."

"I know what you mean."

"But I suppose the day is coming when I may have to make that change." He frowned. It was the first time he'd said that to anyone, although he'd thought it numerous times since his back troubles started.

Grant stopped walking. "You'd give up the farm?"

"I might have to, though I hate the thought of it. I'm sure I could lease the land to another farmer, but I don't think that would give your grandmother and me enough to live on. God willing, we've a lot of years still to live, and we haven't got much in the way of savings. This land's all we've got of any value. You know how it is. Most farmers go from month to month or year to year." He smiled ruefully. "A good year might have meant braces on somebody's teeth or a newer car or a piece of much-needed equipment. A bad year meant using whatever reserves there were and holding on until the next good year."

"It's still the kind of life I want. Wish I could buy it from you."

Andrew felt his heart stutter. "You'd want to buy *this* farm? I thought you were looking farther west and for more than forty acres."

"Grandpa, there's no place I'd rather be than the Henning farm if I could swing the price and you were ready to sell." His grandson's gaze swept over the fields and barnyard. "I love it here. But I'm years away from being able to buy a farm. Any farm."

"I suppose." Andrew's gaze went to the house, and he lost himself in thought for a long while. Finally, he said, "You know, I was always going to remodel our home, add on more rooms, maybe even tear it down and build a whole new one. Would've been nice if I could have done that for your grandmother."

"The place must've been bursting at the seams when your kids were little."

"Yes. Helen's mother lived with us, too, until she passed."

"That's a lot of people under one roof."

"It was indeed." He nodded, picturing his family in his mind. "Now it's next to impossible to get everybody back to the farm at the same time. They're all rushing this way and that. Things were simpler when your dad and his brothers and sisters were young and at home."

Andrew shook his head slowly. He'd become a sentimental fool, starting to think the past was better than the present. That was an old man's game. Had the Great Depression been simple? Had World War II been easy? Of course not.

He looked at Grant. "We'd better get over to that shed. The day's heating up. You need to get to work, and I need to find a comfy bit of shade to sit in where I can observe and advise."

The two of them laughed as they walked on.

Chapter 6

Holly was hurrying toward the sanctuary doorways on Sunday when she heard someone call her name. She stopped and turned to see Kelly Foreman, the women's ministry leader, coming to meet her.

"So glad I caught you." Kelly gave her a quick hug. "You look good."

"Thanks."

"Listen. I heard that you're helping ladies from Lighthouse with cooking lessons. I was wondering if you'd be willing to do something similar with our MOPS gals."

"MOPS?"

"Mothers of Preschoolers. We have a group that meets here at the church. A lot of these moms are just kids themselves. Some don't know anything about how to prepare good meals for their little ones. Especially on teeny-tiny budgets."

"I don't know that I could do another class like that every week."

"Oh, I didn't mean every week. Once a month would be awesome. Or even once every quarter. We could do it in the church kitchen. The program provides child care, so the moms would be free to really pay attention."

A brief tug of war took place in Holly's heart. She loved the lessons she gave on Monday mornings at the restaurant. Those weekly sessions had saved her from giving in to despair. Perhaps she would feel the same way about helping with the MOPS gals. But adding one more thing to her schedule felt impossible.

"Don't answer me now," Kelly said. "Pray about it and let me know. You've got my number."

"Okay. I will."

Kelly's gaze shifted, and her expression said she'd seen someone else she wanted to talk to. With a tiny wave, she was off again.

A few moments later, bulletin in hand, Holly stepped through the sanctuary doors. As the service hadn't started yet, many people were still standing, milling about, visiting with friends. She was greeted with smiles and waves as she slowly made her way toward her usual row of chairs.

Holly had made Covenant Fellowship her church home soon after buying the house on Jefferson Street. She'd visited several churches after her move to Boise, and all had made her welcome. Most had pastors who preached good sermons. But she'd known on her first Sunday at Covenant that this was where she belonged.

She was about to sit down when a man in the aisle up ahead turned. Jed Henning. Even though he'd told her he had family who attended Covenant, she hadn't expected to see him here. Maybe because he hadn't responded to Trixie's less than subtle suggestion.

He stepped toward her. "Morning, Holly."

"Good morning."

"I forgot to ask which service you attended, so I wasn't sure

I'd see you." He glanced around the sanctuary. "Big enough we could have missed each other."

She nodded.

"Let me introduce you to my family." He cupped his hand beneath her elbow and drew her several rows forward. Seeing her, two men rose to their feet, the older a man who looked to be in his seventies, the younger a man who appeared to be close to the same age as Jed.

"Grant, Ben, this is Holly Stanford. Holly, my cousin Ben Henning and his grandfather, Grant Henning."

Grant grinned. "Jed's landlady?"

"One and the same."

"I've seen you here before, haven't I?"

"Maybe." She glanced behind her. "Most Sundays I sit back there."

"Well, this is a pleasure. I can't believe Jed is living in that apartment, all of these years later, and here you and I go to the same church. What are the odds?"

"I'm sorry. The odds?" She looked from one man to the other.

"Didn't Jed tell you? My grandparents lived in your basement apartment as newlyweds. And now he's staying there."

Her gaze locked back on Jed. "No, he didn't tell me."

"Long story," he answered. "I'll tell you about it later."

Grant motioned to the row of chairs. "Join us. Please." The two men immediately moved two spaces to their left.

No one awaited her several rows back, and she decided that refusing the older man's request would be rude, so she nodded and took the open seat between Grant and Jed.

The worship band members began taking their places on the stage. At the same time, the lights in the sanctuary dimmed.

Voices throughout the large room faded as many scurried to their own seats. When the music began, Holly rose to her feet, singing. Beside her, Jed joined in. He had a good voice. A strong voice.

A wave of sadness swept over her, not completely unexpected. These same emotions had come and gone over the past year, although less frequently in recent months. Her throat tightened, catching the words in her throat. If she'd been alone, she would have slipped from the row of chairs and escaped to the restroom where she could take refuge in a stall, hidden away from prying eyes. Where she could have given in to the tears. But she wasn't alone. She couldn't leave without asking Jed to move out of her way, and for some reason, having him see that she was fighting tears seemed worse than staying where she was.

O God. O God. O God. Please.

She'd been doing much better. She'd been getting stronger with the passage of time. The feelings of betrayal and of distrust had lessened, slowly but surely. Or so she'd believed. She hadn't wept in church in months. Was it due to the growing stress over the restaurant, to the lack of money, to the constant decision making? Or was it because, even as she stood between these two men, she knew she had to face all her troubles on her own?

I hate this the most, God. I hate being weak. I hate being afraid. I hate not being in control of my emotions, of crying for no reason. That's not me. Or it didn't used to be. Don't let it be me. Change me, please.

Following the morning service, Jed accepted Grant's invitation out to lunch, but Ben wasn't able to join them. He had to pick up his fiancée at the airport. Holly would have been invited, too, but she'd hurried away at the end of the service, leaving Jed wondering if he'd said something wrong.

Once Jed and Grant were seated in a booth at a restaurant not far from the church, Jed asked, "How soon's Ben's wedding?"

"Late September. It's going to be a cowboy service. Bride and groom on horseback. Maybe the minister too. Lucky for me, the guests are allowed to sit in chairs if they so choose."

"I've heard of couples getting married while skydiving or scuba diving. Never pictured a wedding with horses."

"I'm told it isn't unheard of. I guess you can even buy horseback wedding packages in places like Vegas and the Smoky Mountains. Probably around these parts too." Grant chuckled. "This wedding will be far more casual than those specialty ones. Ben and Ashley are determined to keep the costs down."

"Will it be at the farm?"

"Yes. And we're praying the weather'll be good."

"I hope to see it for myself."

A waiter arrived with water and to take their orders. When they were alone again, Grant said, "Do you plan to still be in Boise in September?"

"I doubt it." Silently Jed added, *I hope not*. "But it's a quick flight from Tacoma, so that's not an issue. If I'm invited, I'll be there."

"Of course you're invited. Hopefully your folks and Chris will be here too." Grant took a sip from his water glass.

Uncertainty tightened Jed's chest for a few seconds. What should he say? *The truth,* his heart answered. "Grant, you know what's going on with my parents, don't you?"

The confused expression on his cousin's face told Jed that he didn't.

"They've separated."

Grant's eyes widened. "No," he whispered.

"Yes. A few months ago."

"I didn't know. No one's said a word about it."

"Dad's kept it quiet. He hopes he and Mom can reconcile."

"Do you think they can?"

Jed shook his head. "I don't know. I'm not sure what the trouble is. They fought a lot about Chris when he was still at home, but that was a while ago. Maybe they just grew apart. Maybe one of them—"

"Don't try to tell me more, son. It's their business. Not mine. I shouldn't have asked. But I'll pray for them."

Praying was more than Jed had done. About any of it. About his parents' marriage. About his brother. About work or his personal life, what there was of it. The knowledge shamed him. He called himself a Christian, but he hadn't been living as one. At least not in the way he wanted. He hadn't made church a priority in a long while. He hadn't read his Bible on a daily basis. He was making an effort to change that, and he hoped it would become more of a habit as time passed.

"Have you met Ashley yet?" Grant asked, obviously wanting a change of subject.

"No. Not yet. She wasn't at the farm the day I was there."

"You'll like her."

"I'm sure I will. One thing for sure, Ben loves her. It's written all over his face when he talks about her."

"Indeed." Grant took another sip of water. "Your landlady seems nice too."

Jed cocked an eyebrow, wondering at the abrupt change of subject. Was the older man trying to play the part of matchmaker?

That wouldn't be wise. Nonetheless, Jed had spent a pleasant time with Holly and her sister two days earlier. He couldn't contradict Grant's assessment. "She *is* nice."

"I hope you won't mind if I drop by the apartment sometime. I'd love a look at it myself. Who would have thought a descendant of Andrew and Helen Henning would be staying there almost a hundred years later?" Grant shook his head, chuckling softly.

"It's temporary, but yes, it is kind of a surprise that I've wound up there."

Over lunch their conversation shifted to other members of the family. Eventually Jed shared about the boxes he'd started to go through, and even without seeing the photographs and letters, Grant was able to answer some of the questions they'd stirred to life.

"One more reason for me to come by for a visit," the older man said. "If I'd known those boxes have been moldering in a garage all this time, I would have claimed them ages ago. How did your dad even find out about them?"

"Not sure, to be honest. I didn't ask."

Grant gave him a thoughtful look. "Perhaps watching his own family break apart, your father is in need of the comfort his roots can provide. Going through those old photos and letters may be just the balm he needs."

Jed's first instinct was to reject the notion, but then he wasn't feeling generous when it came to his dad. Jed would be back in Tacoma right now if his father hadn't demanded something be done about Chris and, as usual, given Jed the task of fixing things.

"Son, relationships can be messy. No marriage is easy all the time. Don't judge your parents too harshly. You can't know the whole picture. You don't have all the facts, no matter how much you might think you do."

Again, Jed wanted to argue. Again, he bit back the words.

"For everything, there is a season," Grant said softly.

The comment made Jed wonder about the season he was in. Was it just about finding his brother and trying to repair their relationship? Or was there more to it than that? He hoped God would help him figure it out soon.

Sunday, July 13, 1969

It was Andrew's first Sunday in church since his back troubles had begun. Getting into the church and to their regular pew was somewhat of an ordeal because so many friends and neighbors stopped him to ask how he was doing. He grew tired of answering, "Good. Good. Lots better." Grant must have sensed his grandfather's growing frustration, because he stepped in front of Andrew, shielding him from view, which allowed them to go the last few rows without interruption.

Andrew sighed as he sank onto the pew. Normally he liked to sit on the center aisle. This time he let his grandson have that position. It might prevent more questions about his health. Besides, this way he had a beautiful girl on each side of him, Charlotte on his left and Helen on his right.

He stayed seated for the opening hymn, but only because Helen told him he must. He knew it was for the best. Getting up and down was the trickiest part of his ailment. Still, sitting while singing praises to God felt wrong. He preferred to feel fully engaged in the hymns, and that required standing.

Peter Atwater, an elder in the church, rose and went to stand in the pulpit. "The reading today is from Psalm 71."

Andrew looked down at the Bible on his lap. It was getting old, like he was. The cover was worn and comfortable after forty years of use. Forty years. How was that possible? He opened it, quickly finding the Psalms.

"In thee, O Lord, do I put my trust: let me never be put to confusion. Deliver me in thy righteousness, and cause me to escape: incline thine ear unto me, and save me. Be thou my strong habitation, whereunto I may continually resort."

With a finger under the text, Andrew followed along, letting the words speak to his heart as only the Word of God could. He felt himself putting his trust in the Lord once again. He sensed God inclining His ear. How wonderful to understand that he dwelled in the strong habitation of Christ forever and ever. His body might weaken. It might fail him. But the Lord wouldn't.

"My praise shall be continually of thee. I am as a wonder unto many; but thou art my strong refuge. Let my mouth be filled with thy praise and with thy honour all the day. Cast me not off in the time of old age; Forsake me not when my strength faileth."

While Peter read on, Andrew stopped and stared at the ninth verse. He had learned long ago that God's Word was living and active. It was able to speak into a man's heart in a supernatural way. It wasn't an audible voice that told Andrew God wasn't finished with him. He didn't hear actual words assuring him that he wasn't being cast off or forsaken in his old age and failing strength. And yet he knew the truth of it all the same. Knew it in that secret place deep in his soul. Even if Andrew was never strong again, even if he had to admit to being old, God wasn't finished with him. Not yet. As long as Andrew drew breath, God had a plan and a purpose for him.

Father, help me see what that plan and purpose is.

With that silent prayer, he pulled his attention back to the service.

An hour later, the final strains of the last hymn repeating in his heart, Andrew left the church with his family. They received two invitations to dine with other families, but he declined them both. He was fully aware that Grant and Charlotte wanted time together, just the two of them, which they wouldn't have if they were guests in someone else's house.

In the Jeep, Charlotte leaned forward, placing a hand on Andrew's left shoulder. "Thanks for letting us go straight home."

Andrew reached across his chest with his right arm and placed his hand over Charlotte's. He didn't say anything. No response was required.

Helen started the Jeep. "Besides, we have a fine roast waiting for us. It should be perfect by the time we get there."

Much later, after Sunday dinner had been eaten and the dishes washed and put away, Andrew and Helen sat on the front porch while Grant and Charlotte strolled over to the pasture fence where they watched the horses. Every so often, one of them leaned close to the other for a kiss.

"Did you hear her call the farm home?" Andrew asked, his gaze on his grandson and his fiancée.

"Mmm."

"Grant loves the place."

"Mmm."

"He would buy it if he had the money."

"I'm sorry, dear. What did you say?"

He turned his head to look at his wife. There was an idea stirring inside of him, one that hadn't taken complete form. He would have to wait until it did before he said more. "Nothing important. I've been thinking about the future. That's all."

Helen's eyebrows rose in question.

He decided to change the subject. "Grant's got himself a fine girl in Charlotte."

Her face softened. "He certainly does." She looked toward the young couple. "I hope they'll be as happy as we've been."

"They'll have their ups and downs."

She took hold of his hand. "But I pray they'll have more ups. Charlotte will do better than I did. She won't make foolish choices."

Andrew saw the flicker of sorrow cross Helen's face. He knew she was remembering the darkest time of their marriage. The premature birth and loss of their first child. The depression that overwhelmed her in the weeks that followed. Her eventual involvement with another man. Her plans to leave Andrew, and the despair that followed when the affair ended. By God's grace Andrew and Helen had come through that time. Their marriage had survived and eventually flourished. They'd both received God's forgiveness. And yet Andrew was aware there were moments, like now, when shame pierced Helen's heart.

He squeezed her hand, hoping to let her know, without words, that he saw her feelings, that he understood them, and that he loved her.

His gaze returned to the couple standing by the fence. They were young and in love, and the world seemed a wonderful place. The future seemed bright. But life was often difficult. It was true for every person, every couple, every generation. Andrew's generation had been challenged by the Great Depression and World War II. Grant's generation now faced the war in Vietnam and the temptations of LSD, marijuana, and other drugs, not to mention what had been labeled the "sexual revolution" or even "free love."

Oh, how foolish people could be at times. Love wasn't free. It came at a cost. Real love required sacrifice. He and Helen had experienced that. Charlotte and Grant would have to experience it, too, sooner or later. Their problems might be different from Andrew's and Helen's, but they would have to face them all the same.

"Where did you go?" Helen asked softly.

He looked at her again. "Nowhere." He squeezed her hand a second time. "I'm right where I'm supposed to be."

Chapter 7

Holly loved the quiet of the restaurant kitchen early in the morning. Sweet Caroline's didn't open until eleven, which meant she and the women from Lighthouse who took her cooking classes had until ten each Monday before they had to be out of the way for the kitchen staff to begin preparing for the day.

After hanging up her jacket, Holly tied on an apron. This morning they were going to bake fish and make tartar sauce from scratch, a healthier option than frozen fish sticks purchased at the grocery store.

Moving comfortably around the large room, she assembled all of the ingredients, save for what needed to be refrigerated. As she prepared, she prayed for the young women who would walk through the back door. She rarely had the same small group in consecutive weeks. Often they were a mix of familiar faces and newcomers. Most of the young women she'd worked with over the past months were still girls, really, although many also had a child, sometimes two. Too many had escaped abusive relationships. Frequently the stories she heard from them brought tears to her eyes. Their stories also made her grateful for the family she'd been blessed with. They made her realize that her own problems, no matter how large they seemed, were small by comparison. Even being jilted was better than what some had endured. Holding these classes had saved her, in many ways, from her own heartbreak.

She heard muffled voices coming from outside moments before the rear door opened and three young women entered. For a change, she recognized all of them. "Good morning." She smiled, truly glad to see them.

Adele Turner, a nineteen-year-old with dark hair and enormous brown eyes, was the only one who didn't return Holly's smile. Adele rarely smiled—and when she did, she hid it behind a cupped hand. Her ex-boyfriend's fist had broken off several of her front teeth. That had been the night she'd escaped with the clothes on her back and little else. Now she was waiting for the aid money that would allow her to get dentures.

Madalyn Hargrove, at twenty-seven, was the oldest of the three. Her husband was in prison for something to do with drugs. She and her two children had lived in their car for a number of months before they landed at the women's shelter. Madalyn worked as a maid at a local motel, but she hoped to become a good enough cook that she might work in a restaurant and be able to support her son and daughter on her own.

The last girl was Willow Flynn. Willow was tall and rail thin, looking as if a strong gust of wind would blow her over. Straight blonde hair, worn past her shoulders, framed a delicate face. She was twenty years old and the mother of a two-year-old son. She'd never mentioned the boy's father during her cooking sessions with Holly. Then again, she rarely offered information without someone prying it out of her.

"What are we making today?" Adele asked as she washed her hands.

"Baked fish."

"What kind of fish?" Madalyn asked.

"Tilapia."

Adele wrinkled her nose. "That's a weird name. Is it any good?"

"It's good. I promise."

The three young women formed a semicircle on the opposite side of the worktable from Holly, who began to talk about ingredients. She'd learned to take nothing for granted in these cooking sessions. What she thought was simple and self-explanatory—especially since Holly had started helping her mom in the kitchen when she was six—wasn't so simple for many of the women who attended the classes.

Before long they were cutting the fillets into smaller pieces, crushing cornflakes, dipping the fish in the flour-and-egg mixture followed by the coating of cornflakes. Then onto the baking sheets and into the oven the fish went. While it baked, Holly showed the women how to make the tartar sauce.

"The best part is," she said when the fish were out of the oven, "a four-ounce portion of this fish with two tablespoons of the sauce we made is still less than three hundred calories. It's high in protein too. And even little kids will like it."

Madalyn was the first to take a bite. Her expression was dubious as she lifted the fork to her mouth, but after a moment she nodded. "This *is* good."

The other two women tried the food. They quickly agreed with Madalyn, and pleasure washed over Holly as she watched them finish eating the fish on their plates.

Soon after, the back door opened, and Zachary came inside.

Holly checked her watch. "Are we running late?"

"No. I'm early."

"We'll be cleaned up and out of your way in a bit."

"No worries." Zachary reached for an apron. "In fact, let me give you a hand."

~

Jed tried to remember another time in his life—other than summers when he was a kid—when he hadn't been focused on either school studies or work. Being in Boise, outside of an office environment, made him antsy. His most pressing task at present was to work things out with his brother, and that couldn't begin until the two of them were able to talk. Over the past three days, Jed had placed several more calls to Chris, but so far there'd been no answer, and his messages had been ignored.

Tired of staring at the four walls of the apartment, he drove into town, then walked around awhile, finally entering a bistro where he ordered a Coke. Now he twirled the straw in the soda glass, wondering if he should try to call Chris one more time. Would trying make the situation better or worse?

Music played from speakers in the ceiling, the tune vaguely familiar. It was a rap song. Chris liked rap. He'd played it all the time when the brothers still lived at home.

"Chris!" Jed banged on his brother's door. "Turn that down. I'm trying to study."

He heard no response, and that made him angry. He was a couple of weeks away from his senior-year final exams. He needed to focus. How could he do that with Chris's stupid music making the entire house throb?

"Chris! Turn it down, or I'll do it for you."

The door flew open, revealing his kid brother. "Can't you leave me alone?"

At another time, Jed might have found the question funny. After all, for most of the past ten years, all Chris had wanted was to tag along with Jed everywhere. He'd been the definition of a pest. And now Chris was the one wanting Jed to leave him alone?

"I need to study. Turn the music down, will you? It makes my whole room shake."

Chris raked his long hair back from his face. "All right. Keep your shirt on."

Jed glowered at his brother before turning away. By the time he reached his bedroom door, the volume had been lowered. No doubt Chris was back in front of his computer screen, playing some stupid video game instead of doing his own homework. If he wasn't careful, he would end up having to repeat a grade.

But that wasn't Jed's problem. In a few short weeks, he would be living in a house with a bunch of friends, all of them headed for the university. He wouldn't have to worry about what his kid brother was up to. He wouldn't know when Chris had another fight with their parents. Not that Jed would have to be told about the fights. All those three did was fight lately. It seemed to Jed that Chris was spoiling for trouble all the time. If it was up to Chris, he would stay in his room, wearing a grubby T-shirt and jeans and sneakers, and play games until he passed out on the floor from exhaustion.

Jed sank onto the chair at the desk in his room and stared down at the textbook. But for just a moment he remembered what Chris used to be like—the chubby-cheeked little guy who idolized his big brother. Sometimes he missed that kid. He really did.

Half an hour later, Jed pulled the rental car into the garage behind Holly's house. Leaving through the garage's side door, he noticed the hinges on it were loose. The entire door wobbled when he opened it. A closer look revealed that a number of the screws needed tightening. An easy enough fix. He looked around the garage for some tools and found a few items in a battered toolbox: a hammer, a wrench, a jar of nails and another jar of screws, and two screwdrivers, one of them a Phillips. The Phillips-head screwdriver was all he needed.

He was tightening the last screw on the bottom hinge when Holly pulled her car into the garage. He straightened and waited as she got out.

"Is something wrong?"

He held up the screwdriver. "Not anymore."

Her gaze shifted to the door. "You fixed it?"

"Sure. Didn't take much."

"Thanks. I've been meaning to do that for months." She shrugged. "But then I forget it as soon as I go inside."

He offered a brief smile.

She opened the hatch of her SUV, then stood there, staring inside. Jed had the feeling she was trying to talk herself into something. Or maybe out of it.

The feeling increased when she glanced in his direction.

Finally, she retrieved two canvas bags. "Have you eaten?"

"No."

"Do you like tilapia?"

"Sure. I guess."

"I have leftovers from my class this morning. Would you care to have some?"

Jed liked fish well enough, but it was Holly's company that enticed him. Normally he preferred his own company. He was good with solitude. It allowed him to think, to make plans. But right now he'd rather be distracted. "I'd like that. Thanks." He reached to take the bags from her hands.

Together they followed the walkway to the side of the house. Holly climbed the few steps ahead of him and opened the door to the house. Jed followed her inside, setting the bags on the kitchen island.

"Leftovers from a class," he said. "What class is that?"

"I instruct women from one of the local shelters on how to cook healthy foods for their families. We cover lots of different things, but that's the main focus."

Jed took a seat on a kitchen stool. "How'd you get involved in that?"

Holly paused, pressing her palms against the counter as she looked at him. "It's a long story. I went through a bad patch a year ago. A failed relationship that left me . . . sad." She was silent a moment before continuing, "I was about to reopen Sweet Caroline's when things . . . fell apart. Everything about opening the restaurant was harder than I'd expected."

"I know what it's like to get a business up and running." Something in her expression made him wonder if he understood as much as he thought he did.

She drew a deep breath. "I'm not sure what would have happened if I hadn't been asked to give these lessons. Maybe I would've drowned in a sea of self-pity. Or maybe I would have gotten lost in anger and bitterness. All I know is it helped me to have others to think about for a few hours each week. Mondays have been a good reminder of how blessed I am."

"Or maybe I would have gotten lost in anger and bitterness." He'd been angry and bitter because of Chris, and if he was honest, he'd felt sorry for himself too. He'd wanted his brother to be punished, and instead Jed stood to lose his business if he couldn't get Chris to meet with him. Their dad had placed all of the responsibility on Jed's shoulders. It seemed unfair. Jed had studied hard. He'd worked hard. But his brother was getting off scot-free. Or so it seemed.

"Mondays have been a good reminder of how blessed I am." Holly's words echoing in his mind made him feel ashamed. If his world came crashing down around his ears, even if he lost Laffriot and had to start over, he was still blessed. He had a large and loving family. He had a home and food. Maybe he needed to get over himself.

"Are you okay?" Holly asked softly.

"Sorry." He met her gaze. "Yeah. I'm okay. Just thinking."

She nodded. "Why don't you set the table while I whip up our dinner?" She pointed. "You'll find everything you need in those two cupboards, and that's the silverware drawer." She indicated the drawer with another motion of her hand. "Then you can tell me about your ancestors who used to live in my basement. I've been dying of curiosity ever since I heard about the connection."

Jed was thankful she hadn't asked what he'd been thinking. He would much rather tell her about the letter that had brought him to this address, ending with him as her renter. He knew that story had a good ending. He wasn't so sure about the one involving him and Chris.

Sunday, July 20, 1969

Along with much of the world, Andrew and Helen listened when Neil Armstrong's voice came across the airwaves, saying, "The *Eagle* has landed."

Helen shook her head. "I never thought we would actually make it there."

Andrew had to agree. When President Kennedy had set the goal of Americans going to the moon in that decade, he'd thought it an impossible dream. But why? In Andrew's lifetime, horse-drawn vehicles had been replaced by automobiles, travel in airplanes had become commonplace, and polio had been all but eliminated. Why hadn't he believed man could make it to the moon? Then he wondered what else he would see if he lived another twenty or even thirty years. He pictured his older grandchildren. In some ways, it was hard to believe their generation, with its unisex attire, long hair, and a desire to tune in and drop out—whatever that meant—would accomplish anything of consequence. So what would they see in their lifetimes in a world that often seemed to be going to the devil in a handbasket?

Drawing his Bible from the nearby shelf, he closed his eyes and began to pray for all eight of his grandchildren—from the oldest at twenty-four to the youngest at only one year of age—asking the Father to draw each one of them to Jesus. *Keep them close to You, Lord. Keep them close.*

Six and a half hours later, Grant joined his grandparents in the living room to witness Armstrong leave the lunar module for the first time. The television transmission was grainy, the audio crackly, as the astronaut descended the ladder. They all held their breaths until Armstrong's large white boot touched the moon's surface. "That's one small step for man, one giant leap for mankind."

"Wow," Grant uttered.

"Amen," Andrew responded.

The two men looked at each other, grinning.

"If it weren't for my bad back," Andrew said, "I'd get up and do a jig."

Helen shot him a frown. "Don't you do anything so foolish." But the smile that appeared in the corners of her mouth removed any strength from the warning.

"Don't worry, my girl. I haven't lost complete use of my faculties."

Although the moonwalk continued, the poor quality of the transmission made it easy for Andrew's attention to wander. He brought up a few matters concerning the farm with Grant while Helen went to the kitchen to do some final tidying up. A short while later, the older couple left their grandson to finish watching the momentous occasion on the television while they retired for the night. A lifetime habit of "early to bed, early to rise" was hard to break. It didn't matter if it was daylight until ten o'clock at this time of year. He and Helen were ready to turn in well before then.

Even moving slowly for the sake of his back, it wasn't long before his teeth were brushed and he was clad in his cotton pajamas. He slid between the sheets on the bed, bid his wife goodnight with a kiss on her cheek, and turned off the bedside lamp. A soft sigh escaped him as he turned onto his side. Then he said his silent goodnight to God, as was also his habit.

Lord, it was a miraculous day for the astronauts, and it was a good day for the Hennings too. Thanks for seeing us through it. Thanks for another day to try to serve my own generation by Your will. I don't feel as able as I've felt in the past, so help me do whatever I can without complaint. I'm trying not to be impatient with the process. I'm trying to wait on You as You would have me. But sometimes I feel useless. Grant has taken on so much while I must sit on the porch. So, if it be Your will, please heal my back. But no matter what, thanks again for this good day. Amen.

Chapter 8

Seated on the living room sofa, Trixie fixed Holly with her gaze. "Holly Stanford, you *like* him."

Holly shrugged, pretending the comment meant nothing to her, but she definitely regretted telling her sister that Jed had fixed her garage door, let alone about the dinner she'd shared with him afterward.

"Don't try to fool me or yourself. You *really* like him."

"Jed Henning is a nice man. You know that from the night you met him. And yes, he's attractive. I can't deny it. But I hardly know him, and I'm not likely to get to know him better. He won't be here that long. He's going back to Washington."

"No." Trixie shook her head. "You're interested in him."

Holly blew out a breath. "I'm not, Trix. I'm too busy with the restaurant and trying to keep my head above water. I don't want to be involved with anybody. I've been down that road and it didn't work. I don't—" She stopped the confession from leaving her mouth, but finished silently, *I don't trust myself. I don't trust my judgment.*

"You know, sis. There are more ways to fix a broken heart besides working until you drop. You can't swear off all relationships because Nathan was a bad egg." Trixie twisted a strand of hair. "And there is something to be said for that pull of attraction, even before you know a guy well. When I met Brett, everything inside of me went *zing*!"

"Good for you. I'm glad you felt that way about him. But you and I are different." She spoke firmly, leaving no doubt that she wanted to put an end to the subject. It brought up too many bad memories. She didn't want a repeat of last Sunday, the sadness, the threat of tears. She might risk being friendly with a man, with someone like Jed. But she wouldn't risk her heart again, no matter how nice he was.

With determination, she picked up another bridal magazine from the coffee table and opened it. "What do you think about this dress?" She pointed to the first one, not caring what it looked like.

Trixie wouldn't be so easily distracted. "I remember, you know."

"Remember what?"

"How devastated you were."

Holly stiffened.

"I was here. I stayed with you for several weeks after Nathan broke things off. Remember? You cried yourself to sleep every night. It didn't matter how much you tried to muffle the sound in your pillow. I could still hear you through the bedroom wall."

"What has that to do with anything? I'm over it. I'm long over Nathan."

"Not completely. He's the reason you've closed yourself off. You've locked up your emotions. It's like you've given up on the possibility of a real relationship. Given up on finding a real love.

It's as if you don't think you can have it or maybe that you think you don't deserve it. But you do deserve it. It was Nathan who didn't deserve you."

Holly stood, fearing her sister's words might shatter her resolve. "This conversation has gotten out of control." She walked into the kitchen where she filled a glass with water and stood near the refrigerator, drinking it.

"Sis, I love you. That's all." Trixie now stood in the archway between living room and kitchen.

Holly put the glass on the counter. "I know you do."

"I'll try not to interfere anymore."

Holly's smile was bittersweet. She shook her head, knowing Trixie might try but she would never succeed. Her younger sister was, by nature, the one who wanted to be certain that everyone was as happy as she was, even if she was clueless about how to make it happen. "Come on, Trix. Let's get back to those magazines. There's a lot to get done."

The look in Trixie's eyes said she knew she'd been forgiven. But, as if to be sure, she crossed the kitchen to give Holly a tight hug.

Jed stared at the short list of names on the screen of his laptop—names of his brother's friends, people he thought Chris might trust with his whereabouts. Most of them, however, had been high school buddies. He wasn't sure how many Chris had remained in touch with in the years since leaving school.

"We're strangers, Chris and me," he whispered, leaning back in his chair.

How much of the drifting apart was his fault? Could he have been more patient? Could he have said something or done something to straighten out his younger brother before it got this bad between them?

Or maybe he'd said too much. Maybe he'd butted in when he shouldn't have.

He released a breath of frustration. Waste made him angry, and Chris had done nothing but waste his life and his talent. He was smart. Way smarter than he let on. He knew computers forward and backward. And his imagination. Whew. With or without all the Red Bull he chugged, Chris was always creating something new in his head. His mind raced at a hundred miles an hour. But he never would have done anything about any of that genius without Jed. It was Jed who'd harnessed Chris's creativity and actually done something with it. Without Jed, *Caliban* would be nothing but an idea among dozens of others on his brother's computer.

And where was his thanks for that?

"Get things right with your brother," his dad's voice echoed in his memory. *"And I don't mean simply getting him back to work. I mean what's wrong between you two personally."*

Jed rose and began pacing the small living room. How was he supposed to fix something he didn't understand? He didn't know what was wrong between him and Chris, beyond that they were two entirely different personalities. How was he supposed to fix that? He was who he was, and Chris was who he was. Had their dad given that truth any consideration? Apparently not. Maybe he should tell his dad to go ahead and shut Laffriot down. Maybe he should—

His train of thought was broken by the ring of his phone.

Seeing the call was from his cousin, he answered it, glad for any distraction.

"Hey, Ben."

"Hi, Jed. Have I interrupted anything?"

"Nothing important." He walked to the sofa and sat. "What's up?"

"Ashley wants to have you out to the farm for dinner on Saturday. Can you make it?"

"Sure. What time?"

"Come about three so I can show you around since we didn't have time for that when you were out last. We'll plan to eat about six or six thirty."

"Okay. Sounds good to me."

"Hey, why don't you bring Holly? Ashley'd like to get to know her since the three of us go to the same church."

Jed hesitated. The truth was he'd like to spend more time in Holly's company. He'd thought about asking her out to dinner, but he knew it wasn't a good idea. She'd been hurt by somebody. A failed relationship that had left her sad, she'd said. He suspected that her sadness ran deeper than she wanted to let on. Probably not a good idea to form any sort of relationship with her. Last thing he wanted was to be the rebound guy. Besides, he didn't have a great track record when it came to dating. He'd been called a bona fide workaholic by an old girlfriend, and the last woman he'd taken out had compared him to a character in some movie, saying that his idea of a long-term relationship was giving his date time enough to order dessert.

"It was Ashley's idea," Ben added, drawing Jed's attention to the present. "She's new enough at Covenant that she's still making friends."

"All right. I'll ask Holly. I'll let her know it isn't a date. Just getting to know more people from the church."

"Sure. Whatever you say. And so you know, dinner won't be anything fancy. Ashley's all about what's easiest when it comes to cooking. Both of us would rather be out with the horses than messing around in the kitchen."

Jed decided to keep quiet about Holly's cooking skills. He wouldn't want Ashley to be intimidated. "Whatever it is, it'll be fine with me."

Ben asked if there was any news of Chris, and Jed told him they'd talked for a minute but that was all. He still didn't know where his brother was or what his plans were.

After they ended the call, Jed checked the time as he set down the phone. Seven o'clock. Holly should be done eating her dinner by now. Should he call her or go to her back door? Back door, he decided. It would be better to ask her face-to-face. Especially since he wanted her to know this was dinner with her tenant and a couple of soon-to-be friends. Nothing more.

He frowned. Would it be so awful if it *was* a date? Holly was the most appealing woman he'd met in a long while, and right now nobody could call him a workaholic. Would it be so terrible to enjoy time with a beautiful woman? Then again, Jed wasn't a catch-and-release kind of guy. He was in Boise temporarily, and five hundred miles separated this city from Tacoma. Once he found Chris, life would go back to normal. He'd be putting in long hours again.

So that was that. Friendship was the only option.

Decision made, he headed out of his apartment and up to the back door of the main house. He drew a quick breath and knocked. It wasn't a long wait before Holly opened the door.

"Hope I'm not disturbing you," he said.

"Is your power out again?"

He shook his head. "No."

Her brows raised slightly as she waited for him to say more.

"Come in, Jed," came Trixie's voice—he recognized it at once—from inside the house. "Don't just stand there on the steps."

A smile touched the corners of Holly's mouth, then was gone. So fast, he wasn't sure it had been there. "Yes, please come in." She turned and walked away, leaving the door open.

He waited a moment, then followed her inside.

Trixie stood in the kitchen, leaning a hip against the center island. "It's great to see you." She made it sound as if it had been years instead of six days.

"Thanks. You too. How are the wedding plans?"

"That's why I'm here. Holly and I were going over wedding cake ideas and looking at all the bride magazines I could find."

Jed took a half step back. "Sounds like I'm intruding after all."

"No, you're not. We're done. I was about to head home." Trixie tipped her head slightly to one side.

Jed had the sudden feeling that he was being measured, studied, put under a microscope. Not a comfortable sensation.

Trixie turned her gaze on Holly. "Don't forget what I said earlier." Then she grabbed a stack of magazines from a table near the door and let herself out.

Holly released an audible breath. "Our mom says everybody's left winded in Trixie's wake. And it's true."

"I believe it."

She smiled again. "She's so happy she's contagious."

"Lucky girl."

"Yes." Her smile faded. "Yes, she is a lucky girl."

Her wistful tone caused his chest to tighten. It made him want to bring the smile back. "I came to ask if you'd like to join me for dinner on Saturday at Ben's farm. Ashley, his fiancée, will be there, and she's cooking dinner. Ben hoped we could make it a foursome, especially since the three of you attend the same church. And me, too, while I'm in Boise."

"I don't know." She gave her head a slow shake. "I've got so many things to do. I should get caught up on my bookkeeping, and I—"

"You'd be doing me a favor," he interrupted. "Seriously. I'll feel like the odd man out if I'm there with only the two of them. They're like your sister. Up to their ears in wedding plans."

He watched as she considered the invitation. One thing that made him good at his job was his ability to read people. What he saw in Holly's expression was trepidation, maybe even distrust. It seemed she was going to decline his invitation. But a look of resolve entered her eyes. Her mouth firmed. Then she nodded. "All right. It sounds nice. I'll go with you. What time?"

"We'll plan to leave here about two twenty."

"I'll be ready."

Monday, July 21, 1969

After the excitement of the moon landing, the following day seemed uneventful. That morning, Grant drove into Boise for his day job as usual, and after lunch Helen baked a raspberry pie. Knowing her husband well, she warned him not to sneak a slice before dinner.

Now, as the afternoon waned, the two of them sat in the living room, Andrew with the folded newspaper on his lap, still unread, while Helen knitted something. A fan hummed in the corner of the room where it sat, summer after summer, faithfully moving the air.

"I think we should have Grant buy us one of those coolers that go in the window."

His wife looked up. "Really?"

"Mmm."

"Seems an expense we don't need. We've gotten by with fans right enough all these years."

As a young man, Andrew had promised Helen the world. He'd promised her travel to foreign places. He'd planned to give her a large home in the city, complete with a servant or two. But their lives hadn't turned out that way. While he'd found contentment on the farm—much to his own surprise—he'd feared the same wouldn't be true for his wife. He'd feared she wouldn't be content with the life or with him. And for a time, his fears had been justified. She'd lost her way, and he'd nearly lost her forever. But somehow, miraculously, she'd learned to love him again, to love the life they shared.

I'm blessed.

He looked down and unfolded the newspaper. Usually he read the paper first thing in the morning, but the headlines had been all about the *Eagle* landing and the astronauts walking on the moon. Since he'd seen all that for himself the previous night, he'd decided the paper could wait.

He scanned the articles on the first page, then moved inside. After a few moments he said, "That's not good."

"What, dear?"

"It says here that consumer prices have risen 6.4 percent since the beginning of the year. The worst since '51. Probably couldn't afford that cooler for the window anyway."

Helen didn't answer him.

He read a few more lines before a strange unease caused him to lower his paper. Helen sat with the knitting gone still in her lap. She wore an odd expression, one he couldn't describe. He spoke her name, but she didn't meet his gaze, didn't move. She sat still, eyes unfocused.

"Helen?" He put the paper aside. "What is it?"

At last she spoke, but the words made no sense to him. It was as if she spoke another language.

He got up from the chair. Ignoring the stab of pain in his back, he went to her, placing a hand on her shoulder. Up close, he finally understood why her expression looked odd. The left side of her face drooped.

"Oh, God," he whispered, heart hammering. "Help her."

He turned away and went to the telephone to call for an ambulance. It seemed both forever and no time at all before he was able to return to her. By the time he did, the droop in her face had lessened some. Focus had returned to her eyes.

"An ambulance is on its way," he told her, once again placing his hand on her shoulder.

"I . . . I don't need an ambulance."

Realizing his knees felt weak, he sat on the sofa beside her. "They're coming anyway."

"I felt odd, but whatever it was, it's gone." She looked at her left hand, raising it a few inches and lowering it again to her lap. "Really, Andrew. I'm all right."

"Just stay put."

"Don't make a fuss."

She looked normal. She sounded normal. She talked clearly. Maybe he'd imagined the distress she'd been in minutes before.

No. He hadn't imagined it. Something had been very wrong, and he needed to know what.

Chapter 9

Jed called his mom on Saturday morning, as he'd done the previous three Saturdays since arriving in Boise.

After the usual words of greeting, she said, "I talked to your dad earlier. He planned to go out on the sailboat this afternoon, but it's raining cats and dogs, so he won't be going. You should call him."

"Yeah." He felt a sting of guilt, especially after his conversation with Grant the previous Sunday. "I should. I'll do that next."

"Good."

"It's beautiful here. Lots of sunshine. It's supposed to hit close to seventy degrees this afternoon." He rose from the sofa and went to the door, opening it to the pleasant weather he'd told her about.

"Spring in Boise was always lovely."

"Are you ever sorry you and Dad moved?"

"No. Except for being farther away from our families. That's the only thing I ever minded."

"I'm going out to Ben's place later today. He's going to show me his equine therapy operation. I didn't get a chance to look around last time I was there."

"Has the farm changed a lot?"

"Judging by the photos I've been going through from the thirties and forties, the house is pretty much the same and the barn too. But there are some new outbuildings and pastures where crops used to be."

"Do you remember going out there with Ben when you were kids?"

"A little. Mostly I remember that one horse we both liked to ride."

"Yes. I remember him too. I think his name was Rover."

Jed closed the door and leaned his back against it. "Ben's fiancée's going to fix us dinner. This will be my first chance to meet her."

"I'm glad you're getting to spend time with Ben while you're there." There was a small catch in her voice.

He understood why, of course. She was thinking about Chris. "I haven't talked to him again, but I've tried plenty. He's back to not taking my calls."

"I thought that by now—" She broke off suddenly.

He didn't hear his mom's tears through the phone, but he felt them in his chest. He would gladly strangle his brother if he could find him. It was one thing for Chris to leave Jed and Laffriot in the lurch. Hurting their mom this way was unforgivable. It didn't matter so much that Chris cut himself off from Jed, but doing the same to their mom was another. "I'll find out where he is, Mom. I'll make sure he lets you know he's okay." He hoped he was telling the truth.

"Thanks, honey. I . . . I'd better get off the phone."

"Sure."

"Take care of yourself. I love you. Give my love to Ben and his Ashley."

"I will. Love you too. Talk to you next week."

As soon as the call ended, he punched his brother's name and listened to the phone ring. It went to voice mail as usual. "Listen, Chris. Stop being such a selfish—" He stopped himself before he called his brother something he shouldn't. Taking a breath, he continued, "Call Mom. It's killing her, not knowing where you are or what's happening to you. I just got off the phone with her, and she was crying. Be mad at me all you want, but she doesn't deserve this." He took the phone away from his ear, prepared to hit End, then pulled it back. "Man up, bro, and meet with me. This has gone on long enough."

He returned to the sofa and sat on it, anger tightening his gut. Words he'd wanted to say to his brother, names he'd wanted to call him, roiled in his head. Hateful words. Punishing words. Accusing words. But as he sat there, other words drifted into his head from the past.

"You're being too hard on him, Thomas." Jed's mom looked at his dad, pleading in her eyes. "Chris isn't like you."

"He should be if he wants to get anywhere in this world."

Jed took a step back into the hallway. He didn't want to end up in the middle of his parents' latest argument about his kid brother. It seemed like all they did was fight about Chris. Good thing it wouldn't be much longer before Jed was gone from home and he didn't have to hear it anymore.

"And if I'm too hard on him," his dad continued, "then you're too easy. You've coddled him, Gloria."

"I haven't. I've respected his personality."

Jed turned and headed toward the back door. He had a date, and he didn't want to be late. Emily Granger might just be the prettiest girl at the high school. He couldn't believe he hadn't noticed her until last week. Sure, she was a couple of grades behind him, but sophomores and seniors shared the same hallways. He must've been sleepwalking through them not to have seen her before almost the end of the term.

He stepped outside, closing the door quietly behind him. He turned to see Chris sitting on the back steps, a cigarette in hand. "You trying to get grounded?"

His brother took a drag, then snubbed the butt of the cigarette on the step before tossing it out into the lawn. "You off on your date?"

"Yeah."

"With Emily Granger."

"Yeah. How'd you know?"

"Word gets around." Chris stood, shoving his fingers in his back pockets as soon as he was up. "How'd you meet her?"

Jed shrugged. "Usual way. Walked up and introduced myself."

An odd expression crossed Chris's face. Not belligerent, as was most often the case. No, more sad or disappointed or . . . or lost. For a second, something caught in Jed's chest. Should he ask Chris what was wrong? No. He didn't have time for that.

His anger cooled by the memory of that long-ago evening, Jed lowered his gaze to the items on the coffee table. After a while, he picked up Andrew Henning's Bible. He'd been reading a chapter or two a day from it, always pausing when he came to an underline or a note or a date in the margin. Sometimes he could tell why Andrew had selected a specific verse. Often he couldn't know, only guess. On occasion, a word in the margin would make no sense to him at all. One thing that did make sense? This Bible had been personal and meaningful to his great-grandfather. Now it had begun to feel personal and meaningful to him too. In fact, holding it made him ashamed of what he'd wanted to say to his brother only minutes before.

Opening the Holy Book, he returned to a chapter he'd read earlier in the week, the one in Luke about the prodigal son. In the margin, Andrew had written two names, along with a few brief words of prayer: *Bring the prodigal home to You, Lord.* The first name was Oscar. Jed knew that had been Andrew's middle child, the one who'd died in the closing days of World War II. The second was Ben's mom's name. Jed didn't know Wendy Henning's entire history, but he knew she'd never married and had remained estranged from most of the family, even to this day. Apparently, Andrew had prayed for his great-granddaughter the same way he'd prayed for his son.

Jed took a moment to reread the words of Jesus as He told the story of the two sons. When done, he closed his eyes and asked God's forgiveness. Too often he'd been self-righteous when it came to Chris—and to his dad—and he regretted it. He wanted that to change. "Bring the prodigal home to You, Jesus," he whispered as he opened his eyes again. Then he picked up a nearby pen and wrote Chris's name in the margin of the Bible, right beneath the other two names. Afterward, he set the Bible aside, grabbed his phone, and punched his dad's name in his Favorites directory.

Holly was ready—more than ready, if she was honest with herself—by the time Jed knocked on her back door. On her way to answer it, she grabbed her purse and sweater. It was warm enough outside right now, but spring in Idaho guaranteed that the temperature would cool off quickly come evening.

Jed grinned when he saw her, and she felt a wonderful-terrible flutter in her stomach at the sight of him. He wore jeans and a snug black T-shirt and had a jacket slung over his shoulder, hooked on the index finger of his left hand. He could have been posing for an ad in a magazine. He was that handsome.

For several good, sound, logical reasons, she knew it wasn't wise to let herself feel anything for Jed. Friendship at the absolute most. Even that came with risks. Feeling more than that was a guaranteed doorway to pain. However, Trixie was right. She had closed herself off from life. She didn't want to give in to fear. She'd done too much of that over the last year. Jed seemed a nice man, and he was only in Boise temporarily. So how dangerous could he be?

"All set?" he asked.

She nodded.

"Let's go, then. We've got a perfect day for a visit to the old farm."

She stepped outside and pulled the door closed behind her. As she turned the key in the lock, she said, "I feel like I'm playing hooky."

"Why's that?"

"I'm not at the restaurant. I usually am at this time on a Saturday."

They walked toward the garage. "People tell me it's good to take time off every now and then. Not that I have a whole lot of experience with it. Running my own company, I've often worked eighty-hour weeks. But I've been thinking maybe that's not so healthy. Maybe I need to pay attention to other things."

"But it *was* important in the beginning, as you got your business off the ground. Right?"

"Yeah, it was."

"And then it got easier?"

"Sure. It got easier." He stopped beside his car and opened the passenger door.

She didn't get in at once. Instead, she looked up into his eyes. "Did you begin your business because you were passionate about it?"

"Passionate?" One of his eyebrows rose higher than the other.

"Was it something you always wanted to do?"

"Sure." He gave a small shrug. "I always wanted to run my own company. It didn't matter so much what, exactly. That came about because of my brother. He's a whiz with computers and program and design. He's creative too. I'm the one with the business acumen."

"You're lucky to have each other," she said before slipping onto the passenger seat.

He was silent a moment before saying, "Yeah. I guess you're right." Then he closed the door.

If only I had someone to do this with me, maybe I wouldn't hate the restaurant so much.

She frowned. Did she hate the restaurant, or did she hate the overwhelming amount of work, the lack of money, and the worries that went with it all? She wasn't sure. It was difficult to sort through her feelings.

Jed slid onto the seat to her left. "Ready for a day of fun?"

"Yes," she answered, willing it to be true, willing herself to cast off her cares for a few hours.

They drove out of the city, the suburbs spreading for miles

and miles to the south and west, eating up what had once been farmland. It amazed Holly how much the area had changed over the years. Growth and a robust economy were good things for businesses. Good for restaurants—like hers. All she needed was a way to make more people discover Sweet Caroline's.

Look at me. I can't go more than fifteen minutes without my thoughts going back to it.

Holly turned toward Jed, as much as the seat belt allowed. "Tell me about where you live. Are you in the city or out in the suburbs?"

"City. I bought a place with a great view, but to be honest, I'm not there a lot. I spend more time at the office complex than anywhere else."

"Hobbies?"

He gave his head a slight shake. "Not really. I run. Does that count as a hobby?"

"I don't think so."

"I don't think so either."

"Do you have a girlfriend?" Her cheeks warmed with embarrassment the instant the words were out of her mouth. She'd wanted to change the direction of her thoughts, but not this way. "Sorry. Not my business."

He glanced over at her, then back at the road. Something in his profile told her he was choosing his words carefully. At last he answered, "No. I don't have a girlfriend. I haven't had a lot of luck in that department."

Holly found it hard to believe there wasn't someone waiting for him back in Washington. In addition to being incredibly good looking, Jed had an easy charm. He must draw women like a magnet. Just the kind of man she should avoid.

"One more thing, Holly," he said, his voice low. "I wouldn't have asked you to come out to Ben's farm with me if I was seeing someone back home."

She felt even more embarrassed now. "Of course you wouldn't."

He looked at her again. "But I like spending time with you."

It wasn't her cheeks that warmed this time. It was something inside of her. Heat coiled in her belly, and she had to look away rather than risk him reading the fear and confusion in her eyes.

A short silence settled between them before Jed said, "That's the Harmony Barn up ahead on the right. You can just now see the sign."

She looked. The sign was made of logs and rough-cut boards. Placed near the road, the name was legible from a good distance away. As they drew closer, she saw additional information in smaller letters, although she couldn't yet read what it said. They passed a row of trees running perpendicular to the road, and the pastures, horses, barn, and other outbuildings came into view.

"Oh my." She wasn't sure what she'd expected, but this was more.

Jed slowed and turned into a driveway. On Holly's right there was a low fence made of lava rock. Up ahead on the left was a small house, white with a yellow front door and matching shutters. Without having met the woman, she was certain Ben's fiancée was responsible for the added color.

"There's Ben." Jed pointed in the direction of the barn as he parked near the house. He got out of the car and came around to open the door for Holly.

"Hey, you two," Ben called as he strode toward them. "Glad you could come out. Holly, good to see you again."

"Thanks for inviting me."

Ben looked toward the house as a young woman stepped onto the front porch, wiping her hands on a towel. "Ashley. Come meet Holly and Jed."

Ashley tossed the towel onto a nearby porch chair and came down the steps. Dressed in a cotton shirt, Levi's, and boots, her hair in a ponytail, she moved with a long, easy stride. Her smile was warm and welcoming. "We're so glad you came." She shook each of their hands in turn. "I'm sorry I wasn't at church to meet you last Sunday, but this will be better anyway. We'll have time to talk. I hear through the grapevine that you're a terrific cook, Holly, so I'd better ask your forgiveness in advance."

Everyone laughed, and Holly believed right then that she and Ashley were destined to become good friends.

Monday, July 21, 1969

"They're called transient ischemic attacks. TIA for short." The doctor looked from Helen in the hospital bed back to Andrew and Grant, the two men standing nearby. "They're often referred to as a mini stroke. A TIA can be a sign of a more devastating stroke in the waiting."

"What can be done about them?" Andrew asked.

"TIA's don't usually have lasting side effects, but they are a warning. There are steps your wife can take to lessen the chances of a stroke. Diet and exercise are among them. I'll make sure you have the necessary information when she is released."

Helen asked, "When will that be, doctor? When can I go home?"

"We'll keep you overnight, Mrs. Henning, but I see no reason to think you won't go home in the morning." He patted her foot beneath the sheet and blanket. "Get some rest. It's the best thing for you now." Then he left the room.

Helen harrumphed. "This is a horrible waste of time and money."

"Better to be safe than sorry." Andrew took hold of her hand. "Try to do what they tell you to do."

She gave him that certain look he knew so well.

He met it with a smile of encouragement that he didn't feel. After a few moments he stepped forward and placed a kiss on her forehead. "We'll go so that you'll rest. Like the doctor ordered."

She frowned at him, making sure he knew how unhappy she was to be stuck there. "What about your dinner?"

"We'll grab something on the way home. Don't worry. We can take care of ourselves for one night."

His parting words haunted him as he and his grandson made their way along the hospital hallways to the elevator and out to Grant's pickup truck. He *could* take care of himself, even with a bad back. But what if . . .

"You okay, Grandpa?"

"Yes." He realized the truck door was open, waiting for him to get in. "Yes, I'm okay."

But he wasn't okay. His thoughts had drifted to the worst that could happen. What if he were to lose Helen for good? He wasn't ready for that. How could he be?

He supposed he thought about death as much as most people his age. He knew he and Helen were far closer to their eternal reward than to their births. He didn't fear death. This world wasn't his real home. But if he were to lose Helen? It was too soon for that. Much too soon.

Not enough years, Lord. We haven't had enough years together. Heal her, please.

Grant waited while Andrew stepped up into the truck, then hurried around to the driver seat.

"I'm not hungry," Andrew said, closing his eyes against twin stabs of pain, one in his back, the other in his heart. "Let's just go home."

They drove through downtown Boise without speaking. Andrew sensed his grandson looking at him with quick glances, but he kept his own gaze fastened straight ahead, his emotions too strong for words. Stopped at a red light, Grant turned the knob on the radio. A familiar song played through the speaker above the noise of the truck's engine. Andrew didn't care for most of what passed for music these days, but he liked Herb Alpert and the Tijuana Brass. And he liked this song.

". . . this guy's in love with you . . ."

Tears sprang to his eyes. *You see this guy, Helen. He's in love with you. He's always been in love with you, and he can't manage without you. Not really.* He drew a ragged breath. *Make me strong, Jesus. Keep me strong for my girl.*

Chapter 10

Jed stood in one of the pastures, running his hand over a tall black gelding's back while Ben explained more of the equine therapy operations. The sun was warm on his shoulders, the hint of a breeze bringing the smells of spring with it.

Ben stopped talking, then asked, "What?"

Jed shook his head, not understanding.

"There's something about the way you looked just then. Made me wonder what you were thinking."

He laughed. "I'm not sure." But that wasn't true. "I was thinking this probably beats working in an office for ten to fourteen hours a day."

"But you love what you do."

"True. I do love it. But I have to admit, this is nice for a change. There's something to be said for sunshine and fresh air and horses. I'd forgotten how much I like it. And what you're doing for the people who come here." He shook his head again. "It's amazing." He didn't add that he envied Ben for having such a strong sense of God's call and direction on his life.

"I can't argue. It is amazing." Ben's gaze moved to the house. "And I never would have managed without Ashley's help."

"I can believe that."

"You don't have to sound so sure." Ben punched him lightly on the arm. "Now come on. My stomach tells me it must be close to dinnertime."

Jed gave the horse one final pat, then turned and fell into step beside his cousin. "Your grandpa said you're doing a horseback wedding here on the farm."

"Yeah. It was Ashley's idea."

"And you'd do whatever it takes to make her happy."

"Guilty as charged."

"Lucky Ben."

Ben's laughter was a sound of agreement. He was still grinning as they climbed the steps to the porch and went into the house, Ben leading the way. Delicious odors greeted them.

"Hey, you two are just in time." Ashley appeared in the doorway to the kitchen. "Go wash up. We're about to get dinner on the table." She put one hand to the side of her mouth and, in a stage whisper, added, "It's much better than expected, thanks to Holly."

"I didn't do anything," Holly said from somewhere out of view.

Ashley mouthed, *Yes, she did,* before she, too, disappeared from sight.

The two men took turns washing their hands in the bathroom sink, then went to the kitchen table where the meal awaited them—fried chicken, tossed salad, mashed potatoes, gravy, and biscuits.

As Ashley took her seat, she said, "There wouldn't be gravy or biscuits if Holly hadn't been here. And I would have burned the chicken if she hadn't been watching it."

Ben leaned to his right, toward Holly. "Then, may I say, thanks again for coming."

Jed watched the blush rise in Holly's cheeks. He loved the way the extra color made her eyes appear even more blue than usual.

"Let's give thanks so we can eat." Ben offered a hand to the women on either side of him, and Jed completed the circle. After the blessing, the serving dishes quickly began making their rounds.

Jed smiled as he remembered other times in this kitchen with members of his extended family. There'd been one particular rousing game of spoons with so many people crammed into the room they were lucky there'd been enough oxygen to breathe. He didn't recall the rules of the game. Only that at a certain point, spoons had been grabbed from the center of the table, one less than there were people playing. Lots of shouting and laughter had been a large part of the mix. He supposed he'd been no more than seven or eight, so Chris would have been too young to join in, although, knowing his brother, the kid would have tried.

"We haven't registered for gifts yet." Ashley's voice drew Jed's attention back to the present. "But I suppose we should. I don't know what I should ask for. I'm not much of a homemaker. I'd rather be out with Ben and the horses."

Holly glanced around the small kitchen. "Ben doesn't have much in the way of pots and pans. What about you?"

"Even less than he has," Ashley answered with a shrug. "And where would we put them if we had much more?"

"You could hang them from the ceiling over there." Holly indicated the place with a tip of her head. "With the right cookware, it can be attractive. I could give you some suggestions, if you'd like."

Ashley turned toward Ben. "Do you think marriage will domesticate me?"

The look the couple exchanged was filled with love and joy—it was almost palpable—and Jed felt an unexpected flash of envy for what his cousin had found with Ashley.

It had been ages since Holly enjoyed an evening as much as she was enjoying this one. Ben and Ashley were easy to know and easy to be with. She liked them both and was convinced friendship with them had already begun.

Since moving from Thunder Creek to Boise, Holly had gained plenty of friendly acquaintances, especially at her new church, but so far she hadn't made any close friends. That was her own fault, of course. She'd been focused on other things, mostly keeping her restaurant afloat. But it would be nice to have somebody other than her sisters and parents to call when she felt stressed or to go with to a movie or a sporting event or something.

Her gaze shifted to Jed, observing him as the foursome lingered around the table. The evidence of dinner had long since been cleared away. All that remained were mugs of decaf coffee along with plenty of laughter as Ben and Jed shared memories from their childhoods. The Hennings were a large family. She'd lost count of the many aunts, uncles, and cousins—first, second, and third, as well as a few once-, twice-, and thrice-removed varieties. Lots of the memories the two men shared were set here in this house and on the surrounding acreage, back when it had been a working farm.

It was obvious that Jed enjoyed reminiscing about his family.

Holly could see it in his eyes and hear it in his voice. But there were moments when she glimpsed something despondent, too, as if his thoughts had gone some place less happy for an instant. She wondered what was behind it.

Jed looked at the clock on the wall, and genuine surprise crossed his face. "Is that really the time?"

"On the nose," Ben answered.

Jed's gaze shifted to Holly. "I'd better get you home."

She hated for the evening to end but knew he was right. Turning toward Ben and Ashley, she said, "Thanks for such a wonderful evening. I loved learning about your therapy barn. Maybe next time you do a fund-raiser, I could donate some desserts to sell."

"That would be fabulous." Ashley took Ben's hand. "Let's not forget that offer."

He nodded. "We won't."

Jed stood, then stepped over to hold Holly's chair for her. The simple gesture made her feel pampered. How long had it been since she'd felt that way? Or even trusted a man enough to let him make her feel that way?

"Thanks," she whispered, her pulse suddenly erratic.

Jed led the way into the narrow entry where Holly collected her purse and sweater from a small table. Ben and Ashley followed them out onto the porch.

"We'll see you at church in the morning," Ashley said.

"See you there," Jed returned as he and Holly descended the steps.

At the car, Jed reached to open the door for her, then stopped. "Look."

She followed his gaze toward the west. The sun had dropped

from sight, its final rays painting scattered clouds in shades of lavender, pink, and peach. "Beautiful."

"Yes."

"My mom calls a sky like that God's finger painting." She turned from the sunset to look at Jed again.

"Good description." His eyes shifted to her.

The way he looked at her made her feel seen, truly seen. Made her think he was the type of man who could care, the type of man who could be honest and steady and true. A more trusting Holly would have been tempted to lean forward and kiss him over the top of the car door. The woman she had once been might have done that. But she wasn't that same Holly. She didn't trust herself. Jed was likable in many ways, but he wasn't worth the risk. No, she'd worked too hard to piece her wounded heart back together to be careless with it now.

Lowering her gaze, she sank onto the car seat. *Oh, please don't let him guess my thoughts.*

"Thanks for joining me tonight," Jed said as he got behind the wheel and started the car.

"It was fun. Ben and Ashley make a great couple."

"That's what I think. Fascinating what they're doing with the farm. Maybe next time we visit there'll be an equine therapy session in progress. That would be interesting to see."

"*Next time*"? "*We*"? This was Trixie's fault. Her little sister had put crazy notions in her head that made those words mean more than they should. Holly didn't want or need romantic complications in her life. Especially the kind that couldn't have a happy ending. She'd been there, done that, and owned the T-shirt.

Saturday, July 26, 1969

Andrew kept a close eye on Helen in the days immediately after she came home from the hospital. And not only Andrew. Their children along with their spouses, not to mention most of their grandchildren, came out to the farm to check on her.

"Will everyone stop fussing?" Helen said several times each day. "I'm perfectly all right."

No one paid attention to that command.

Their son Ben, back from one of his flights, came to the farm on Saturday. He sat with Andrew at the kitchen table, sipping coffee while his wife visited with Helen, Grant, and Charlotte in the living room.

"You should sell the farm, Dad."

"I'm not ready for that." He didn't tell his eldest boy that he'd thought the same thing not all that long ago. But it wasn't what he wanted, and it wasn't what Helen wanted either.

"It's too much for you. Who knows how long you'll have trouble with your back? Maybe for the rest of your life. Especially if you don't take proper care of yourself. And Mom shouldn't be doing all that she does either. You could get a nice price for this property, enough to settle into a retirement community and live in comfort."

"Your mother would hate it. She likes it here. We both do."

Ben leaned slightly forward. "How is she, really?"

"She seems herself. She's trying to follow the doctor's orders. More exercise. Changes in her diet, such as less meat and more vegetables. She's taking a walk each morning. Not long ones yet, but long enough. Grant goes with her before he leaves for work."

"Sounds good. But what if she has another one of those TIA things? Or a full-out stroke? What if she was paralyzed and bedridden? You wouldn't be able to take care of her by yourself."

Borrowing trouble. It was hard not to do. Hard for everyone. All Andrew could do was shake his head.

"You're way out here in the boonies, Dad. How long did it take for the ambulance to get here after you called them? How long before they got her to the hospital?"

"I'm really not sure. Felt like forever." He remembered the ambulance ride into Boise. He'd been allowed to accompany his wife, holding her hand the entire way, his heart screaming as loud as the siren.

"See? If you were in a retirement community, help would be much closer at hand."

Grant walked into the kitchen. For a moment he looked at his dad and granddad at the table, and then he moved to the coffeepot and refilled his mug.

Andrew sighed as his gaze returned to Ben. "I don't want your mother to be unhappy, and I'm afraid leaving the farm, leaving this house, would make her so. All her memories are tied up here. We talked about it before, and she made certain I knew she didn't want that. Not as long as we could possibly stay."

"Are you talking about selling the farm again?" Grant asked, taking one of the empty chairs.

"Your father thinks we should."

"But I'm here. You don't have to worry about anything except taking care of Grandma."

Ben cleared his throat. "You won't be here forever, Grant. You're getting married in the fall."

"Well . . ." Grant drew out the word. "Maybe Charlotte and I should move in here after the wedding."

Ben gaped for a moment. "You must be joking."

"I'm not."

"What would Charlotte think?"

"She says she's okay with it, Dad. We talked about it already."

Andrew remembered moving into this house as a newlywed, with his in-laws. Overall, the two couples had gotten along well. Still, it hadn't been ideal. Especially when being the woman of the house had passed from his mother-in-law to his wife. It had been a strain at times.

Grant looked Andrew in the eyes, his gaze serious. "Grandpa, you and Grandma raised five kids in this house, and your mother-in-law lived with you for a lot of that time. That was eight people living in this house. Why couldn't four of us do it? There's three bedrooms down here, plus the loft bedroom."

"But there's only one bathroom, and the living room and kitchen are small."

"Charlotte and I don't need a lot of room. We're not gonna have much between the two of us, even with wedding gifts." He leaned forward, his coffee mug on the table, pressed between his hands. "And maybe we could figure out a way for us to buy the farm eventually so it wouldn't have to leave the family."

Andrew felt a quickening in his chest. That same idea had been swirling around in his mind for a couple of weeks.

"You two are crazy." Ben rose from his chair. "But you're going to do what you're going to do. I've learned that through the years." He headed into the living room.

Andrew drew a steadying breath. "You're sure Charlotte's willing?" he asked Grant. "What if your grandmother takes a turn for the worst? Running the house could fall on your bride's shoulders. And it's different being a guest in a home and sharing a home, even among those who love one another."

"She can handle it. *We* can handle it."

"Well, then. We have a lot to pray about, you and I. Don't we?"

Chapter 11

Jed was glad Holly agreed to ride with him to church the next morning. They were headed to the same destination. It was simply common sense to go together. At least that's what he told himself as they walked toward the entry doors. Inside, he asked if she would like something from the coffee bar.

She shook her head. "No, thanks."

"Well, I need a tall one. I got up too late to make my own. Wait for me here?"

This time she nodded.

He got into the queue, feeling impatient. Was it eagerness for his morning shot of caffeine or that he wanted to get back to Holly? They'd had a great time yesterday with Ben and Ashley, but something had changed between saying their goodbyes to their hosts at the farm and arriving at Holly's house. She'd seemed withdrawn and even reluctant to look at him. Maybe it shouldn't matter so much, but he didn't like the idea of her pulling away from him, from their budding friendship.

The reaction puzzled him. His relationships with women had always come second, first to his higher education, then to his work. More than one of the women he'd dated through the years—attractive women, nice women, interesting women—had grown tired of waiting for him to become more involved. Some had told him their feelings. Others had simply disappeared. And, to be honest, he'd never minded much.

But when it came to Holly, he did mind. He didn't want her to disappear from his life, even though he couldn't say she was actually in it to start with. How strange was that?

He glanced over his shoulder and discovered Holly talking to a girl with a toddler in her arms. Holly smiled as she touched the little boy's cheek, then said something to the young mother. At least he assumed she was the mom. Maybe she was a sister to the little boy.

His turn to order arrived, and he gave his full attention to the volunteer barista behind the counter. A short while later, a tall black coffee in hand, he made his way back to Holly. The younger woman was still talking to her. As he stepped close, they both turned to look at him.

"Jed, I want you to meet Willow Flynn and her son, AJ. Willow has taken my cooking classes recently. This is her first time at Covenant Fellowship. Willow, this is a friend of mine, Jed Henning. He's visiting Boise, so he's new to Covenant too."

"Hi, Willow. Nice to meet you." Jed didn't offer his hand since both of hers were busy holding her wriggling toddler.

Willow didn't return the greeting immediately. She simply stared at him, her light-blue eyes seeming almost too big for her face. Her complexion was so pale he wondered if she'd ever been in the sun, even for a minute. Finally, she said, "I . . . I'd better find the nursery. AJ wants down."

"Sure." Holly glanced at Jed. "I'm going to show her to the children's wing. We'll join you in the sanctuary in a few."

"Okay." He watched them go, an even more troubled feeling settling in his chest. The way Willow had looked at him. Had Holly said something negative about him to the younger woman? But why would she? Still, he had the distinct sensation that Willow had wanted to get away from him.

"Hey, Jed."

He turned toward Ben's voice. His cousin had his arm around Ashley's shoulders as the two of them walked toward him.

"Holly didn't come with you?" Ashley asked, sounding disappointed.

"No. She's here. She's showing someone to the children's wing."

"I know Grandpa's already here," Ben said. "I saw his car outside. Shall we join him or wait here for Holly?"

"She said she'd meet us in the sanctuary."

The threesome moved in that direction, stopping every so often to speak to someone. The exchanges made it obvious how well liked Ben and Ashley were within this congregation. It reminded Jed once again how separate he'd kept himself for so many years, even within the body of Christ. His life had been almost 100 percent about work, and even there he'd formed only a few friendships. By his own choice. He'd been the one to set up boundaries with others.

Including with his brother.

His gaze darted to the entrance of the children's wing. He didn't like it that Holly had seemed to pull away from him, and yet he'd been doing that very thing for years—and to the people he loved.

It needs to change. I need to change.

He was still mulling over that thought when they arrived at the row of chairs where Grant Henning awaited them.

"Holly?" Willow held her son tight against her chest. "I think I'll stay in here with AJ. They said I could do that and watch the service on the screen. You don't mind, do you?" Her expression was anxious.

"Are you sure? AJ will be fine. There're lots of kids for him to play with, and you could sit with me. I'd love to introduce you to my friends."

"No. I'm sure. I want to stay here."

Something told Holly not to press too hard. It was enough that Willow had come to church that morning of her own accord. "All right. Would you like me to come for you afterward? We could give you a ride back to the shelter."

"No, thanks. We'll walk back on the Greenbelt. It's a pretty day."

"If you're sure."

"I'm sure."

Holly gave a little wave to AJ, then made her way out of the children's wing. She told herself not to be disappointed by Willow's decision. She'd issued many invitations to the women who came to her cooking classes, but none had accepted until today. Willow was here, even if she'd chosen to stay in the nursery. That was something.

She made it into the sanctuary as the worship team began leading the first praise song and soon reached the chair that had been saved for her between Ashley and Jed. Ashley gave her hand a squeeze of welcome. Holly returned it before setting her purse and Bible on the chair. Then she faced the stage and closed her eyes, joining in the worship.

"It's not too late," Jed said as he opened the door of his car for Holly. "We could still meet the others at the restaurant for lunch."

"Sorry. I can't. I have things I must do this afternoon."

He was tempted to say she worked too much but stopped himself. Who was he to talk? If he hadn't come to Boise to look for Chris, if his dad hadn't suspended operations, he would be thinking about work even if he wasn't at the office on a Sunday afternoon.

"Besides," Holly added, "Trixie's coming over later."

Jed got into the car and started the engine. "More wedding plans?"

"Of course." She laughed softly. "It's all-consuming for my sister, and she seems to want me involved with everything. I should have said all I could do was bake the cake. I never should have agreed to be maid of honor too."

"From what I can tell, it's hard to say no to Trixie."

She laughed again, this time with gusto. "You said a mouthful."

"I envy how close you two are." He hadn't meant to say that.

"You aren't close with your brother?" Sympathy had replaced humor in her voice.

"We were close when we were little. But we grew apart later. It got . . . complicated between us."

"It happens."

He frowned at the road ahead. "My dad seems to think it's up to me to fix things. I guess that's because I'm the older brother. But it's hard to fix something when you don't know why it's broken."

As the words left his mouth, he wondered if they were true.

Did he *really* not know why the relationship with his brother was broken? He'd made his impatience with Chris obvious, not only to his brother but to everybody else who worked at Laffriot. He'd tried to force Chris to be more responsible, more ambitious. *More like me.* The thought made him wince.

"I've been too hard on him. Too hard for too long a time."

"I'm sorry," she said softly. "I can tell you're unhappy about it."

Funny, he hadn't thought he was unhappy about it. He'd been angry and irritated. He'd had plenty of reasons to be. But he hadn't thought he cared that the two of them were no longer close. Until now.

"Oh, look. Trixie's already here. I wasn't expecting her this soon."

Jed turned into the alley and parked his car in the garage. By the time they stepped into the backyard, Trixie awaited them by the back door.

"You're early," Holly called to her sister.

"I know." Trixie's gaze went to Jed. "I was with a younger cousin of ours yesterday. His name's Ricky. Do you know what he likes to do most? He's a gamer. Isn't that what you call people who are serious about playing electronic games? Role-playing and shooting and blowing things up and slaying the villain and all that?"

Jed shrugged.

Trixie grinned. "You should have seen Ricky's face when I happened to mention the name of Holly's new tenant. He said, 'You mean the Laffriot guy?' After that, he couldn't shut up about you." Trixie turned toward Holly, then looked at Jed again. "This guy's famous."

"Famous?" It was Holly's turn to look at him.

"Not me. My company, maybe."

"That's not what Ricky says. He says the game you released last year is the best he's ever played. He says you're a genius."

Jed felt tension tightening his jaw. Chris was the genius. Jed's business plans had put the company on the map, but the game itself had been dreamed up by Chris, developed by Chris, perfected by Chris. But some kid in Idaho didn't know that. He knew about Laffriot. He knew about Jed. But Chris wasn't on the boy's radar.

And that was Jed's fault.

His jaw was throbbing now. "I'd better leave you two to your wedding plans." Without waiting for a response, he turned and headed toward the apartment stairwell.

Saturday, August 2, 1969

Andrew sat on a bale of hay. He swiveled the cane between his hands as he watched Grant doctoring a wound on the back leg of the large buckskin called Two-Bits. Even with the doors open at both ends of the barn, the air was still and warm. The dog days of summer were upon them for sure.

He wished he could join his grandson in the stall. He wished he could bend down and pick up the gelding's leg. For that matter, he wished he could saddle the horse and go for a ride, even if it was only a circle around the borders of the farm. He hoped his days in the saddle weren't gone for good. Only this morning, he'd looked in the mirror and taken note of his gray hair. Like many other things in life, turning gray had happened so slowly he'd hardly noticed. From dark to salt-and-pepper to stone-colored. From young man to middle-aged to senior citizen. In the blink of an eye.

Grant set the horse's hoof down and looked at his grandfather. "Are Aunt Francine and Pat still up at the house?"

"Yes. I think they plan to stay until after lunch."

"I suppose Aunt Francine let you know what she thinks about me and Charlotte living here after the wedding."

"Of course. Who hasn't shared their opinion?" He heard the voices of his children in his head. Nobody seemed to think it was a good idea. Nobody except for him and Helen, Grant and Charlotte.

"Grandpa, does it matter what the others say as long as the four of us are good with it?"

Andrew gave the cane a good spin. "Perhaps not. On the other hand, I want to make certain I'm not being selfish, thinking of only what will make me happy. I have to ask, is it fair to you to start off your married life living with your grandparents? Even if it's for a good reason and the ultimate outcome you desire."

"I've already answered that question. And if you don't believe Charlotte feels the same way, ask her."

He was about to say he would do that when his granddaughter Pat ran into the barn.

"Grandpa, something's wrong with Grandma."

He rose quickly, grimacing at the pain, and hurried toward the house. When he arrived in the kitchen, he found Helen looking shaken and tired, but the worst of the episode seemed to be over. According to what the physician at the hospital had said, that was one sign it wasn't a stroke. TIAs lasted a shorter time, and the effects didn't remain long either.

Francine stood near her mother at the kitchen table. "Dad?" She looked at him, fear in her eyes.

He nodded to show he understood what hadn't been said.

"Don't you . . . dare call . . . for an ambulance." Helen didn't lift her gaze from her hands, folded on the table. "There is nothing . . . they can do for me . . . but tell me to rest."

Francine leaned forward, trying to force her mother to see her. "You should at least call your doctor. What if this is more serious than last time?"

Andrew went to his wife's other side and managed to kneel down so he could study her face. He tried to hide the concern he felt. Instead, he wanted to reassure her.

"Please." Tears brimmed in her eyes. "No hospital."

He nodded. "Into bed, then."

Francine helped Andrew get Helen to the bedroom, but afterward, he shooed his daughter away while he helped his wife remove her clothes, put on her nightgown, and get into bed. Then he sat on a nearby chair and waited for her to drift off to sleep.

God, he prayed, *she knows You. She loves You. Be merciful to her and to us.*

When he was sure she slept, he went to the living room where the others waited for him. "She's resting."

"Dad, it isn't even two weeks since this happened the first time."

"I'm aware of that, Francine."

"It scared me, seeing her like that."

"I know." He sank onto his favorite chair. Although not the same chair he used to call his favorite, it was in the same spot the other one had been. During the war years, he'd been able to reach out and turn on the radio. That radio was long since gone. But the old bookshelf remained nearby, filled with a collection of books. It was comforting to see the familiar items beside him.

"Dad."

He pulled his attention to his daughter.

"I've been doing some research, and I think you should take Mom to see a vascular neurologist. They have experience in the diagnosis and management of strokes."

"Your mother didn't have a stroke. A transient ischemic attack is similar but still different. That's what we were told."

Francine leaned forward and took hold of his right hand. "But a TIA is often a sign that a stroke could be next."

Andrew heard her words. He even knew she was right. But he wanted to resist acknowledging it as long as possible. It would become too real once he did that.

"Why don't I ask around for recommendations for a neurologist in Boise? There must be someone good who can answer our questions. I'm sure the doctor who cared for her in the hospital was competent, but I want her to see a specialist. Please."

Was he a coward because he didn't want to ask those questions aloud to another physician? But he knew the answer. He had to ask. Like it or not, he had to ask.

O Lord, help us. Have mercy on us.

Chapter 12

Willow Flynn came alone to Sweet Caroline's on Monday morning. While Holly was delighted to see her, it was a disappointment when more women didn't come for lessons. Still, she'd learned not to take it personally. The gals at the shelter often had other commitments that couldn't be shifted to another day or time.

"I'm glad you're here," Holly said as Willow tied the apron around her waist. "I looked for you after the service yesterday, just in case you changed your mind about a ride home."

"We left as soon as the pastor finished his prayer."

"I hope you'll want to come back again."

Willow gave a slight nod. "Maybe."

Leaving well enough alone, Holly turned toward the items on the counter. "We're making a Tex-Mex skillet today. I hope you're hungry. The recipe serves eight, and there are only two of us. Why don't you start by washing those vegetables?" She pointed at the lettuce, green bell pepper, tomato, and jalapeño.

Except for brief words of instruction from Holly every now and then, the two women were silent as Willow shredded, diced, minced, and grated the various items on the work counter. It wasn't until the lean ground beef was browning in a large skillet that Willow spoke again. "Your . . . friend . . . The one who was with you yesterday. Have you known him long?"

"Jed?" She looked at Willow, wondering what prompted the question, but the younger woman was concentrating on the meat in the skillet, stirring it with a wooden spoon. "No, I haven't known him long."

"How did you meet him?"

Willow didn't seem like a gamer, but Holly had to wonder if she'd recognized Jed's name the same way Ricky had. "My house has a basement apartment," she answered. "He's renting it."

"I thought you said he was visiting."

"He is. He only rented the apartment for three months."

"An apartment," Willow said as she turned to look at Holly. "If he's only staying for three months, does that mean the apartment will be up for rent again?"

Holly might not know why Willow asked about Jed, but she definitely understood her interest in the apartment. The young mother must hope for a place of her own to rent once she was ready to leave the shelter. Low-income housing was at a premium in the valley. To be honest, it was closer to nonexistent, which made things difficult for a single mother like Willow. She doubted the girl could afford the rent that Holly required. Rather than get Willow's hopes up, Holly pointed to the other items on the counter. "We need to get everything into the skillet now."

Conversation ended as Willow added the frozen corn, beans, water, and spices to the browned meat. While the mixture simmered, Holly showed her how to make the salsa, adding jalapeño and a pinch of salt to the grated tomato and onion. Before long, the two women sat at a small table to sample the results of the morning's efforts. Holly watched Willow take her first bite. A moment later a smile blossomed on the younger woman's face.

"This is really good."

"Surprised?"

"No. Everything you teach us how to make is good."

"Thanks. I appreciate that."

"I'm not just sayin' it to be nice. It is always good. And it makes me happy to know I can make healthier food for AJ instead of giving him mac and cheese from a box."

The compliment brought a mist of tears to Holly's eyes. She was so often miserable when working at the restaurant. But never in these few hours on a Monday. Blinking back the tears, she asked, "Do you think it's too spicy for AJ?"

Willow took another bite and waited until she swallowed before answering. "I don't think so. I wouldn't use the salsa for his meal, but I think he'd like the rest."

"He's such a cute little boy. I hope he enjoyed being in the nursery at church."

"He did. I wasn't sure how he'd like it. He can be real shy around strangers. Even other kids his age. He's never been around many people up until we got to the shelter."

Holly silently debated her next question. She wanted to know where AJ's father was, why he wasn't helping to support his little family. But she decided to try to find out in a less direct way. "Does AJ look like his dad?"

Sadness filled Willow's eyes. "Yes. A little." There was a small catch in her voice.

"I'm sorry. Was that too personal?"

"No." Willow shook her head slowly.

Holly knew the younger woman's answer wasn't completely

the truth. The question *had* been too personal. She also knew Willow wasn't going to say more about the man who'd fathered AJ. Not this time anyway.

Jed sat on the apartment sofa, Great-Grandpa Andrew's Bible open on his lap, staring at the three names in the margin next to the story of the prodigal son. Andrew's now-familiar hand had scrawled both Oscar and Wendy. Jed had written his brother's name. He placed a finger on it, his chest aching as he wondered what he could have done in the past to have altered the way things were now.

He'd lain awake a lot of the night, remembering Trixie's declaration of his fame. Sure, he'd had a lot to do with the success of Laffriot. It took business sense to successfully launch a start-up. It took good management. It took strategic thinking. But without Chris . . .

His gaze shifted to the Bible story, and he saw himself, even more clearly than he had before, in the person of the older brother who refused to celebrate the return of the younger. Maybe Jed had been jealous. Maybe he'd been rigid. Maybe he'd been selfish. Whatever the reasons for his thoughts and actions, he didn't much care for the results of his recent introspection.

Hands now folded on the open Bible, he began to talk to God. No fancy words. No attempt to quote Scripture. No pontificating, as Grandpa Andy would have called it. Jed had asked for forgiveness before, but this time was different. His prayer was earnest, raw. He wanted to change the type of man he'd become. He wasn't sure how to accomplish it, but he knew he couldn't do it without God's help. There was more at stake here than the survival of his company. More even than the restoration of the relationship with his brother. God wanted his full attention, his full surrender. Jed had kept a tight grip on his life—personal, spiritual, and professional—for many years. Was he ready to loosen that grip and let God take full control?

"Make me ready, God. Please."

His phone vibrated on the coffee table. He kept his eyes closed, trying to ignore it, but finally he had to look. Chris's name was on the screen. He grabbed the phone, swiping to answer the call.

"Chris?"

"Yeah. It's me."

He drew a quick breath. "I'm glad you called me back." His gaze alighted on his brother's name in the margin of the open Bible.

"I talked to Mom."

"Good. That's good."

"You might as well know. I'm not going back to Washington. I've got my reasons."

Panic started to rise in Jed's chest. He pushed it down. "Will you meet with me? Just to talk. You pick the time and place, and I'll be there."

"I'm surprised you're still in Boise. You've hardly left Laffriot's offices, even for a few hours, let alone for days."

"We've temporarily shut down operations." Jed winced, knowing it sounded as if he'd had something to say about the situation. Time to be more honest. He couldn't fix anything if he wasn't honest. "It was Dad's idea."

"Because of me?"

"It's more complicated than that."

"Really?"

"Give me half an hour. In person. Please."

Chris was silent. Maybe it was Jed's last word that gave him pause. He couldn't blame Chris if it was. After all, when had Jed last said "please" to his brother? In the business setting, his MO was more demanding, more about barking orders. Maybe that was his MO beyond the business setting too.

"Half an hour, Chris. Anywhere you say."

"All right," his brother said at last. "Thursday night. I'll text you the time and place."

"Okay." Part of him wanted to insist they meet sooner. He'd waited all this time already. Why three more days? He managed to swallow the words. Or maybe it was God who stopped them in his throat. "See you Thursday."

"Later." The phone went silent.

It was a start. He would be thankful for the start.

Sunday, August 3, 1969

Andrew and Helen stayed home from church that Sunday. With his wife still in bed, Andrew read aloud from the Bible. He began in the Psalms, then at her request moved to the book of James. "'My brethren, count it all joy when ye fall into divers temptations; Knowing this, that the trying of your faith worketh patience. But let patience have her perfect work, that ye may be perfect and entire, wanting nothing.'" He continued to read for another five minutes before Helen interrupted him softly.

"We must be patient."

He looked up, but her eyes were closed.

"There is a purpose for all suffering," she added in a whisper.

A purpose for all suffering. Yes, he knew it was true. Trials had entered their lives more than once through the years, and God had taught him many lessons through them. His times of greatest growth had come because of the valleys, not the mountaintops. And yet he resisted the trials, fought against them, wanted to make them go away. His response should be to look to Jesus in the first instant and to trust Him completely for the outcome, but all he could think about was what it might cost him. And what if he couldn't bear the cost?

An invisible hand seemed to rest upon his shoulder. He heard the whisper of the Comforter, reminding him that he wouldn't be alone, no matter the trial. The burden wasn't his to carry. He shouldn't even try.

He reached for a pad of paper and a pen on the night table and wrote on it:

> Whatever suffering is allowed into my life—whether my own fault, an attack of the enemy, or because I live in a fallen

world—God's ultimate purpose is for the trial to make me more like Jesus.

He tore the paper from the pad, folded it, and pressed it into the gutter of the Bible before he turned the page.

Chapter 13

Holly stood in her kitchen, staring at the red mixing bowl on the counter, not far from the beautiful new range. More than anything, she wanted to forget the list of chores that awaited her, now that she was back from the restaurant, and lose herself in creating something super sweet and super yummy. Or maybe something as simple as a batch of sugar cookies with bright-colored icing. Or how about some funky-looking cupcakes? She sniffed the air, as if hoping to catch a scent of vanilla. It wasn't there, and she couldn't conjure it in her imagination.

A sigh escaped her as she looked around the kitchen again. When was the last time she'd baked anything just for fun? That was one of the reasons she'd purchased her new range, so she could experiment with new recipes, new cake designs, new flavors and shapes and frostings. But where was she supposed to find those hours? Steal them from sleep? Take them from the restaurant?

She frowned. It wasn't right, the pattern she'd fallen into over the past year. Apart from church on Sundays and her Monday mornings with the women from the shelter, her waking hours were mostly about keeping the restaurant afloat, filling in for servers, ordering supplies, an endless stream of paperwork. There was no joy in any of that. The restaurant was a millstone around her neck. There had to be a better way than simply getting through the day and hoping she would swim instead of sink. But how did she find it?

Releasing another sigh, she grabbed the trash bag out of the kitchen can, then carried it from room to room, emptying more trash into it as she went. After tying the bag closed, she took up a box of recyclables and headed outside. She was dropping the items in their respective bins when the garage door opened and Jed stepped into view, a canvas grocery bag in each hand. He stopped when he saw her.

"Hey, Holly."

"Hi."

He glanced toward the house, then back at her. "Listen, I owe you an apology."

"Me? Why?"

"I was rude yesterday. When your sister brought up Laffriot and I left like I did."

"You weren't rude."

"Yes, I was." He gave his head a slow shake. "Trixie's comments caught me off guard. I . . . I'm feeling a bit defensive about my company right now."

She nodded to let him know she listened.

"Look." He raked a hand through his hair, a gesture of frustration. "I told you my brother and I aren't in a good place. One of the reasons is because of Laffriot." A frown knitted his brows. "I'm just starting to figure out some of the things that went wrong between us, but the business is definitely one of the reasons we don't get along. So it's kind of a sore spot with me. Anyway, I'm sorry for the way I walked out."

Strange. She hadn't realized, until this moment, how bothered she'd been by his abrupt departure.

"There's something else I'd like to say. I've been successful in business. Your sister told you that. But I haven't been good in personal relationships. God's shown me that since I came to Boise."

Holly couldn't relate to the succeeding in business part, but she could about failing at personal relationships. She nodded, hoping he read the empathy in her eyes.

"I'm hoping I can change things. Make things better with Chris. Maybe become a better man in other ways."

Nerves tumbled in her stomach. She wasn't sure why. Perhaps his words felt too personal.

He took a small step forward. "I like you, Holly. From the start I've liked you. I don't know if it could be anything more than friendship, but I'm wondering if . . ."

Her mouth went dry. Her throat constricted.

"It's complicated. Right? You live in Boise. I live in Tacoma. But I'd like to see if we might become more than friends."

The last man Holly was attracted to had fooled her, then dumped her. He'd left her struggling emotionally and financially. He'd left her afraid to take risks. She didn't want to be hurt like that again. She couldn't trust her judgment. She would be a fool to consider it, especially with a man who lived and worked on the opposite side of the neighboring state.

"Holly Stanford, you like *him,"* Trixie's voice whispered in her memory.

Like him or not, she didn't want to be foolish. She hadn't

time for romance. Relationships took work. They took time and attention. She didn't have either of those to give.

Again her little sister's words returned: *"You've closed yourself off. You've locked up your emotions."*

It wasn't easy, but Holly could remember a time when she'd been fearless, when she'd been eager to take on the world, ready to risk it all to achieve her dreams. She didn't want to be the woman who shrank back from life. If only . . .

"Let me take you out to dinner one night this week."

Her heart fluttered erratically. Did she dare say yes? This would be a date. This would be the first step in seeing if they could be more than friends. Did she want that? Why would she? It was a situation rife with danger. She was better off alone. She couldn't trust her feelings.

"Shall we say Wednesday at six?" he prompted softly.

"Okay." The word escaped her, against her will.

"Wednesday it is, then. I'll make reservations and pick you up at your back door."

O God, don't let this be a mistake. Don't let me regret meeting him. Don't let him make a fool of me.

There was a kindness in his eyes as he watched her, almost as if he had read her desperate prayer. She hoped she was wrong. She wasn't ready for him to know her that well.

It surprised Jed, how much his mood was improved by his brief encounter with Holly, and his footsteps felt lighter as he descended the steps and entered his apartment. He walked straight to the kitchen, where he quickly emptied the two shopping bags, perishables into the fridge and the remainder of the groceries into one of the small cabinets.

Once finished, he returned to the living room and opened his laptop. There were half a dozen emails awaiting him. Three of them could wait. The fourth was an offer to buy Laffriot. A good offer, based on dollars alone. This wasn't an unusual occurrence. Ever since the success of *Caliban*, other game companies—larger and with longer histories—had come calling, hoping to absorb Laffriot. Jed had rejected the offers without consideration. His plan had been to take Laffriot from a small start-up to a global company. Why sell when he was only getting started?

But if we sold it, I wouldn't have to go back to Tacoma.

Sell Laffriot? Only a month ago, his dad's threat of doing that had made Jed go ballistic.

His gaze rose to the ceiling of his apartment. He hadn't heard any footsteps since he'd left Holly out by the garage. But then, he never heard much noise from upstairs. She moved as quietly as that cat of hers. What was she up to now? he wondered. Had she already eaten her supper, or was she dining late? Or maybe she was soaking away the day in a bubble bath.

That thought brought an unwelcome image with it. Appealing but unwelcome. Tempting but unwelcome. At least for a guy who was trying to get his walk with the Lord back on track.

With a shake of his head, he lowered his gaze. He'd better distract himself and quick. He reached into one of the nearby boxes he'd brought with him from his cousin's garage and pulled out the first packet of envelopes. The top letter had brought him to see this apartment. He took it from the envelope and read it once again. It made him wish, not for the first time, that he could remember Andrew Henning. Even more, he wished he could sit down with his great-grandfather and ask for advice. Something about the tone of this letter—in addition to Andrew's well-used Bible—told Jed he would have received wise and godly counsel from this man. From all he'd heard, family had been of utmost importance to his great-grandfather. Maybe he could have asked him how to fix things with Chris.

What went wrong between us, Lord? When did it really start? What part did I play in it? I need to know. Otherwise, how can I make it right?

Jed frowned. He wasn't someone who asked for advice. Not often, anyway. He liked making his own way, making his own decisions, even making his own mistakes so he could learn from them. But he'd also been someone who'd tried to tell his younger brother how he should live. He'd offered plenty of advice that hadn't been wanted. Worse, he'd tried to control Chris's behavior once the two of them started working together. It didn't matter that he'd been convinced he did it to help his brother. He'd been in the wrong.

He leaned back on the sofa.

I'll tell him I was wrong when I see him.

But would that be enough to set things right?

Monday, August 4, 1969

A fly buzzed near the screened door as Andrew climbed the porch step on his return from the mailbox. He was about to open the door when he heard a vehicle approaching the house. Turning, he recognized Charlotte's black Pontiac Bonneville. A quick glance at his wristwatch told him Grant wouldn't be back to the farm for another two hours or so.

"Hi, Grandpa Andrew," Charlotte called as she got out of the car.

"What a nice surprise."

"For me too. I didn't expect to have the afternoon off."

"You know Grant won't be here until close to six."

She came up the steps. "I know. I came to see you and Grandma Helen."

He loved it that she hadn't waited until after the wedding to begin calling them Grandma and Grandpa. "I think Helen's still napping. Would you like some lemonade?"

"No, thanks. I'm okay." She glanced at the porch chairs. "Shall we sit out here?"

"If that's what you'd like. Not bad here in the shade."

A hot breeze caused the trees to sway in a lazy sort of dance. The horses stood near the water trough, heads low and tails swishing at flies. Chester rose from his spot beneath the porch swing and came to rest his muzzle on Charlotte's thigh.

"Hello there." She scratched the dog behind the ears. "What a good boy."

"You know his weak spot."

"Don't I, though." She bent at the waist and touched her forehead to the dog's. "We're best friends. Aren't we, Chester?"

Andrew's daughters had loved the farm, but neither of them had been what could be called a tomboy. Charlotte, on the other hand, seemed made for rough and noisy activities. He suspected she would rather be hauling around bales of hay or driving a tractor than baking a pie in the kitchen. She and Grant were going to do well together, even if they might live on peanut-butter-and-jelly sandwiches.

Charlotte straightened. "Grant told me you're still nervous about newlyweds sharing the house with you. But isn't that what you did when you were first married?"

"Things were a lot different back then. Especially after the market crashed and the Great Depression began. Families of several generations used to share houses all the time. You young people today are different." He shook his head. "I'm afraid it would be asking too much of you."

"Grandpa, Grant and I share a dream of owning a farm, of raising crops and animals, and eventually having us some kids who'll grow up on horseback and love the earth like we do. It's hard to buy the kind of place we want." Her eyes swept the barnyard. "A place like this. You don't want to leave it, and we want to become a part of it. I think it can work for all of us."

Andrew mulled over her impassioned words. He remembered a few differences of opinion that he'd had with his father-in-law. What if he and Grant couldn't agree about planting or harvesting? Who would be making the decisions then?

And yet his heart told him this was the right choice. It would be best for Helen, best for him, and best for Grant and Charlette too. Oh, how he wanted to believe that.

Chapter 14

At five forty-five on Wednesday evening, only one word could describe Holly. Terrified.

It didn't help that she'd told Trixie about her upcoming date with Jed.

After squealing like a teenager, her sister had cried, "I knew it!"

Holly had pulled the phone away from her ringing ear.

"I feel good about this," Trixie had continued, excitement lingering in her voice. "I feel good about him. You deserve somebody special in your life."

Remembering the phone call, Holly stared into the bedroom mirror, wishing she hadn't mentioned anything to Trixie. Wishing she hadn't agreed to go out with Jed. She wanted nothing so much as to call it off. It was more than nerves. Fear churned inside of her. She already liked Jed more than she should. What if she let him into her heart, only to have him break it?

"Shame on you," she said to her reflection. "You didn't used to be a coward. You *aren't* a coward. He's nice. You like his company. It's a dinner. It needn't be anything more. You can be strong enough to risk one dinner." She turned away from the mirror and reached for her sweater that lay on the foot of the bed.

"Meow." Pumpkin jumped onto the bed, stepping on the knit garment.

"Don't you start." Holly scratched the cat behind the ears before gently pushing her away.

Pumpkin protested with a soft growl.

"I love you too."

She stroked the cat's head once, then left the bedroom. In the kitchen, she got a drink of water and was setting the glass on the counter beside the sink when a rap sounded on the back door. Nerves exploded in her stomach a second time as she went to answer it.

"Wow." Jed grinned. "You look amazing."

She glanced down, her mind blank. For that split second, she'd forgotten what she wore. Oh yes. She'd chosen one of her favorite dresses, one that Trixie said was the same shade of blue as her eyes. "Thanks." She didn't say that he, too, looked amazing in his burgundy-colored dress shirt and a pair of dark trousers. Even more handsome than usual.

Don't do this. Don't like him too much. Be careful.

"Ready?"

She nodded. "Let me get my things." A few moments later she returned with her purse and sweater. As she stepped outside, she caught the scent of lilacs in bloom, brought from the neighbor's yard on a gentle breeze. She paused long enough to close her eyes and take a deep breath through her nose. When she released it, it came out on a sigh of pleasure.

Jed's soft laughter caused her to look at him. "I'm guessing you either love spring or love lilacs."

"Both." She smiled, despite her anxiety.

"Me too."

For some reason, that caused her fears to calm somewhat.

Jed had made a reservation for them at an upscale Boise restaurant. Holly had heard lots of great reviews of the Riverfront, but she'd never been there before. Nathan hadn't been one for fancy dining, and this wasn't the sort of place a girl came to alone, even if she could afford it—which Holly could not.

Candlelight flickered at each table, and piano music wafted through the air, giving the large dining area a romantic ambiance. Their table was located beside a window overlooking the river. Early-evening sunlight glittered off the rippling water that flowed past them. Cottonwood branches on the opposite side of the river danced as birds landed and flew away again. People strolled on the Greenbelt pathway, enjoying the balmy evening.

"This is nice," Holly said as she looked across the table at Jed.

"Yeah, it is. Ben told me about it. I think it's where he popped the question to Ashley."

"Really?" She easily imagined the scene, and it brought back that unsettled feeling to her stomach. She picked up the menu and began to peruse it.

"If money wasn't an object, would you rather run a restaurant like this one instead of Sweet Caroline's?"

She laid the menu down. "No. I'd rather own a bake shop. I'd rather design wedding cakes. That's what I planned to do. Owning a restaurant just sort of happened to me."

He cocked an eyebrow.

"I told you I inherited it from an uncle."

"Yeah."

"It was closed for years after my aunt passed away. I thought about selling the building, but then . . ." She hesitated, unsure how transparent she wanted to be. But there was something in the way he watched her, something in his eyes, that made her want to be honest with him, even if she wasn't ready to trust her feelings. "Nathan was the one who convinced me I should re-open it."

"Nathan?"

"My ex-fiancé." She glanced out the window. "He was going to manage the restaurant while I did my cake thing, as he called it."

"What happened?" Jed's voice was soft.

Her throat narrowed. "He changed his mind. About me. About marriage. About everything."

"I'm sorry, Holly."

"It's all right." She looked at him again, lifting her chin and stiffening her spine at the same time. "I'm all right. And I mean to make certain that Sweet Caroline's will be all right too. There's a lot of food-service competition in Boise, but we're gaining loyal customers. We'll manage." She wished she felt as confident as she tried to sound.

"What about that cake-baking business you wanted to start?"

She shrugged. "Someday, maybe."

Jed saw something in Holly's expression that made him want to rescue her. An unfamiliar and unwelcome notion. Did women even want to be rescued these days? She'd probably shut him down if he tried. Thinking that made him glad when the server came to take their order. The interruption gave him time to think of something else to talk about.

He was certain Holly had no interest in electronic gaming, and he knew he wasn't interested in cooking or baking. He already knew she loved her cat. His preferred pet was a dog, although he hadn't had space in his life to own one in a long while. Maybe he would change that when he went home.

By the time the server left the table, Jed had decided the safest place to start was to ask a few questions about her family and where she'd grown up. His decision worked out well. Over dinner, they took turns talking about their parents, memories from childhood, school experiences, and even their individual causes of teenaged angst. They each shared how they'd come to faith in Christ, discovering similarities and differences in their respective journeys. They learned they both enjoyed reading fiction, although Holly's favorites were historical novels while Jed preferred suspense and mystery. They each liked to hike, but both had to admit it had been ages since they'd taken the time to do so.

Jed couldn't remember when he'd spent this much time getting to know a woman—and enjoyed it too. He didn't ask Holly questions in order to avoid silence. He asked because he wanted to hear her answers. Listening to her gave him pleasure. Had he ever felt that way before? He didn't think so.

Was this what it felt like to really fall for a woman—as in feeling something more than mere infatuation or sexual attraction?

"Gradually, then suddenly."

The line in his head was a quote from a Hemingway novel. The character had been talking about bankruptcy, saying it happened gradually and then suddenly. It seemed to Jed that the line also applied to falling in love. And it seemed to him that he was in the "gradually" stage.

Twilight blanketed the valley by the time he walked Holly toward the back door of her house. "Thanks for tonight," he said as they paused at the bottom of the steps. "This was nice."

"Yes." A hesitant smile played in the corners of her mouth.

He wondered if he should lean in to kiss her. He wanted to. A lot. But he remembered that fragile, wary look she'd worn more than once. He didn't want to be the cause of its return.

Instead of a kiss, he reached out, took her hand, and gave it a gentle squeeze. "Weather's supposed to stay nice. How about a hike on Sunday after church?"

Her smile was less hesitant now. "I'd like that."

"Well . . ." He released her hand. "Good night, Holly."

"Good night."

Saturday, September 20, 1969

On the day before the wedding of Charlotte Kincaid and Grant Henning, Grant drove a U-Haul truck up to the farmhouse at eleven o'clock in the morning. One of his cousins, Michael Valentine, was in the U-Haul with him. A car and a pickup, holding various other Henning relatives, followed the U-Haul into the barnyard. They couldn't have asked for a better moving day. After three days of rain, today had dawned with clear skies and no wind.

"Hey, Grandpa," Grant called as he dropped to the ground.

"Morning."

Michael called a greeting too. Soon after, so did Francine and her husband, son, and daughter, followed by Andrew and Helen's youngest son, Andy.

"Quite the crew." Andrew grinned at his family. It wasn't all of them, but it was enough to make it feel like a holiday gathering. "Where's Charlotte?"

Grant answered, "She won't be joining us. Too many last-minute wedding details."

"Does anybody want coffee and a cinnamon roll? Helen made a fresh pot and baked the rolls special."

"Isn't Mom supposed to be resting?" Andy asked as he came up the steps.

"As if I could keep her down if she doesn't want to be." He shrugged. "She says she feels fine. And it has been six weeks since that last episode."

Andrew didn't fail to see the worry that crossed Francine's face. His youngest daughter had called over a week ago with several more recommendations for neurologists, but no appointment had been made. Helen had said she didn't have the time, what with all the changes going on. According to her, after the wedding would be soon enough to make an appointment. Andrew had been forced to acquiesce.

The family trooped inside. Coffee was poured and cinnamon rolls were set on dessert plates. Andy and Francine kissed their mom. Next came the grandkids, from oldest to youngest, to give Helen more loving attention. Andrew exchanged a look with his wife, letting her know he understood. It was good to have the house full of their voices. Silence wasn't all it was cracked up to be.

In no time the young men had eaten their cinnamon rolls—not even a crumb or smear of frosting left on their plates—so they headed outside. Soon the back of the U-Haul was open, and boxes and furniture began to be moved into the first empty bedroom. Everyone but Helen pitched in; her job was to sit quietly and observe. There was plenty of laughter and good-natured banter as the bed was set up, then moved from one position to another and back again because no one could decide how Charlotte would want the room arranged.

Andrew had learned an old proverb from his mother that said many hands made light work. It was as true that day as ever. By one o'clock, the moving was done and the U-Haul was empty. Helen prepared sandwiches for Grant and the rest of the family to eat before they started back to town. And then, after a flurry of goodbyes, they were gone.

Andrew and Helen stood on the porch, his arm around her shoulders, until long after the last car was out of sight. Soft sounds remained. The *thwap* of the dog's tail on the porch. Leaves, already beginning to turn with the season, rustling in a gentle breeze. Clucking of the chickens. They were sounds that brought comfort to Andrew, as familiar to him as the beat of his own heart.

"Our life is about to change again," Helen said, pressing her head into his shoulder.

"Change is the only constant. Isn't that what they say?"

She laughed softly, a sound of agreement.

He kissed the top of her head. How many countless times had he done that through the years? Back when her hair was dark and abundant. How many times had they stood on this porch together, watching loved ones drive away but knowing they had one another to hold on to? So many years. So many memories.

"We'll have an early dinner." Helen patted his chest with one hand. "Don't forget. Lawrence Welk's on tonight."

"In color."

She gave him a look.

"Weren't you paying attention earlier? Grant insisted the new color set they got for a wedding present go in the living room."

They turned in unison and reentered the house. Helen paused long enough to look at the television console that now took up a good portion of one wall.

"Awfully big, isn't it?"

"We can't very well make them put it in their bedroom. Even less space in there. We'll get used to it."

Her expression was pensive as she took in the rest of the rearranged furniture.

He stepped closer. "Not having second thoughts, are you?"

"Second thoughts?" She took one step back and met his gaze. "About Grant and Charlotte being here?"

He nodded.

"Heavens, no." A fleeting smile crossed her lips. "Now, I'd best get into the kitchen. Lots to do before bedtime. Tomorrow's a big day."

"Our second grandchild getting married." Andrew shook his head slowly.

"Not to mention that our first great-grandchild will arrive soon."

"Great-grandchild. Maybe you should start calling me your old man."

She laughed, this time giving him a small push on the arm. "And sound like a hippie? Not a chance. Besides, it would give you permission to call me your old lady, and I'll not put up with that nonsense."

"Have I told you how pretty you are when you get your back up?" He kissed her on the lips before she hurried into the kitchen to start dinner preparations.

Chapter 15

"Spill," Trixie demanded. "I want all the details."

Holly leaned back in the booth. The lunch customers at Sweet Caroline's had left, and the sisters could talk in peace. "It was nice."

"Nice?" Trixie's eyebrows rose.

"The Riverfront is spectacular, both the ambience and the food. I ordered the salmon, which was amazing. I'd love to have the recipe."

"I wasn't asking about the ambience or the food. What about your date?"

Holly gave her head a slow shake. "Jed's nice too."

"Sis, you're impossible."

"I know." She laughed, feeling a lightness in spirit that she hadn't felt in more than a year. Taking pity, she told her sister what she wanted to know. "We talked a bit about our families and about where we each went to school. We discovered things we have in common and things we don't. I . . . I told him about Nathan."

"You're kidding." The teasing tone was gone from Trixie's voice. "Wow. That was a big step."

"I know. I didn't say a lot, but enough for him to understand. He's a good listener."

"I knew I was right about him."

"Maybe."

"He's nice. He's a good listener. You had a good time. You like him. He likes you. Sounds perfect."

"Liking is one thing. Friendship is okay. Nobody says it'll be anything more than that. I'm not sure I want it to be more than that. I'm not sure he does either."

"Holly, you may be older than me, but you don't know much about men. Have you noticed the way he looks at you?"

It frightened her, thinking Trixie might be right. It frightened her even more, thinking she wanted her sister to be right. "Don't."

"Don't what?"

"Don't read too much into it. I . . . I'm not ready."

A frown pinched Trixie's eyebrows, and her lips thinned as she pressed them together. It was a look Holly had seen before, one that said her younger sister was not going to give up.

"Trix, every girl can't be as lucky as you. Brett's a great guy, and the two of you have something special."

Her sister's posture relaxed a little. "Yeah, he is great. The thing is he's great for *me*. But there's a guy somewhere who'll be just as great for you. He wasn't Nathan. Maybe he's Jed."

Holly dreaded the wanting that hummed in her heart. How had she let herself care this much for someone she'd known only a matter of weeks? She'd put a wall of protection around her heart ever since Nathan walked out on her. But somehow Jed had caused her to lower her guard, if only a fraction.

"Oh, Trixie," she whispered. "I'm scared. He doesn't even

live in Boise. Even if I wanted more, we're already set up for failure."

Her sister took hold of her hand. "Caring for someone isn't a bad thing, even if it doesn't work out between you two. You need to live again, Holly. Nathan was a Class 1 jerk. So, lesson learned. Move on. You need to let yourself feel things, both good and bad. Bottling it up isn't healthy."

Holly swallowed hard, blinking away unexpected tears. She both loved and hated that Trixie understood her so well.

"Did Jed ask you out again?"

"Yes." She nodded as she drew a deep breath and released it. "We're going on a hike on Sunday."

"Well, then. Cheer up. Give the guy a chance. Give yourself a chance." Trixie squeezed Holly's hand. "You haven't given up trying to make this restaurant succeed. You have all kinds of faith in the women you're teaching how to cook. Now you need to have some faith in yourself and your ability to live life to the fullest."

Holly smiled through her tears. "Have I told you how much I love you?"

"How could you help it?" Trixie gave her head a saucy toss, eyes twinkling.

The two of them broke into laughter, and Holly would have sworn she felt her faith in the future increase.

Jed entered the dimly lit bar and grill a little before seven on Thursday evening. Music played from speakers in the ceiling. The air smelled of fried foods. He squinted, waiting for his eyes to adjust, then looked for his brother. Chris wasn't there.

No surprise. When's he ever on time?

He shook his head, displeased with the thought. Wouldn't do him any good to have a negative attitude from the get-go.

He stepped deeper into the room. After another quick look around, he chose an empty booth with a clear view of the entrance. A server came to the table, and he ordered a Diet Coke to sip while he waited.

Jed had prayed about this meeting for the past three days. He'd prayed that he would keep his temper in check. He'd prayed for patience. He'd prayed for wisdom and understanding. Trouble was, he didn't know what any of that was supposed to look like. He thought of his brother's name, now written in their great-grandfather's Bible. Jed had meant it when he wrote it in the margin. He wanted the prodigal to come home. Home to the family, if not home to Laffriot. Their dad had been the catalyst for this hoped-for reconciliation, but Jed wanted a better relationship with Chris. More than he'd known.

The bar's door opened, and a guy entered, his right arm draped over the shoulders of his girl. Both of them wore leather jackets, white T-shirts, and jeans. In their early twenties, they had eyes only for each other. It was a wonder they made it to a booth without running over someone or something.

Thoughts of Holly resurfaced. Memories of her tentative smile, of her melodic laugh, of the wariness that came and went from her pretty eyes, of her generosity to others, of the way she adored her younger sister. Holly Stanford was special. She was—

The door to the bar opened again. This time it was Chris who stepped into the establishment. Like Jed before him, he squinted, as if unable to see clearly yet. Jed stood, drawing his brother's gaze. His expression didn't change as he started to walk in Jed's direction.

"Thanks for coming, Chris." He took a step forward, as if he would give his brother a hug.

Chris sidestepped, keeping the embrace from happening.

Jed sat down on his side of the booth, any hope he'd had of an easy reunion evaporating. "Would you like something to drink? Or eat?"

Chris nodded at the Diet Coke. "One of those'd be okay."

"I'll get it for you." As he stood, Jed took a moment to study his brother. He looked tired, dark circles etched beneath his eyes. Was he thinner too? Jed couldn't be sure. Chris had always favored a loose-fit clothing style.

He went to the bar and ordered the beverage. It gave him time to say another quick prayer. A few minutes later, he returned to the booth, drink in hand. He set the glass in front of his brother before sitting opposite him.

Chris gave him a level gaze. "Your meeting. Your agenda." His words dripped with animosity.

A quick retort popped into Jed's head. He managed to quash it before it reached his lips and ruined everything. Instead, he drew a slow, deep breath and released it. "You said on the phone that you're not going back home. Do you plan to stay in Boise?"

"For now."

"Boise's got a lot going for it."

"Yeah."

Another breath. "Look. I'm sorry about the things I said the last time we were together. I stepped over the line."

Chris's eyes widened for a moment, then darkened with suspicion.

"Laffriot never would've got off the ground without you. You're right about that. I may know business and finances, but without your creativity, we never could've launched *Caliban*." He shook his head, lowering his gaze to the Diet Coke in his right hand. "The company needs you, but I need my brother more." The truth of the confession pierced his chest, and he looked up again. "I didn't realize how far apart we'd grown. I'm not even sure how it happened or why it started. But I know I rode you hard the last couple of years, and I'm sorry for that."

"You think I can't take it when you come down on me. You still see me as some dopey kid, don't you?"

Jed wanted to deny it but couldn't.

Chris leaned forward. "I was okay with you doing better than me in school. I handled it when the girl I liked so much only had eyes for you."

"What girl?"

Chris ignored the interruption. "I got used to Dad boasting to everybody about your achievements and nobody thinking I'd amount to anything. Heck. They were right. I'm not wired the way you are. And I'm okay with it now. I don't want to be you. I want to be me. Took me a while to figure that out, but I'm good with it."

His brother's demeanor changed as he talked. His shoulders seemed less tense. His voice wasn't filled with the same defensiveness. Jed didn't dare hope that one brief meeting would fix all that was wrong between them, but he could hope this was a start.

Chris pulled his phone from his pocket and looked at the screen. "I've gotta go."

You agreed to give me half an hour. Somehow Jed managed not to say those words aloud. Instead, he asked, "Can we meet again? Soon?"

"Depends." Chris took a few quick swallows of his beverage before standing. "My work schedule's crazy right now, and I've got some other stuff to deal with. I'll see what I can work out."

Work schedule? Where was Chris working? What was he doing? Where was he living? What did he have to deal with in Boise?

"I'll text you," his brother added, then walked away.

A few weeks ago, Jed would have gone after him. He would have grabbed his brother by the arm and forced him to stay. He would have told him what to do, and he would have demanded answers to all his questions. But this time he sat still, watching the door close behind Chris.

God, bring him home. Bring us both home. Bring us back as brothers, and bring us back to You.

Sunday, September 21, 1969

The day of the wedding was as beautiful as anyone could want, as was the interior of the church. The afternoon sun sent shafts of light through the stained-glass windows. Autumn-colored flowers of gold and red and orange decorated the ends of the pews on the center aisle, as well as the altar area.

As soft music played, a flower girl and two bridesmaids walked the length of the church. Then, with the louder chords of the bridal march, Charlotte stepped into view, holding her father's arm. Family and friends all rose to watch as they made their way toward Grant, who waited for his bride near the altar steps.

Andrew grew misty-eyed. He'd never considered himself sentimental. He wasn't afraid to show love for his family. Others would, no doubt, call him affectionate and tender. But sentimental? No, he'd never thought so.

But as the bride came down the aisle, waves of nostalgia washed over him. Wedding snapshots flashed in his memory even as the photographer's camera flashed in reality. He and Helen's wedding in October of 1929. Louisa's wedding in 1944. Ben's wedding soon after he'd returned from Europe in 1945. Francine's wedding in 1950. Finally, their youngest, Andy Jr., in 1964. It had all happened so fast. Life was a whirlwind. His parents had warned him. They'd said that the years went by in the blink of an eye, but he hadn't believed them. Why would he when just getting through four years of college had seemed to take forever? But here he was, on the other end of that lifetime, knowing how right they'd been.

Helen's grip on his arm tightened while she dabbed at her eyes with a handkerchief held in her free hand. Blast if he didn't think he could use a handkerchief himself.

Chapter 16

Holly didn't go to the restaurant that Saturday. Her sister's wedding was mere weeks away, and she had yet to settle on a cake design. Holly had decided Zachary could manage the restaurant without her for the day. In many ways, he seemed to manage better than Holly ever did. He was more than a great cook. He was calm in the midst of any storm. She envied him that.

A little before noon, Holly reached for her phone, opened the camera app, and took several photos from different angles. Then she texted them to Trixie, along with the question: Thoughts on this naked cake? (Means not frosted all over.)

It wasn't long before she got Trixie's reply: Love it! Different. Can you add flowers to the berries?

Holly put down her phone and went into the spare bedroom. In a basket in the closet, she found different kinds of artificial flowers. She grabbed several bunches and returned to the kitchen. There she placed the various blooms on different layers as well as the stand and took a couple more photos.

Text to Trixie: Examples only. Can match your bouquet.

Text to Holly: Perfect. Love it. Naked cake. Scandalous for a wedding?

Holly laughed before texting back that she thought it was okay. When Trixie didn't send another reply, Holly returned her attention to the cake. It really was pretty, garnished with blueberries, raspberries, strawberries, and blackberries. Simple, yet elegant.

She picked up the nearby bowl and carried it to the sink. Before washing it, she ran her index finger around the bottom, scraping up the remaining frosting. She closed her eyes as she put her finger between her lips and let the vanilla buttercream flavor burst to life in her mouth. How long had it been since she'd allowed herself this much pleasure? Ages. Ages and ages. It was more than simply a day off. It was more even than getting to bake and play with designs. She felt a strange kind of freedom. Happiness, even. Worries awaited her, but for this moment she refused to let them enter her mind.

Turning, she looked at the cake again. Of all of her different ideas for Trixie's wedding cake, she liked this one the best. Of course this was a smaller version of the one she would make for the day itself.

After removing the artificial flowers, she lifted the cake stand with both hands and carefully carried the confection down to the extra refrigerator in the basement. There it would stay for a couple of hours before she drove it over to the Lighthouse women and children's shelter.

As she left the basement, her gaze went to the connecting doorway to the apartment, and she wondered what Jed was doing today. Their paths hadn't crossed much since their dinner at the Riverfront three days earlier. One of them always seemed to be returning when the other one was headed out somewhere. Smiles and a few exchanged pleasantries hadn't been enough for Holly. She'd missed his company. Missed it more than she should, but she no longer tried to deny how much she liked him, even if the feelings still frightened her.

Letting out a breath, she climbed the stairs. At the landing, she flicked off the basement light. Pumpkin's demanding meow drew Holly into the utility room, where she dispensed a few cat treats into a bowl across from the washer and dryer. She was rewarded with a loud purr of approval and a head rub.

"You're welcome, baby." She gave the cat's coat a few strokes before returning to the kitchen. "Alexa, play my 1960s favorites."

To the words and music of "You've Lost That Lovin' Feelin'," Holly slow danced around the kitchen until she reached the sink. After wetting a cloth under the faucet, she began the task of cleaning up from her baking session. Her choice of music was thanks to her mom's influence. When Holly was a girl, she and her mom had cooked and baked to the music of the sixties and seventies. Holly had never outgrown the habit. She could name more song titles and more artists from those two decades than she could from the first two decades of the twenty-first century. Her friends in school had thought her a bit strange because of it. She didn't care.

By the time the Beach Boys began to sing "Good Vibrations," the dishes and pans had been washed, dried, and put away, the counters wiped down, and the floor swept. Holly glanced around the room, loving her cheery kitchen. Then, swirling the dish towel over her head, she spun and gyrated around the island, letting the beat decide her movements.

Back from a late-morning run along the Greenbelt, Jed grinned as he watched Holly dance past the kitchen windows. He couldn't see all of her movements from where he stood on the sidewalk, but he saw enough to love it. It was too adorable. No, *she* was too adorable. Leaning slightly forward, he strained to hear the music. Nothing except for the thrum of the bass.

Holly's dancing stopped suddenly, and her gaze met Jed's through the glass. He guessed there might be a blush rising in her cheeks. His smile broadened as he waved. A heartbeat later, he moved toward the back door. She met him there.

"What was the song?" he asked, still grinning.

"'Good Vibrations.'"

"The Beach Boys?"

She was definitely blushing. "Yes."

"Before your time. That's for sure."

"Before your time too." She seemed to relax, and her laughter came easily. "My mom always listened to her favorite music when we baked. Her favorites became my favorites. At least in the kitchen."

Jed leaned his forearm on the doorjamb. "Holly Stanford, you're full of surprises."

"I think I like that."

"I think I do too." He also liked the ease with which she met his gaze, the absence of the all-too-common wariness in her eyes.

She took a step back, opening the door fully. "Do you have time to come in?"

"As a matter of fact, I do." He followed her inside.

"I made a cake for Trixie to consider," she said when she reached the island. "It got a thumbs-up. This one's much smaller than she'll need for the wedding, but it gave her the idea."

A hint of vanilla lingered in the air, but no sign of baking could be seen in the kitchen. Jed motioned around the room. "Where's the cake? Did you eat it already?"

"No." She gave him a playful punch on the arm. "It's in the basement fridge. I'm going to take it over to the Lighthouse in a little bit." She paused for a moment, then added, "Would you like to come with me?"

What he would like to do was lean in and kiss her, but he settled for "Sure."

Something flickered in her eyes. Had she guessed his real desire? And would she have welcomed the kiss? Maybe, but he didn't want to rush her. He didn't want to make the wrong move and hurt her. He would never want to hurt her.

She broke eye contact, lowering her gaze. "I . . . I'd better change my clothes before we go." She untied the apron and pulled it over her head. "Meet me at the back door in half an hour?"

"I'll be there."

Holly hadn't taken more than a few steps toward the hallway before Jed made himself scarce. Once down in his basement apartment, he peeled off his shirt on the way to the bathroom, where he showered off the morning. As he lathered on the soap, he closed his eyes, remembering the way Holly had looked as she danced around the kitchen. A moment later he realized he was whistling "Good Vibrations." He laughed at himself, feeling in great spirits. He'd been looking forward to the hike tomorrow. This afternoon was a bonus.

The half hour she'd requested wasn't up yet as he closed his apartment door behind him. That didn't matter. He found her waiting for him, holding a cake in a large cardboard box with both hands.

"Want me to take that for you?" He held out his hands.

"I've got it. But you can open the hatch of my car for me."

He moved ahead. Both garage door and hatch were open in short order.

"Thanks." She set the cake box on a foam mat in the center of the level surface.

"So that's what Trixie's cake's going to look like?"

"Yes." She closed the hatch. "Only bigger."

"Nice."

She smiled at him. "Tastes good too."

"Didn't doubt it."

They looked at each other for a moment more, then turned in unison toward their respective sides of the SUV.

The light banter the two of them had begun to exchange surprised Jed every time it happened. He'd never felt such ease with a woman. What was it about Holly that made the difference? He glanced over at her. She drove with her hands at nine and three. Her eyes were focused on the road ahead, breaking only to check both ways at the cross streets. A defensive driver. Even that seemed adorable to Jed.

Man, I've got it bad. He grinned as he looked out the passenger window. *And I'm not the least bit sorry.*

Thursday, September 25, 1969

Andrew answered the phone call that came at five in the morning, not long after he'd risen for the day. It was Louisa, their eldest daughter. Her daughter-in-law, Michael's wife, was in labor.

"Shari's pains started early yesterday, and I'm getting worried." The strain in Louisa's voice punctuated her words. "It's gone on so long. Will you pray?"

"We'll get dressed and drive into Boise. Your mother and I will do our praying on the way."

"I don't think you should come. It isn't good for Mom. The doctor said she should avoid stress."

"Do you think I could keep her away after this phone call? Do you think she won't already be worried?"

Silence filled the line.

"We'll be there as soon as we can."

"Okay. If you think you should. Thanks, Dad."

After hanging up the phone, Andrew turned to find Helen watching from the bedroom doorway.

"Shari's in labor?"

"Yes, and it doesn't seem to be going well."

"Oh no." Sorrow flitted across her face.

He embraced her. The decades hadn't erased the heartbreak over their stillborn son. The memories assailed Andrew as if it had happened yesterday. Helen's pain. The blood and the fear. The baby who'd never had a chance to know or be known. The loss had rocked their world far beyond that night. It had threatened to break their marriage in two. Only by God's grace had they made it through that difficult time.

"I told Louisa we'd come to the hospital right away."

"Yes. We'll hurry."

Grant and Charlotte were still away on their honeymoon, but Grant had arranged for a neighbor to feed the horses and gather the eggs. All Andrew needed to do, after getting dressed, was to pour kibble into Chester's bowl and make sure there was fresh water beside it. His own breakfast could wait. He wasn't hungry now.

It was after six before Andrew and Helen entered the hospital waiting room. When their eldest daughter saw them, she jumped up and rushed across the room, almost falling into Andrew's arms. "I'm so glad you're both here." After hugging him tightly, she turned toward her mom.

Helen embraced her. "Why didn't you call us yesterday?"

"We thought it would be better if you didn't know until after it was over. You've been doing too much lately. You're supposed to rest more, and you know how it is." Louisa glanced at Andrew. "Francine will be furious with me for calling you."

Andrew nodded. "And your mother would be furious if you hadn't."

"What have you heard?" Helen asked.

"Nothing. Not for a long time. Michael's still with Shari. Her labor started yesterday morning. It was slow, but it seemed normal. Then all of a sudden—" She broke off abruptly, shaking her head.

Andrew looked around the waiting room. To his right, there were two couples—strangers to him—seated near each other, the women talking softly. They looked to be in their forties, so Andrew assumed at least two of them were about to become grandparents. To his left was Louisa's husband, Samuel, who watched his wife with concerned eyes.

"Let's sit down." Helen hooked her arm through their daughter's and gently guided her back to the chair she'd vacated.

Taking a breath, Andrew moved to sit beside his son-in-law. "Have you been here all night?"

"Yeah." Samuel glanced at his wife again. "Louisa's been here from the start. I came after I finished work yesterday."

Andrew said a silent prayer for mercy and protection, but he didn't promise Samuel that his daughter-in-law or his grandbaby would be all right. He couldn't know what would happen. What he did know was that he trusted God with the end result, even if it turned out to be painful. It was all he knew how to do. Trust and pray. Pray and trust.

A grinning young man—barely into his twenties, by the look of him—bustled into the waiting room. "It's a boy!"

The two couples on the opposite side of the room were on their feet at once. There were hugs and back slaps exchanged and plenty of excited talk. But soon, the new dad led the delighted grandparents out of the room. Only silence was left behind, and Andrew felt the weight of it on his soul.

Please, God. Protect Shari and her unborn child.

Time ticked by with agonizing slowness. Andrew could see the strain of it on the faces of his loved ones. Unable to help ease their worries, he looked down, resting his forearms on his thighs, and prayed some more. Then someone—he couldn't be sure who—sucked in a breath that caused him to look up.

Michael stood in the doorway. Exhaustion was etched on his face, but the smile he wore told Andrew all he needed to know.

Louisa rose and hurried across the room. "Shari's okay?"

"Yes." Michael's gaze took in the others in the waiting area. "It's a girl. And she's a beauty. Complaining about her entrance into the world for all she's worth."

"Thank God." Andrew stood.

While the others talked and celebrated, Andrew's thoughts went back in time again. He'd been twenty-five years old when they lost their firstborn, and the pain of the loss had been keen. He was thankful beyond words that his grandson didn't have to endure the same pain.

"She's in the nursery," Michael said. "Come and see her."

Andrew joined Helen, placing his arm around her back while they exchanged understanding looks. "God is good," he said to her.

"Always," she replied.

Then they followed the proud father and grandparents out of the waiting room.

Chapter 17

Jed was taken to the Lighthouse common room, the only room in the shelter where men were allowed.

"I'll be back as soon as I've brought in the cake," Holly told him, then left him there.

Judging by the exterior, at one time the Lighthouse had housed a church. Extensive remodeling on the interior had removed any resemblance of that use. Perhaps the common room had been part of the sanctuary, but there was no way for him to be certain of that. He stood in the middle of the large room, letting his gaze roam over all of the mismatched furniture—sofas, loveseats, chairs, end tables. Donations, no doubt. Things that people no longer wanted in their homes and had gifted to the shelter. Shelves on two different walls were packed with books, some upright, some in piles. Framed prints hung on the walls. A worn area rug covered much of the floor.

"Who're you?" a young voice demanded from behind him.

Jed turned, his gaze lowering to the dark-haired boy who wore a scowl, distrust written in his eyes.

"You supposed to be in here?"

"Yes, I am." He held out a hand. "I'm Jed. Jed Henning."

The boy looked as if Jed was offering a snake instead of a handshake.

He didn't have much experience with kids, but he knew enough to lower his hand and take a step back, giving the boy some space. "I'm waiting for Miss Stanford. Do you know her?"

"Ethan?" A woman appeared in the doorway, holding hands with a little girl. She looked as if she would say something to the boy, but then she saw Jed. "Oh. I didn't know anyone was in here." Her expression resembled Ethan's. "Are you waiting for someone?"

"I came with Holly. She's in the kitchen, I think." Again he held out a hand. "Jed Henning."

The woman's expression was transformed by a smile. "Holly's friends are always welcome at the Lighthouse. I'm Madalyn Hargrove. That's my son, Ethan." She shook Jed's hand. "And this is my daughter, Olivia."

"Ethan and I were getting acquainted." Jed glanced again at Ethan, but the boy still wore a frown. Apparently Jed's friendship with Holly didn't impress him.

Madalyn motioned toward the nearest chairs. "Let's sit down, shall we, Mr. Henning?"

"Sure. And please, call me Jed."

Madalyn leaned down and said something to her daughter. The girl immediately headed to a corner where there were some toys and books. Ethan followed her there a few moments later.

Before either of the adults could move to the chairs, voices announced the arrival of others. Seconds later, five women entered the common room, along with two young girls around Ethan's age and a toddler, running on pudgy legs to keep up.

"We heard there was cake," one of the women said.

A loud "Yes!" came from the children's corner.

The women began to sit down around the room while talking to one another. Overt glances were cast in Jed's direction. Otherwise he was ignored.

"Hey, everyone." When Madalyn had everyone's attention, she performed quick introductions. The last one was Willow Flynn, now seated in the chair to his right.

Jed thanked God for a familiar face. He'd only met Willow that once at church, and they hadn't said more than a few words to each other. Still, her presence made him feel a little more at ease. He was comfortable in board rooms but not so much in a room full of women and children. He'd be glad when Holly walked through those doors again.

As if in answer to his unspoken hope, Holly wheeled in a silver cart with the cake riding in its center, another woman following behind her. Oohs and aahs resounded around the room. Well deserved, Jed thought. The cake looked different from any wedding cake he'd seen before. No thick frosting spread on the top and sides, but lots of fruit everywhere.

From the lower shelf of the cart, the woman who'd come in with Holly brought out plates, napkins, and forks. Holly, in the meantime, had begun to cut slices of the cake with a knife. Before long, the dessert had been distributed to everyone, Jed included. Seeing what had happened, Willow's toddler ran across the room to her with a squeal of delight. She drew him onto her lap with one hand while keeping the cake out of his reach.

"Me do it. Me do it."

Jed looked at the little boy, the three-word phrase throwing his thoughts back in time to when Chris had been about the same age. Independent and headstrong to the core, Chris had demanded to do everything himself. *"Me do it!"* had been his cry as a two-year-old. From that time on, he hadn't wanted help from anyone. He'd wanted his own way. *"Butt out!"* were the words he'd shouted at Jed not so long ago, but it had meant the same thing as his childhood cry.

"AJ, sit still," Willow commanded the wiggly child. "Sit still or you won't get any cake." The threat worked. AJ quieted.

Chris had rarely obeyed when ordered to do something. Ultimatums had made him even more stubborn. Jed pictured his brother sitting across from him in that bar and grill on Thursday night. Jed hadn't heard from him since. Should he be the one to call or text, or should he wait for Chris to make the next move? All he knew for certain was that he missed his brother. An unexpected emotion.

"Are you all right?" Holly asked softly.

He turned his head, surprised to find her standing in front of him. He blinked, then answered, "Yeah. I'm fine." He held up the dessert plate in his hand and forced a smile. "And I can't wait to taste this."

Holly settled onto a chair to Jed's left and watched him take his first bite of the cake. The smile he turned on her was more genuine than the one from moments before.

"This is amazing." He touched the frosting between the layers of cake with the tines of the fork. "It tastes like about a million calories a bite."

She laughed. "Something like that."

"Holly."

She looked across the room at Adele.

Hand covering her mouth, the girl said, "Can you teach us to make a cake like this on Monday?"

"Not this Monday," she answered, "but maybe in a few weeks."

"Mmm. I can't wait."

It might be the most Holly had heard Adele say at any one time. It made her feel good, seeing the change in the teenager. She wondered how much more Adele would change once she got her new dentures.

To her left, a newcomer to the Lighthouse said, "You're the cooking teacher?"

Holly smiled. "Yes, I am." She held out her hand. "I'm Holly Stanford."

"Camila García."

"It's nice to meet you, Camila. I'd love to have you join us on Monday mornings. Anytime you wish."

"Thank you. I would like that."

"Mostly I teach how to make nutritious meals on a budget, but every so often, desserts find their way into the lessons."

"That is good." A shy smile curved Camila's mouth.

Holly wondered what this young woman's story was, what had brought her to the Lighthouse. She wondered the same thing with every new arrival, but she'd learned to let the women tell what they wanted, without any prompting, in their own time.

Camila's attention was drawn away, giving Holly a chance to look around the room again. Except for AJ, the children had been served their cake at a small table near the dining room entrance. By this time their plates were empty, every trace of frosting licked clean. Most of the adults weren't far behind them.

"Mom," Ethan said, "can we have more?"

"Not now, honey," Madalyn answered. "But maybe after dinner tonight." She rose and went to the table. Probably to make sure hands were clean before the children returned to the toys. She was soon joined by two other women.

As Holly looked around the room one more time, she thanked God that she could be a part of the lives of those who resided here. Bringing over the cake had seemed a small thing to her, but it wasn't small to the people in this room. It brought pleasure and laughter. It was a break in the routine of a Saturday afternoon. It was a kindness that was foreign to too many of them.

"Hey there, buddy."

Holly looked to her right. AJ had left his mom's lap and was standing next to Jed, his hands on Jed's thigh, looking up and grinning. Jed held his plate off to the opposite side, protecting the remaining cake crumbs.

"He likes you," Holly said.

Jed chuckled. "He likes your cake."

She couldn't argue with that. It was the plate that had AJ's attention.

"I'm sorry." Willow set her own plate on the floor before scooping her son up in her arms.

"It's okay. He wasn't bothering me."

AJ wriggled, trying to escape his mom's grasp.

"Really," Jed added. "No worries. My kid brother was like that at his age. Never wanted to be still."

With a sigh of exasperation, Willow let AJ slide to the floor.

Holly decided this was a good time to collect dirty plates and wheel the cart back to the kitchen. When she was almost halfway around the room, moving clockwise, she discovered that Jed had followed her lead and was collecting plates going in the counter-clockwise direction. *Thanks,* she mouthed to him when their gazes met over the cart. He replied with a nod and a grin, and she felt the wall of resistance around her heart slipping away.

Tuesday, September 30, 1969

Andrew stared at the neurologist. "But Dr. Schwimmer, Helen hasn't had any symptoms in almost two months."

"We still need to do the tests, Mr. Henning. The more information we have, the better care we can provide for your wife. My nurse is scheduling the arteriogram right now. It should be in the next week or two. Then we'll have a follow-up appointment soon after the results are back."

Helen rose from her chair. "Thank you, doctor. We appreciate the time you've taken with us."

Frustrated—and more unsettled than he'd been in many weeks—Andrew got up, bid the doctor a good day, and left the office with Helen at his side. They were silent as they walked to the car, both of them trying to digest all that the neurologist had said to them, as well as what he hadn't said.

Once in the Jeep, Helen looked at Andrew. "I'm not afraid."

He wished he could say the same. As the physician had laid out the possibilities, a chill had run through him, settling in his heart, and it had yet to dissipate.

"My love." Helen's hand pressed against the side of his face. "Tomorrow has enough trouble of its own. That's what the Lord told us. We must have faith."

He covered her hand. "I know, but my faith feels rather weak today." He leaned over and kissed her cheek.

"Shall we go to lunch before we drive home?" she asked as he drew back. "Or would you rather eat in our own kitchen?"

Truth be told, he had no appetite, but he would do whatever Helen wanted. "You decide."

"Let's go home, then. I'll make chicken salad sandwiches."

He grinned. "Unless Grant ate the rest of the chicken from Sunday dinner."

"Well, there is that." After a moment she laughed.

He joined her, thankful for something to laugh about, even if it was a small thing. "Let's take the risk."

As he turned the key in the ignition, he realized the chill was gone from his heart. Laughter truly was good medicine.

"Drive by the old apartment on our way out of Boise."

Surprised by the request, he looked at Helen.

"Remember the flowers our landlady had along the sidewalk? They were so beautiful that fall when we first moved in, even that late in the year. Autumn flowers are so vibrant. I want to see if they're still there."

Again, he would do whatever his wife wanted. He turned at the next corner and headed through downtown Boise.

Knowing their destination caused his thoughts to fly back in time. He remembered the blustery winter day when he'd been laid off from his job at the bank. That bank building was no longer standing. It had been demolished a decade ago. He remembered the feelings that had run through him as he'd gone home to tell his wife that he was unemployed. A mixture of fear and bravado. He remembered that basement apartment—the windows that hadn't let in as much light as he liked, the worn rugs on the tiled floor, the tiny shower stall where it was hard to turn around without bruising an elbow. Despite the apartment's drawbacks, he'd loved those few short months they'd lived in it.

He slowed the Jeep as their destination came into sight. A few moments later he pulled to the curb and killed the engine.

Helen released a deep breath. "The flowers are still there. I should plant some like them at the farm." She placed her hand on the door as she stared out the passenger window. "The roof looks new, and so are those shrubs." She pointed.

"It's been almost forty years since we lived there. Lots of things must be new."

"Forty years."

He almost couldn't hear her.

She looked at him, a touch of melancholy in her eyes. "Thanks for humoring me. I haven't seen it since right after the war ended."

He didn't need for her to explain which war, even though American soldiers had marched off to Korea and Vietnam in the years since. For the two of them, war would always mean the Second World War.

"Okay." Her expression brightened. "Now I'm getting hungry. Let's get home so I can make those sandwiches."

"Righto. We're on our way." He started the engine again and pulled away from the curb.

Chapter 18

After church the next day, Jed drove to a trailhead in the Boise foothills, following directions he'd found on the internet, and parked his rental car in a leveled area. Half a dozen other vehicles were parked there already. The temperature had climbed to seventy-five degrees, and wispy clouds, undisturbed by any breeze, were scattered around the blue sky.

"Perfect weather," Holly said as she got out of the car. She was dressed all in yellow, from the visor on her head to her shirt and shorts to the athletic shoes on her feet.

"You're right. Perfect." But he wasn't thinking about the weather when he said it.

Holly slid her arms through the straps of a backpack. "This was a great idea. I've spent way too much time cooped up indoors lately." She drew a deep breath, head back and face toward the sun.

Jed dropped the car keys into a small zippered pocket in his own backpack, and then the two of them set off along the trail.

The foothills in early May were covered in long grasses, wildflowers, bitter brush, and sagebrush. According to Ben, the Boise front served as grazing land in the spring for about twenty-eight thousand sheep. With any luck, they might catch a glimpse of one of the large bands of ewes and lambs.

"If you get near them," his cousin had told him, "pay attention. Those Great Pyrenees they use for herding mean business if they feel the sheep are threatened."

Jed looked up the hillsides. If any sheep were within hiking distance, they were hidden by the rolling hillsides.

"No sheep?" Holly asked, guessing his thoughts.

"I don't see any." He glanced her way. "Grant says he remembers the sheep drives going right through downtown Boise on their way to the mountains when he was younger. That was back in the fifties and sixties. But they were doing the drives for decades before that. Can't imagine what that must have looked like, seeing twenty thousand sheep trotting down Main Street. But then, the population of Boise was a whole lot less fifty years ago."

Holly grinned at him. "Sometimes you sound like a historian."

"Do I?" He chuckled. "Yeah, I guess I do. I never used to care much about history. Did okay in it in school, but it wasn't what I focused on. But these past few weeks, going through the boxes of old family photos and letters I got from a cousin, I have to admit, it's piqued my interest more."

Conversation ended as they followed the trail up a steady incline. The ground was hard and dry beneath their feet, but evidence of earlier spring rains was carved into the earth. When they reached the top of the hill, they paused to take in the view—both in front of them and behind them.

"So pretty," Holly said.

From this vantage point, Jed could see a stretch of the Boise

River as it flowed westward, wending its way through the center of the city and across the valley floor. In Andrew Henning's day, the population of Boise had been about twenty-five thousand, and the valley had been farmland or desert from here to the Oregon border. Now homes and subdivisions were spreading to the south and west, joining one city to another, gobbling up both farmland and desert. In some ways, he envied his great-grandfather that simpler life. Well, maybe not simpler. Andrew had lived through the Great Depression, a second world war, and other tumultuous decades besides. But at least the area had been less crowded.

With a soft laugh, Holly said, "Your roots are showing again."

For a second, he didn't understand what she meant. Then he did, and he laughed with her. "Guilty."

"Do you feel the same way about where you live now?"

He thought about the question before answering. "There's lots to love about where I live. It's beautiful. Greener because of all the rain. The forests are different. The ocean is close by." He looked over the valley again. "But there's something about all this that makes me feel like I've come home. It's hard to put my finger on why."

In unspoken agreement, they turned and began walking again, following the trail higher and higher. A couple of times they were passed by mountain bikers. Another time they met three hikers with their dogs. Greetings were exchanged. "Beautiful day." "Great weather." "Nice dog." It was almost another hour before bleating sounds punctuated the silence, telling Jed and Holly that they were about to get their earlier wish. They crested the hillside and saw them: a band of sheep grazing in a long, narrow draw.

"Look." Jed pointed. An enormous white dog had stopped to

stare at them, assessing whether or not they were a threat. "He's got my attention."

"Mine too."

Jed removed the phone from his pocket and snapped photos of the dog, the sheep, and finally, a herder on horseback who rode into view before he was done. Then, when she wasn't looking his way, he snapped a few of Holly and knew he would spend a lot more time looking at those photos than the ones of the herd.

While Jed took his photos, Holly removed the water bottle from her backpack and took several big swallows. It had been too long since she'd done something like this, since she'd gotten away from work and her phone and her worries. Time to simply breathe deeply and enjoy the beauty of God's creation.

"Thanks, Jed."

He looked over at her.

"I needed this."

"Me too." He smiled.

In that moment she realized she wasn't afraid. She knew she could still get hurt. She knew she might even be wrong about Jed. He might not be all that he appeared to be, all that she wanted him to be. She knew he might be gone in another month or two. But still she wasn't afraid. She almost wished—

A bike came sailing over the rise, its tires leaving the ground. Jed grabbed Holly with both arms to pull her out of the way an instant before the bike would have hit her. They went down together, Jed taking the brunt of the fall. Holly heard dogs barking and lifted her head from Jed's chest to see two Great Pyrenees charging across the draw in their direction. Thankfully, a sharp command from the sheepherder stopped the dogs.

"Dude. You two okay?"

She turned her head, squinting into the sun, to see the cyclist standing beside them, a gloved hand outstretched.

"Sorry 'bout that. Didn't mean to run you down."

Reluctantly, she took his hand and let him pull her up. Jed got to his feet right behind her.

"You okay?" the cyclist repeated.

"Yeah," Jed answered. "We're fine."

"You sure?"

"I'm sure." He looked at Holly, and she nodded.

"Okay, then. Again, real sorry." In no time the guy was back on his bike and riding away, as if the encounter never happened.

Holly watched him go. "I don't think he even noticed the sheep."

Jed made a sound halfway between a laugh and a grunt.

She looked at him again. "Turn around."

When he complied, she brushed the dirt, twigs, and pebbles from the back of his shirt. That's when she noticed his right elbow was bloody. "Hey, you *are* hurt. You're bleeding." She touched him, just above the scrape.

He lifted his arm, bending it and stretching to see what she meant, but he couldn't contort quite far enough. "You sure?"

"I'm sure." Holly looked for her water bottle. She'd dropped it when Jed grabbed her. She found it beneath a sagebrush. Next she withdrew a clean cloth from the backpack. It only took her a few moments more to cleanse the wound, dry it, spread some ointment over it, and then top it off with a bandage.

"Good grief, woman. What all do you have in that backpack?"

She laughed. "It's good to be prepared."

"Were you a Girl Scout?"

"No. But my family loved to go biking, hiking, and camping, and my dad taught his daughters well."

"I can see that."

This time his smile made a shiver run down her spine. A pleasurable kind of shiver. One of anticipation. Something flickered in his eyes. Understanding, perhaps. With it his smile faded. His eyes seemed to darken as he gazed intently into hers. His right hand rose to cup her cheek, the flat of his hand gentle against her skin. She couldn't help but press into it. She was tempted to close her eyes, but she didn't want to break the look passing between them. His face drew closer. Was this happening?

"Holly." He whispered her name, as soft as a caress.

She feared her knees would buckle. *Breathe,* she reminded herself. *Just breathe.*

When their lips met, she closed her eyes and gave herself over to the wonderful sensations that swirled through her. She hadn't known how much she'd wanted to be kissed by him until it happened.

His hand moved from the side of her face to the small of her back, freeing her to lift her arms to encircle his neck. At the same time, she rose on tiptoes, wanting more, wanting all. Her former fears, her excessive caution—it was all forgotten.

Of course, the kiss had to end eventually. It was Jed who drew back first, forcing Holly to look at him again. His dark eyes seemed to smolder, and her stomach tumbled in response. Then a slow smile tipped the corners of his mouth.

"This isn't the setting where I expected that to happen."

"You *expected* me to kiss you?" Amusement filled her question, and she realized how happy she felt. Happier than she'd felt in such a long time.

"Imagined it, then."

"Oh, you've been imagining it."

His voice deepened. "More than you know, Ms. Stanford. More than you know."

She laughed aloud.

Jed glanced toward the band of sheep, and she followed his gaze to discover the sheepherder watching them and grinning. Jed gave the man a wave. "We have an audience."

"So I see." She waved to the sheepherder too. "It's only fair, I suppose. You were taking pictures of him and his sheep."

Jed chuckled. "At least he doesn't have a camera." He looked at her again. "Come on. We'd better start back to the car."

She wished she could refuse. She wished they could stay right there and she could relive the kiss all over again. But then he placed his arm around her shoulders, and she realized she would have gone with him wherever he wanted to go.

Saturday, October 25, 1969

The entire Henning family gathered for Andrew and Helen's fortieth wedding anniversary. Andrew would have preferred to celebrate at the farm, but their family was too big for that these days. Thankfully, Francine and Roger lived in a large home in the foothills overlooking Boise that could handle the four Henning children and their spouses, their eight grandchildren—two of whom were married—plus one adorable great-granddaughter.

The spacious kitchen rang with the voices of women as they prepared the celebration meal. Andrew observed the seeming chaos from the safety of a doorway.

"Enter that room," Ben said from behind him, "and you'll be taking your life into your hands."

Andrew chuckled as he turned. "Look at your mother. She loves being right in the center of things, even when they won't let her lift a finger."

"She's happiest in the kitchen. Feeding her family is one of the ways she expresses her love."

"You've always understood that about her, haven't you?"

"Yeah. Right from the start. Of course, we three were mighty hungry back when we came to stay with you."

As if it were yesterday, Andrew remembered the day the three Tandy orphans had arrived at the farm, the tallest, towheaded Ben, protecting his younger brother and sister, suspicious of the strangers who'd offered them a home.

"How is Mom? How is she really?"

"She seems okay. There hasn't been anything to alarm us since she had that TIA in early August. The doctors have run some extra tests, to be on the safe side. A waste of good money, she called them."

He smiled, her voice clear in his mind as she'd sputtered those words again and again. With a nod, he added, "Now we're waiting for the results. We have an appointment for that next week."

"What about you? How's your back?"

Andrew shrugged. "Tolerable." Was that a lie or an expression of faith? He wasn't sure. Maybe a little of both. He still had to move with care. He still couldn't carry anything too heavy. The way he felt now might be as good as it would ever get, according to a friend who had back troubles of his own.

"Hey, everyone," Louisa called from the dining room. "Find your places. Dinner's ready. There's room for twelve in here and eight at the table in the living room. Mom. Dad. You're both at the big table."

Andrew moved to join Helen in the kitchen. She slipped her hand into the crook of his arm. He remembered that moment on their wedding day, as the minister proclaimed them man and wife, when she'd done the very same thing. Forty years ago.

He leaned close and whispered, "I love you, Helen Greyson Henning. I've never stopped loving you. I never will."

She tipped her head, and he saw tears swimming in her eyes, despite the smile that curved her mouth.

I never will, he repeated silently. *Never.*

Chapter 19

Five women from the shelter attended the next morning's class at the restaurant. After a warm welcome, Holly told them what they would be preparing that day, as usual. She assigned stations, as usual. She dispensed ingredients, as usual. Everything was as usual as far as she was concerned.

"Something's different about you today," Madalyn said.

Holly stopped to look at her. "What do you mean?"

"Not sure. But something's different."

Holly tried to shake off the words, but her heart fluttered, as if it wanted to give her away. Because Madalyn was right. She *was* different. Jed's kiss yesterday had changed her. She felt more hopeful, more carefree, more alive, more . . . something.

"Are you in love?" Willow asked from Holly's right side.

She turned her head. In love? No. That wasn't possible. She cared for Jed. She was attracted to him. His kiss had thrilled her. But love?

Willow watched her with a steady gaze. "With Jed Henning."

I love Jed. She tried out the words in her head. *Do I love him? No, it's too soon, even if I wanted it to be true. And I don't want it to be true. Do I?*

"He's a good man, isn't he?" Willow prompted.

"I think so. I mean yes, I'm sure he is a good man."

"Is he a man who loves his family? Would he do anything for them?"

"Yes, I believe he would. Family's what brought him to Boise."

"Then I'm glad for you." Willow lowered her eyes to the mozzarella cheese and grater before her.

Laughter from the opposite end of the worktable drew Holly's attention, and soon after she moved away from Willow's side to answer a question from one of the other women. But in the back of her mind, she didn't forget her own question: *Is it possible I love him?*

Every moment of her time with Jed yesterday had been special. The hike. The weather. The kiss. The early fast-food dinner they'd shared before going home. Even their parting words before each had returned to their separate living quarters.

Am I in love with him?

Even if it was love, could she trust those feelings? Didn't the Bible say the heart was deceptive above all else? She'd been in love with Nathan and that had ended in disaster. Nathan had given her plenty of clues to let her know something wasn't right between them, that he wasn't the man she'd believed him to be. She'd seen and ignored all those clues because she'd loved him. Or thought it was love. How could she be sure of what she felt for Jed?

Slowly, she became aware that the kitchen had fallen silent. Then she realized her students were all looking toward the back entrance. She followed their gazes—and there stood the man at the center of her thoughts, the door closing behind him. Her pulse quickened.

Sorry, Jed mouthed.

Feeling ridiculously happy to see him, her doubts evaporating, she walked across the kitchen. She didn't need to define her feelings, she decided. She could simply enjoy them.

"Didn't mean to intrude, but curiosity got the better of me." He smiled that slow smile of his. "I wanted to see what you're doing with these lessons. Or am I banned because I'm male?"

She wished she could kiss him. Instead, she faced the small group of women. "Anybody object to Jed joining us?"

Shaking heads confirmed what she'd suspected. Perhaps it helped that they'd all met him on Saturday in the Lighthouse common room.

She faced Jed a second time. "There's an apron over there." She pointed. "And you can wash your hands in that sink."

"I'm here to watch."

"No one just watches in my class." She gave him a sassy smile, feeling happier by the second. "Apron, sir."

Someone behind Holly laughed. She suspected it was Willow, but she didn't look to see if she was right. It was more fun to watch Jed's expression as he tried to decide whether or not to comply with her command. In the end he did. However, there was a mischievous look in his eyes that said he would be thinking up an appropriate payback for the future.

Once he donned the apron and washed his hands, Holly led him to a spot at the work counter. Handing him a knife, she said, "Your job is to slice the mushrooms really thin. And don't cut yourself."

He cocked an eyebrow. "You think I don't know how to use a knife?"

She didn't answer him. Instead, she directed her comments

to the whole kitchen. "Since there are six of you now, let's break into groups of three, and each group will complete the lasagna recipe. We should have plenty of the ingredients. I'll get the extra bowls and pans we'll need."

Jed was surprised how much he enjoyed the next hour and a half. He'd spent so much time at work that he was lucky to know where the kitchen in his home was. He was used to takeout and delivered meals and rarely prepared anything more than coffee. But he hadn't lied. He could slice, dice, and chop when required.

While the lasagna baked in the oven, four of the women cleaned up the counters. Jed washed the dishes and utensils, and Willow dried them. No one rushed with their duties since they had a forty-five-minute wait. Small conversations took place around the large room, the sound pleasant.

"Do you like to cook too?" Willow put the last of the dirty items into the dishwater.

He shrugged. "I enjoyed this morning. But it isn't much fun to cook for one. I don't see making a recipe like this for myself."

"I know." A shadow passed over her face. Then she smiled softly. "But my little boy is growing up, so when I leave the shelter, I won't be cooking for one. AJ loves lots of the things Holly's taught us to make, and he's got a healthy appetite."

"Mom says Chris and I tried to eat her out of house and home when we were little."

"Chris is your brother." It didn't sound like a question.

"Yeah. My kid brother."

"You're close?"

He let a bowl settle back to the bottom of the suds-filled sink. "We were, once. I'd like us to be again. That's why I'm in Boise. To see if we can figure things out." A few weeks ago, that would have been mostly a lie. He'd come to Boise because he was forced to. He'd come to try to save his company. But the words weren't a lie now. He really did want to figure things out with Chris, if his brother would give him the chance.

"It isn't easy, figuring things out." She spoke softly, almost to herself.

"No. It isn't."

"I hope it works out for you. I'll bet your brother does too. Whether or not he knows it."

"Thanks." He held out the rinsed bowl to her, and she took it with the towel in her hands.

The oven timer chimed, putting an end to their conversation.

"We'll let it cool about ten minutes," Holly said as she removed the pans of lasagna from the oven, "before we cut into it. To lower your costs when making this recipe, you can use frozen spinach instead of fresh. And even if you're making it for only one or two people, you can cut it up in single-size portions and freeze it for later. If you do that, be sure you use airtight containers. That will keep it good for up to about three months."

Willow leaned closer to Jed. "Looks like you can make it for yourself after all." Then she moved away.

Smiling to himself, wondering if he ever might make lasagna in his kitchen back home, Jed let the water out of the sink, then rinsed away the last of the suds with a spray of fresh water. Holly joined him before he'd finished.

"What did you say to Willow?"

He raised an eyebrow in her direction.

"She hardly talks to anybody. Even to me. But she sure seems to have warmed up to you."

"Huh. Don't think it was anything I said. She seems like a nice girl."

Holly leaned closer and lowered her voice even more. "Should I be jealous?" The teasing lilt was back.

"No need." He wasn't teasing. "She can't hold a candle to you."

Holly blushed, and it made him grin.

"Isn't it ten minutes yet?" Madalyn asked. "We're ready to try it out."

Jed and Holly turned from the sink, and while Holly headed toward the cooling lasagna, Jed wondered if she noticed the knowing looks on the faces of the other women.

Tuesday, October 28, 1969

"An arteriovenous malformation of the brain."

The words reverberated in Andrew's mind.

Dr. Schwimmer leaned back in his desk chair, his expression grim. "You should take time to think about this." His gaze moved from Helen to Andrew and back again.

"Amenable to surgery, but high risk of sequellae or death."

Andrew gave his head a slow shake, trying to clear it, to make sense of it all. The medical terminology was beyond him. The word *death* was not. "If she'd had the test sooner?"

"It wouldn't have made any difference."

"Should we get a second opinion?"

"That is certainly your prerogative, Mr. Henning. In my professional opinion, you won't get different answers. However, you and your wife should make your decision based on as much information as possible. If you feel you want to see another neurologist, I can make some recommendations."

Andrew looked at Helen. "We could go to Seattle or Salt Lake. There might be—"

She put her left hand on top of his right, silencing him with the gentle touch. "Dr. Schwimmer, we'll go home and pray about it. Thank you for explaining things so that I can understand what you're telling me."

"You're very welcome, Mrs. Henning." The physician didn't say he was sorry, yet the words were in his eyes.

Andrew stood, then took Helen's arm and tenderly drew her to her feet. With a nod toward the doctor, he turned his wife toward the door to the office, and they walked out in silence. Much as they'd done four weeks earlier.

Outside on the sidewalk, Helen stopped and tipped her head back, eyes closed. Sunlight bathed her face.

"You're as beautiful now as you were as a young girl."

She smiled but didn't open her eyes or lower her head.

"It's true."

His wife was sixty-one years old, yet her face was still surprisingly smooth. Oh, there were small lines around her eyes and the corners of her mouth, but nothing like other women her age. Her hair—once richly dark—had turned silver over the past decade. She wore it short now and had it permed to try to disguise how much thinner it was. Yes, she'd changed through the years, but she truly was as beautiful as she'd been when he'd seen her the first time.

"Come on." He took her arm again. "Let's go home."

She looked at him now, the smile slowly fading from her lips. "Andrew, I'm not going to have the surgery."

His heart seemed to stop beating.

"If I survived it, I would most likely be handicapped. Perhaps severely. The doctor made that clear. That isn't how I want to end my days with you."

"But without the surgery—"

"I know. I might have weeks. I might have months. I might even have longer."

He'd known. Somewhere down deep in his soul, he'd known from the moment of that first TIA what the results would be, and that he couldn't stop it from happening.

"I'm going to choose to live fully while I can. No babying myself for fear of causing a rupture of the . . . What did Dr. Schwimmer call it?"

"An AVM." Saying it tasted like sawdust in his mouth.

Helen touched his cheek with her fingertips. "In God's book are written all the days that were ordained for me. They were written in it before I was born."

"I'm supposed to be the strong one. I'm supposed to support you." The pain in his chest told him how truly weak he was.

"You're very old-fashioned, Mr. Henning." Her tone was teasing, as if they hadn't just received devastating news. "And I love you for it."

He opened his arms, and she stepped into his embrace, resting the side of her face against his chest.

"'In God I have put my trust,'" she quoted softly. "'I shall not be afraid.'"

"In God *we* have put *our* trust. *We* shall not be afraid."

But a nugget of fear had lodged in his chest, despite him willing it to go away.

Chapter 20

Jed's pulse jumped when he saw his dad's ID on the phone screen, unsure what the call might mean. More than a month had passed since Thomas Henning issued his ultimatum. Had his patience reached its limit? Jed had emailed his dad last week after he saw Chris. Not that he'd had any details to share, but at least he'd been able to say there'd been a face-to-face meeting.

"Morning, Dad," he answered.

"Good morning, Jed." He cleared his throat, then in his all-business voice, he said, "I wanted you to know that operations will start up again at Laffriot on Monday."

He released a breath he hadn't known he held. "That's . . . unexpected."

"I was wrong."

His dad's simple statement surprised Jed. He couldn't recall hearing his father say those exact words before.

"I was wrong to put all of the responsibility for what's gone wrong with Chris on you. I was even more wrong to mix my displeasure about a personal situation with business. I've never done that before. I shouldn't have done it now."

Should Jed say thanks? Should he say that he agreed? He wasn't sure, so he kept silent.

"Your mom helped me see all that."

"Mom did?" He raked the fingers of his free hand through his hair. "I didn't know you two were talking."

His dad took an audible breath. "You and Chris aren't the only ones who need to make things right. I've said I wanted to reconcile with your mother, but I haven't done much of anything to make that happen. I'm trying to change that now."

"I . . . I'm glad to hear it, Dad. Do you want me to come back to Tacoma?"

"No. That's not necessary. Not yet. You've got good people at Laffriot. Get things worked out with Chris first. Then, hopefully, you can come back together."

Strange. He was relieved that he wasn't expected to return immediately. He wasn't ready to go back to Washington. And it wasn't just because he wanted to accomplish what his dad had sent him to do in Boise. It was because he wasn't ready to say goodbye to Holly. He didn't know if he'd ever be ready to say goodbye to Holly.

"Have you talked to him again?" his dad asked, intruding on Jed's wandering thoughts.

"Not yet. He said he'd text me. I'm giving him some space."

"Don't let it drag out too long."

"I won't." He worried his lip a moment, then said, "Dad, I never knew Chris felt like he was being compared to me and always came up short. Shoot. He even said something about me taking a girl he liked from him. I don't know who he was talking about. I thought he lacked ambition. I thought he was rebellious and a screwup. But I never thought he was—" He pictured his brother's expression. "Hurt?"

"Chris was always more sensitive than you. I saw it as a weakness. I was wrong about that too. I've told him I'm sorry for it. Not sure he believed me, but I am."

Jed was trying to figure out what to say to that when he heard a knock.

"Hey, Dad, somebody's at my door. Hold on, and I'll see who it is."

"No. That's okay. I've got other calls to make. Let me know when you talk to Chris again."

"Okay. I will."

He punched End, slipped the phone into his pocket, and headed for the door. When he pulled it open, he discovered Willow Flynn standing on the other side, AJ in her arms.

"Hi, Jed."

What on earth was she doing there?

"Can I come in and talk to you a minute?"

He hesitated, unsure. He didn't know this young woman. Not really. Was it smart to be alone with her? In today's world, a man had to be careful.

"Please. It's important."

He frowned. What could be so important that it brought her to his door? Perhaps he should suggest they meet some other time. But something about the way she looked at him wouldn't let him send her away.

"Uh, sure." He took a step back, making room for her to enter. "Come on in."

Willow moved to the center of the small living room, her eyes taking in the two windows high on the walls, the sparse furnishings, and finally the photos spread out on the coffee table. She moved closer to them, her gaze unwavering. After a moment she picked one of them up.

He walked over to see which photo had caught her interest. "That's me and my kid brother, Chris."

"How old were you?"

"He was fourteen. I was eighteen. We were on a family camping trip just before I started my first year of college."

"Down," AJ demanded as he tried to wriggle free. "Want down."

Willow looked at Jed, questioning.

"Sure. He can't hurt anything. I'll put the photos out of reach." He quickly did so. "Want some coffee or water or anything?"

"No. I'm good."

Jed motioned toward the chair, and Willow settled onto it while keeping an eye on her son. Jed sat on the far side of the sofa, still wondering why she was there. As the wait for her explanation lengthened, he began to feel her tension. It unsettled him.

At long last she spoke. "You're lucky to have family. A family that loves each other."

He nodded.

"I don't have anybody. Except for AJ."

He wanted to ask about the boy's father but thought better of it.

"I came up through the foster-care system. I don't remember my real parents much. They were both into drugs, and the state took me when I was pretty young."

Jed remembered Holly saying how quiet Willow was, how little she said to others. Why was she telling him all this?

"I was barely eighteen when I met . . . when I met AJ's father. Eighteen, afraid, and . . . and confused. I was invisible and—" Her voice caught but she pressed on. "Lonely and unloved. But AJ's dad made me feel special. Cared for." Unshed tears glittered in her eyes.

Sympathy welled within Jed's chest. He wanted to help in some way but didn't know how.

"I fell for him hard. We were together about five months, and then I . . . I found out I was pregnant." Her gaze lowered to the coffee table between them, and she drew in a slow, deep breath. "He said . . . He said he wasn't ready to be a father. He didn't tell me I had to get an abortion, but that's what he wanted. I couldn't do it. I packed up what little I owned and left. I ended up living on the streets. Then somebody told me I'd be better off in Boise, so I caught a ride here." She looked toward her son. "It's where AJ was born. He's the best thing that ever happened to me." She smiled as she said it, although there were tears in her eyes.

"What about his father? Shouldn't he help support his son? Does he know where you and AJ are?"

"He didn't for a long time. I didn't think he would care one way or the other. He didn't want me to have the baby, so why would he want to know where we were? But after I ended up in the shelter, I was encouraged to make contact. I finally did a few months ago."

An odd feeling tightened Jed's chest. As if he was waiting for the proverbial second shoe to drop. Which made no sense at all. Nothing she'd said concerned him.

Willow pulled a tissue from her pocket, dried her eyes, and blew her nose. Then she held out her arms. "AJ, come to Mommy." The toddler raced over to her. She pulled him onto her lap, holding him close. Then she looked at Jed as she ran a hand over the little boy's hair. "His given name is Andrew Jedidiah."

"'Andrew Jedidiah,'" he echoed softly, that odd feeling in his chest turning into a tight band as reality began to seep in.

"Andrew for his great-great-grandfather. Jedidiah for his uncle."

"Andrew Jedidiah . . . Henning."

"Yes."

Jed took a breath, then said the words he knew were true, no matter how unbelievable they sounded. "AJ is Chris's son."

"Yes."

His eyes went to the boy. The resemblance was clear to him now. The same chubby cheeks. The same impish smile. The same cowlick in his hair. "He giggles like Chris did when he was that age."

"Does he?" She smiled, but her eyes remained sad.

"*Me do it.*" Jed wasn't sure if the voice in his memory belonged to his brother from many years before or to AJ from a few days ago. They sounded so much the same. How could he not have guessed the truth immediately?

He got up and walked to the door. Running his hands over his hair, he tried to make sense of it. Chris was AJ's father. Chris had obviously followed Willow to Boise after learning about his son. That had to be the reason for his moods and his sudden departure. It explained so much. But why hadn't he said anything to his family? Why had he kept it a secret? Maybe if Jed had known . . .

He turned around and saw Willow kiss the top of AJ's head. She held the little boy tight, and Jed wondered if his silence had made her even more nervous. He cleared his throat. "How long have you known I'm Chris's brother?"

"Since the day Holly introduced us at church. Chris talked about you sometimes."

Jed stepped forward. "Why didn't you tell me sooner?"

"I was afraid."

"'Afraid.'" He said the word beneath his breath.

"First Chris came to Boise. Then you. I know your family's got money. Chris always said your father likes to win and likes to do things his way. He said you were the same. I was afraid maybe you'd all try to take AJ from me. I've seen stuff like that happen before. I've seen foster kids get kidnapped by parents and even grandparents. And once a dad with a gun showed up where I was staying. I didn't want anything like that happening to us."

Jed's back stiffened. "Has Chris said he wants to take AJ away from you?"

"No." She shook her head. "He says he wants to be part of his son's life, and he'll do whatever he has to do to make me want that to happen too."

Good for him, Jed thought, an unexpected feeling of pride welling in his chest. Then he asked, "If you were so afraid of the Hennings, why did you decide to tell me all of this?"

A sad smile briefly curved her mouth. "Because I don't want to keep secrets anymore. I don't want to be afraid either. I'm learning stuff, about myself and about God. I'm learning how to be a better person and a better mom. I don't want to run away again. I've made a lot of mistakes. I don't want to make my life worse by lying to anybody. Once I met you, once I got to talk to you, I knew staying quiet would be the same as a lie. I had to tell you who we are. So now you know." Willow rose, shifting her son to ride on her hip. "I need to get back to the Lighthouse. I have a class later this afternoon."

"I could drive you back."

"No, thanks. It's not far." She started toward him and the door.

He put up a hand. "Willow, wait."

She stopped.

"Does Chris know you're telling me about AJ?"

"Yes. We . . . talked last night, and I told him I was going to."

"Is it okay if I let my parents know?"

Trepidation filled her eyes. "I'd like Chris to tell them when he's ready."

"But if he doesn't?"

"Then do whatever you think is right. No more secrets. Remember?"

With a nod, he stepped out of her way.

She walked to the door and let herself out.

Jed stood where he was, mulling the encounter. Of all of the things he'd imagined that might come out of this trip to Boise, discovering Chris had a son hadn't been among them. Would it have made a difference if he'd known? Would he have shown more concern, talked to his brother in a different way, been a better brother?

Grant's comment at their lunch a couple of weeks ago echoed in his memory. *"You can't know the whole picture. You don't have all the facts."* His cousin had been talking about Jed's parents' marriage, but it was just as true about Chris. Jed hadn't known the whole picture. He hadn't had all the facts. But he had them now. Some, at least. And he hoped having them would help him do the right thing when the time came. Whatever that meant.

When Holly got home from the restaurant on Tuesday evening, she discovered Jed sitting on her back stoop. He didn't smile as she walked toward him. He looked . . . unsettled.

"Hi," she said as she drew near.

He stood, his expression serious. "I was hoping we could talk."

She'd been so happy this past week. Happy because of him. She'd loved their dinner out and their hike and the cake sharing at the Lighthouse and his presence at yesterday's cooking class. Was it over already? She'd warned herself not to be careless. Had her hopes been raised only to be dashed in so short a time?

"Sure," she answered him. "Come on in." She unlocked the door and led the way into the kitchen, all the while trying to steel herself against bitter disappointment. Stopping near the center island, she turned to face him. "What's up?"

"Willow came to see me this morning."

His words confused her. "Who came?"

"Willow." He paused, took a breath. "She told me my brother is AJ's father."

Holly had no idea how to reply. All she could do was shake her head. Willow and AJ and Chris Henning? How was that even possible?

Jed glanced toward the living room. "Shall we sit down?"

This time she nodded, and they both moved in that direction. Once they were seated, Jed shared what Willow had told him, then explained more about his estrangement from his brother. After that, he fell silent, his gaze lowered to the floor.

Holly had questioned God often over the past year. She'd wondered why He allowed Nathan to enter her life, then leave it in tatters. She'd wondered why He left her burdened with so much debt and a struggling restaurant she disliked. She'd wondered why He didn't stop her from making foolish choices. But for some reason, she had no questions for Him now. "God brought the two of you together for a purpose."

Jed looked up.

"It has to be a God thing. How else would you have met Willow? You were looking for Chris, not a former girlfriend. You didn't know she existed. And you certainly didn't know he had a son. If you hadn't rented my apartment, you wouldn't have met Willow. It must have happened by design."

He frowned. "I suppose you're right."

She felt a pull at her heart. *Lord, was my only part to introduce him to Willow?* Dread of the answer made her throat constrict.

Jed met her gaze. Unlike yesterday, there was no humor or pleasure in his eyes. "I'd better go. I just . . . thought you should know."

His quick departure seemed answer enough, and with the end in sight, she felt her heart begin to break.

Tuesday, October 28, 1969

That evening Andrew climbed the ladder to the barn's loft, ignoring the spasms in his lower back as he did so. For almost forty years, this loft had been his thinking place and, more often than not, his prayer closet. The dusty smell was comforting to him. He knew the number of steps it took to pace from one end of the loft to the other, and he knew the view from the loft door as well as he knew his own face. Now, having reached the top of the ladder, he moved to that door and opened it. Gloaming blanketed the earth, and the cool air was rich with the particular scents of autumn.

Helen hadn't wanted to tell Grant and Charlotte the results from her recent tests, but since the young couple had known about the doctor's appointment, there hadn't been much choice other than lying to them. That hadn't been an option. So they'd settled for telling them Helen wasn't ready to talk about it yet and to please be patient. Their grandson wasn't a fool. He understood the news had been serious or his grandparents would never have asked for more time before discussing it. But the younger couple had honored the request and asked nothing more.

Tomorrow would be different. Tomorrow they would tell Grant and Charlotte what they knew before making the necessary phone calls to their children, who would then tell their spouses and their own children in the proper way and at the best times.

Watching as darkness deepened beyond the barn, Andrew stepped back and sat on a bale of straw. He took slow, deep breaths and released them.

"Death is a part of life," his mother had once told him.

It was true. As long as the world remained under the curse, death would surround them. Yet death felt wrong. God had created mankind for eternity, and somewhere inside every person, whether or not they acknowledged God, they resisted an end to life because it wasn't part of the divine plan.

Through the years, loved ones had been taken from Andrew. Some had gone slowly, like his parents in old age. Some had gone suddenly, like two of his children, one stillborn, the other taken in the Pacific during the war. He'd lost a good friend in an automobile accident and another to cancer. Those were only a few of the funerals he'd attended in his lifetime.

"We're never ready for death, Lord," he whispered. "Even when we see it coming, we're not ready."

He realized as he sat there, watching the crest of the rising moon appear above the tree line, that he'd expected to be the one to go first. Statistically, women lived longer than men. His father and father-in-law had both passed away before their wives. His old neighbor Hirsch had passed away before his wife, Ida. A husband dying before his wife seemed the more natural order of things. It should have been Andrew himself who was diagnosed with a TIA or an AVM. It should be Andrew himself who was facing the end of life. Not Helen. Not his wife.

Pain wrapped like a belt around his chest, tightening until he could scarcely draw breath.

"How precious also are thy thoughts unto me, O God! how great is the sum of them!"

Psalm 139 had long been a favorite of Andrew's. He found it comforting to know that God had ordained the number of each person's days since before they were born. But accepting that Helen's days were fewer in number than his own came hard. Harder than he'd expected.

"She's my partner in life, Lord. She's been with me in every up and down since the day we married. How will I manage without her?"

A cool breeze entered through the open loft door, causing bits of straw to twirl and tumble across the boards before him. Along with it came a whisper in his heart, a reminder that he wasn't without Helen. She was still with him. Death hadn't visited them yet.

Her words echoed in his memory. *"I'm going to choose to live fully while I can."*

If she chose to live fully, shouldn't he do the same?

He rose and moved to the open door a second time. There, he stared across the barnyard and fields.

"You brought us to a good land, Lord. A very good land. You've given us many good years. You've blessed us beyond measure. We'll live fully together while we can."

For the briefest of moments it seemed he felt the hand of God stroke his head, offering comfort. It was enough for now.

Chapter 21

After a sleepless night, Jed went to see Ben. Even if his cousin didn't have advice, Jed was sure a visit to the Harmony Barn would provide a distraction for a few hours. The air was still cool when he arrived, and before he could walk to the house, he saw Ben rolling a wheelbarrow filled with hay toward one of the paddocks. As Ben set it down, he noticed Jed, straightened, and waved. Then he waited for him to walk his way over.

"Morning, Jed. Didn't expect to see you in the middle of the week. Especially this early."

"I needed to get out and clear my head. This was the logical destination. Can I help with the feeding?"

"Sure." Ben lifted the handles of the wheelbarrow again. "Follow me."

They worked together in silence, tossing hay into feed bins, watching as the horses plunged their muzzles into the food and began to chew. Huffs and occasional stomps punctuated the morning air, but they were calming sounds. By the time the two men made their way to the front porch of the house, Jed was ready to share what he'd learned from Willow. It was easier to tell Ben than it had been Holly. He wasn't sure why. Perhaps because Holly had been Willow's friend first.

"Holly thinks God brought all of this about," he ended. "Caused Willow and me to meet, I mean."

"I have to believe the same. Hard to believe your paths would've crossed otherwise."

Jed knew his cousin's faith ran deep. He wished he could be as sure of his own faith. Sure enough that he could place his life—and the lives of those he cared about—into God's hands and trust completely, no matter what.

I believe, Lord. Help now my unbelief.

Ben leaned forward, resting forearms on thighs, hands clasped. "Now what?"

"I don't know. The ball's in Chris's court at this point. Maybe I could pressure Willow to tell me where he's living or where he's working, but that doesn't feel right to me." He stared toward the paddocks. Some of the horses had finished eating and were moving away from the feed bins. "No sessions today?"

"Nope. Next riding series starts up in June. But you could come by on Saturday if you want to see what it's like when some of our other clients are here."

"Maybe I'll do that." Jed looked at his cousin again. "Do you think I should tell Mom and Dad about Willow and AJ? Or should I leave that to Chris? He must mean to if he's planning to be in the kid's life."

"I don't know, Jed. You need to figure that out for yourself. What's right for your parents. What's right for Chris. What's right for Willow and her son." He shrugged. "What's right for you."

A magpie scolded from a tree at the corner of the house. Both men looked in the direction of the harsh sound.

"That's a lot of figuring out," Jed said.

"Afraid so."

"Do you ever wish God would text you the answers? That way there'd be no guessing or wondering if you're making the right choice. Nice clear words. 'Jed, make this phone call. Say these words. Do it at three o'clock tomorrow.'"

Ben chuckled. "Would be nice." He looked up at the sky for a moment. "But if we had that, we wouldn't need to listen to the Holy Spirit. We wouldn't need faith."

"And without faith, it's impossible to please God," Jed finished.

His cousin nodded.

Jed relaxed against the back of the chair, letting the worry drain out of him, at least for now. He would pray on what to do and wait for direction. He wanted to make the right choices. Right for everyone. He would try to trust God to show him what those right choices were.

Dusty, Ben's yellow lab, got up from his spot beneath the porch swing and came to his master, pushing his head underneath Ben's hand.

"That's a hint," Ben said with a smile as he scratched the dog behind his ear. "I need to get some work done."

"Anything I can help with?"

"Sure. If you want." Ben stood. "Come on."

The empire-style floor-length gown had dropped sleeves and a V-neck. The chiffon bridesmaid's dress had been pretty in the catalog, but Holly hadn't expected it to be this stunning in person.

"Oh, sis." Trixie walked around Holly. "I'm glad you chose the cornflower blue."

"So am I."

"It's perfect on you."

Holly checked out the back of the dress in the mirrors that surrounded her.

The seamstress straightened. "We'll need to take the hem up an inch, but no other alterations are necessary."

Trixie frowned in thought. "I'm not sure what the bridesmaids should wear on their heads. Maybe some flowers. A spray of those tiny white ones, whatever they're called."

"We have some wonderful hair accessories," the seamstress interjected. "Combs and headbands and more. Why don't you come out front and look for yourself?"

Moments later Holly stood alone in the dressing room, staring at the mirror. Yet she no longer saw herself in the bridesmaid's gown of cornflower blue. She remembered herself in her wedding gown, all white satin and lace. She'd only had the dress on in the bridal shop. She and the gown had never made it to the church. The wedding had been canceled before that could happen. For weeks afterward, she'd imagined what had never taken place. She'd seen herself standing beside Nathan, promising to love, honor, and cherish. Even though he'd broken her heart, even though she didn't really want him back, still her imagination had clung to the dream. It had been a huge relief when she hadn't seen herself in the dress anymore.

But now her imagination took wing, and she envisioned herself walking down an aisle toward her groom. Only it wasn't Nathan waiting for her. It was Jed.

"No," she whispered, squeezing her eyes shut. "I won't want

him. I won't let myself fall in love with him. It's over before it started. I knew that yesterday." She pressed her lips into a tight line, determined that those words would be true. It was over before it started. It was over before it started. She wouldn't let herself fall in love with Jed. It was over before it started.

But it wasn't true, and determination wouldn't make it true. She couldn't deny how she felt, no matter how hard she tried.

She opened her eyes and stared at her reflection. "You don't *allow* yourself to care for someone. You don't *let* yourself fall in love. You feel what you feel."

No matter how hard she tried, she couldn't *not* feel what she felt for Jed Henning. She could only control what she did with those feelings—and what she allowed them to do with her. Trixie had helped her see how she'd closed herself off emotionally this past year, and Holly didn't want to revert to that old way of living or thinking. Because Tennyson was right. It was better to have loved and lost than never to have loved at all.

She stepped off the riser and moved closer to the mirror. "Who says you've lost? Why are you so determined to see the half-empty cup instead of the half-full one? When did fearing the worst become your default?" She closed her eyes one more time. "God, I don't want to be that person. I'm Your daughter. I'm a child of the King. Change me. Change my heart and renew my mind. Don't let me be afraid to live, to feel."

"Talking to yourself?" Trixie asked with a lilt of humor in her voice.

Holly turned to face her sister, who stood just inside the dressing room curtain, a few hair accessories in the palm of one hand.

"Praying, actually."

"What about?"

Holly shrugged, not ready to say more. Perhaps she was tired of her younger sister being the one who had the most wisdom, the most common sense, the one who had her life in order. Or perhaps she was waiting for the renewal of her mind to happen first so she could see things the way God wanted her to see them—no matter what happened.

Trixie didn't press for an explanation. Instead, she crossed the room and began to hold the accessories against Holly's hair, trying one, then another. After looking at everything she'd brought into the room, she asked, "What do you think?"

Holly drew a deep breath and focused her attention once more upon her sister. "The first one. Especially if I'm supposed to wear my hair up."

"The first one it is."

Jed stood beneath the shower spray, washing away the dirt, sweat, and bits of hay from his day at the Harmony Barn. He was tired, in the best kind of way, from the work he'd done with his cousin. Ben hadn't given him specific advice, but Jed's spirit had quieted enough now to hear when God spoke to him. At least he believed so.

Once dried off and dressed in clean clothes, he went into the living room and sat on the sofa. This past week, he'd started each day with time reading the Bible and praying. He often picked up his great-grandfather's King James Version, searching out the handwritten notes therein. This time he reached for his own Bible, lying where he'd left it that morning. Using the attached ribbon to find where he'd stopped reading earlier, he opened to

Luke. He'd read only a few chapters when he arrived at the story of Jesus's invitation to His first disciples to follow Him and become catchers of men, ending with: "*When they had brought their boats to land, they left everything and followed Him.*"

At that point Jed felt a need to backtrack a few verses, to the place where Jesus told Simon to go into the deep water and let down the nets there.

"*Simon answered and said, 'Master, we worked hard all night and caught nothing, but I will do as You say and let down the nets.*'"

It occurred to Jed, as he stared at those words, that Simon had believed the instructions were foolish, that they'd made no sense to him since they'd fished all night without success. Still, because Jesus had said to do it—the Jesus he'd heard teaching the crowd—Simon did it.

"Jesus," Jed whispered, "even when what You tell me doesn't make sense, I will do as You say. I want that to be my default response every time." He drew a slow breath and released it. "Just make sure I can tell it's You who's talking."

How Sweet It Is

Thursday, November 13, 1969

The condo in Lincoln City, Oregon, had large windows overlooking the ocean, both in the living room and in the bedroom.

"Oh, Andrew." Staring out at the water, Helen clapped her hands, then crossed them over her heart in a gesture of delight. "It's perfect."

"It's a step up from the place we stayed on our honeymoon."

"How can you say that?" She turned toward him, a scolding look in her eyes. "Our honeymoon was perfect."

He laughed as he draped an arm around her shoulders. "The honeymoon was perfect. The accommodations were less so." He kissed her cheek, noting its softness against his lips. "And the weather back then was surprisingly warm. Not gray, cold, and windy like it's supposed to be this time."

"Windy is perfect for flying kites, and we brought warm coats. Let's go back to the shop we passed on our way through town and buy a kite for each of us."

"Great idea. But let's get unpacked and eat first. I'm starved."

"The shop might be closed if we wait."

"It'll be open again tomorrow morning. Even if we bought them tonight, we can't fly kites in the dark. We'll go to the shop first thing tomorrow. We'll be there when they open. I promise."

She turned fully toward him and stepped into his embrace, pressing her cheek against his chest. "There's so much I want to do."

Andrew knew she meant much more than what she wanted to do during this second honeymoon to the Oregon coast. His chest tight, he kissed the top of her head. "We'll do as much as we can."

Neither one of them moved for a minute, but finally Helen drew back. "Let's get unpacked. I'm hungry too." She gave him a watery smile.

Andrew nodded, then headed out to the Jeep to collect their suitcases. He was determined this trip would be everything Helen hoped it would be. If she wanted to fly kites for seven days straight, that's what they would do. The idea for the second honeymoon had come out of nowhere—or so it seemed to Andrew. They'd been talking about their life together, and memories of the Oregon coast had come up. Suddenly they'd been planning this trip. Two weeks later, here they were.

He smiled as he looked toward the entrance of their condo, glad he hadn't resisted the idea. For much of his life, the farm had made it difficult to travel. It had become a habit to stay home, to never want to be away overnight for any reason. But the demands of the farm were no longer the same. For that matter, the demands were no longer his. They belonged to Grant—and Andrew belonged with Helen wherever she wanted to be.

With a suitcase in each hand, he returned to the condo, making his way straight to the bedroom. Working together, the two of them emptied the suitcases, hanging some clothes in the closet and putting other clothes in drawers, arranging toiletries in the bathroom, setting their Bibles and a few other books on the nightstands. Then, after Helen made certain her hair was in order, they went in search of something to eat.

To Andrew's surprise, his favorite restaurant was still in operation, forty years later. He supposed the exterior had received new coats of paint over the years, and he was fairly certain the signage was different. But the view of the Pacific with its rising tide crashing against the craggy shore was the same, as were all of the wonderful seafood choices on the menu.

"We should have come back long before this," he said after the waitress took their order.

"When would we have done it? Our lives have been so full."

He looked at Helen across the table. "I should have made sure you had more trips to beautiful places. I'm sorry I didn't do that for you."

"Andrew Michael Henning, you stop that right now. I've lived exactly the life I wanted."

Have you? He reached across the table to take hold of her hand. She'd nearly left him once, oh, so many years ago, but they'd weathered that storm, coming out stronger and more in love on the other side. Still, they'd spent their marriage in a small house, raising five kids in it, getting up at the crack of dawn to tend the livestock and raise the crops and weed the vegetable garden and mend the clothes and on and on. They'd never starved or gone without the basic necessities, but they'd never had a lot of excess either. God had faithfully provided what they'd needed. But could he have given his wife more with a little extra effort?

"Exactly the life I wanted." She squeezed his hand.

He squeezed back. "So have I," he managed through a tightening throat. "So have I."

Chapter 22

Pushing hair back from her face, Holly sat on the side of the bed. She felt as tired now as she had when she'd retired for the night. Sleep hadn't come until the wee hours, and even that had been restless. Her mind had churned with thoughts of Jed, with the feelings she was afraid to feel but felt all the same.

She hadn't seen him yesterday. She didn't know if that was because she'd been so busy at the restaurant and then with her sister or if it was because he'd avoided her for some reason. Maybe, after learning about Willow and AJ, he was ready to leave Boise and didn't know how to tell her. But that didn't sound like him. He wasn't a fearful sort. She was the fearful one. Not him.

A glance at the clock told her she was running late. She hurried through her morning routine and was feeding Pumpkin when her phone rang. The cat purred contentedly as Holly set the bowl on the floor, then looked at the phone screen. The call was from the Lighthouse.

"Holly, it's Madalyn. There's been an accident."

"An accident."

"It's Willow. She got scalded in the kitchen. Not even sure

how she did it. They've taken her to the hospital. She asked me to call you. She wants you to go there if you could, please."

"Of course I'll go. Which hospital?"

Madalyn told her, then said, "Hurry. I think she's hurt bad."

"I'm on my way. Five minutes at most."

Her heart pounding, she raced to the bedroom and slipped on some shoes. On her way back to the kitchen, she grabbed her phone, purse, and car keys from the small table in the living room. Then she was out the back door. In her rush, she nearly collided with Jed.

"Whoa!" He steadied her with hands on her upper arms. "What's wrong?"

"It's Willow. She's hurt. I've got to get to the hospital."

"I'll take you."

"I don't want to—"

"I'll take you," he interrupted firmly.

Relief flowed through her. "Thanks."

He guided her to his rental car, and she got into the passenger seat.

"Which hospital?" he asked as he started the engine.

"St. Al's."

He didn't ask for directions, but she supposed he'd driven around Boise enough in recent weeks to know the way. The large hospital complex was easily seen when driving on the connector into the heart of downtown. She was thankful she didn't need to speak, because her thoughts were racing. Wondering how the accident happened. Wondering how serious the young mother's injuries were.

At the hospital Jed found a parking space not far from the entrance to the emergency room. He took her arm as soon as she was out of the car. It was a gentle but steadying touch, and she felt calmer because of it as they passed through the electronic doors.

"I'm here to see Willow Flynn," she told the young man behind the counter. "They brought her in a short while ago. I think by ambulance."

He looked at the computer screen and moved the mouse with his right hand. After a few moments he said, "She's here. Have a seat, and as soon as she's allowed to have visitors, we'll let you know."

Holly nodded, hating the wait, hating not being able to ask questions and get some answers. She moved to the chairs lined up with their backs to the windows.

"Could be a while," Jed said, stating the obvious.

"I know."

"Care to tell me what happened?"

"I don't really know. She got scalded. A kitchen accident, Madalyn said. I assume Willow was boiling water for breakfast." She drew in a shaky breath. "I've seen my share of scald burns. They're not uncommon in the food services industry. Water has to be kept at a high temperature to kill bacteria and properly clean the cookware. If you're not careful . . ." She let her words drift into silence.

"Maybe it's not too bad." He looked toward the doors that separated them from the ER's treatment rooms. "Hopefully you'll be able to see her soon."

Holly wanted to believe it wasn't bad. But if it wasn't, they probably could have treated Willow at the shelter or at an urgent-care facility, not taken her to the hospital. Then again, maybe they were only being extra careful.

Please, God, let that be the reason.

When Jed left his apartment half an hour earlier, he'd wanted to see Holly. He'd wanted to tell her how he felt about her, how much she'd come to mean to him in these past weeks. He'd wanted to see if they could figure out a way to keep seeing each other, even after he returned to Tacoma. It wouldn't be easy. He knew that. He had obligations. She had obligations. But some people managed long-distance relationships.

But he couldn't tell her any of that while sitting beside her in an ER waiting room. He would have to be patient.

"Jed." She looked at him, face tight with worry. "Shouldn't you call Chris and let him know what's happened to her?"

For a moment he couldn't answer. He wasn't sure. Chris knew Willow had planned to tell Jed about AJ, so that wouldn't come as a surprise. Then again, the two of them weren't married. Willow had said Chris wanted to be part of his son's life. She hadn't said Chris wanted to be part of hers. Would Willow even want him to know?

"I think you should," Holly added, softly but firmly.

"Okay." He took out his phone and pressed his brother's name. The call went straight to voice mail. "Chris, it's Jed. I need you to call me when you get this message. It's important." He hung up, his gaze going to Holly. "He didn't answer. Must have turned off his phone while he's at work."

"You didn't tell him it was about Willow."

"I didn't think I should in a voice mail."

Her eyes pleaded with him.

"I'll say more in a text."

He opened his message app and began to type: Willow hurt in

accident. At hospital now with her friend Holly. Call me ASAP.

A whooshing sound sent the message on its way.

"Miss Stanford?"

They both looked toward a woman wearing hospital scrubs who stood in the doorway to the ER.

"Are you Holly Stanford?"

"Yes." She stood.

"Miss Flynn has asked to see you."

Holly looked at Jed.

"Go on," he said. "I'll be right here. Waiting."

Sunday, November 16, 1969

From the deck of the condo, Andrew and Helen watched the storm roll in. Dark, angry clouds roiled and tumbled toward them, and below the deck, the ocean churned and frothed. Whitecaps rode the tops of high waves, crashing against the shore as loud as thunder.

"When the ocean gets high in a storm, don't stand outside watching it," a local had warned Andrew the previous day. "At least one poor fool gets washed out to sea most years somewhere along this coast because he wants to get too close to the action. Some flimsy porch rail isn't going to save a body."

Remembering the advice, Andrew said, "We'd better go in. The rain is going to start any moment."

Once they were inside, they settled onto chairs that faced the window. The glass rattled as the wind continued to rise. The rain came, driven before the storm. Day seemed to turn to night, and Helen rose from her chair long enough to turn on the lights. The roar of the ocean intensified.

When Helen returned, she sat on the arm of Andrew's chair, putting a hand on his shoulder. "It didn't storm like this when we were here before."

"No."

"I kind of like it. Sunny was nice, but this is exciting."

"I'm surprised you remember what the weather was like all those years ago. We hardly left the bedroom, so how can we be sure?"

She feigned a shocked expression. "Mr. Henning. The way you talk."

Laughing, he pulled her off the arm of the chair and onto his lap. Color rose in her cheeks, reminding him of the bride she'd been. Sobering, he kissed her, hoping it transmitted all the love he felt in his heart.

A loud crack of thunder startled them apart. Their gazes went to the window, where water ran in sheets down the glass, blurring the foaming sea.

"Oh my," Helen breathed.

They rose in unison and stepped closer to the window as jagged lightning split the clouds. Andrew counted aloud to see how long it took the thunder to reach them. Even expecting it, the sound made Helen jump. She drew closer to Andrew, seeking protection. Glad to oblige, he placed an arm around her shoulders.

Lord, he prayed silently, *it seems our lives are in the midst of a similar storm. It could end soon. It could go on for a long time. I suspect we shall both grow weary at some point. Perhaps we'll give in to fear. Remind us, Jesus, that You're in the boat with us, even when it's tossed to and fro. We need not be afraid. Joy doesn't come from perfect circumstances. It comes from knowing You. Put a new song in our hearts. A song of praise to You. Restore to us the joy of knowing You, walking with You, talking with You, loving You.*

As if she'd heard his prayer, Helen began to sing "Spirit in the Sky."

The breath caught in Andrew's chest. It was a song of praise. It was also a song about dying. Though he wanted to worship with her, emotions took his throat captive.

After a few refrains, Helen fell silent, her head now resting on Andrew's shoulder, and they watched the storm roll on.

Chapter 23

Jed had a long wait. He checked and answered emails on his phone. He got up and paced the waiting area, from one end to the other. He surfed the internet, looking for information on scald burns, ways to prevent them and ways to treat them. He shot up a few bullet prayers, brief calls for help and for mercy. Glancing at the large clock on the wall again and again, he wondered why time in a hospital waiting area moved so much slower than it did elsewhere.

At long last the doors opened and Holly appeared. She looked pale and wan. He went straight to her, putting an arm around her back.

Voice shaky, she said, "She'll be all right with time, but she's in a lot of pain."

He guided her to a couple of chairs and they sat.

"I wasn't allowed to be with her for long. Fear of infection from the burns, I think. One of the doctors talked to me afterward. I . . . I don't think I understood very much. I couldn't concentrate, I was so upset. She has some full and some . . . partial-thickness burns. That's what he called them. Her hands and arms were scalded and so was a small area on her torso." She touched her stomach. "Here, I think."

"Poor Willow. I'm sorry."

She looked at him. "She's scared, Jed. She's scared about AJ."

"AJ?"

"He was in the kitchen with her. He could have been burned too. And now she won't be able to take care of him until she's healed. That will be a few weeks, at least." Her gaze seemed to intensify. "There are complications. Her care after she's out of the hospital. The fact that she's living in a shelter, technically homeless and unemployed. She's afraid AJ will be taken by child services, that he'll be put into foster care."

"But they wouldn't—"

"You're his uncle. She needs you to take him right now."

"Me?" He drew back, stunned.

"If a family member takes him, then the state shouldn't need to get involved."

"What about Chris? He's his father."

"Chris isn't here. He's on some kind of trip for his job, and she hasn't heard from him in a couple of days. It sounds like they had a fight."

"I can't take AJ. I don't know anything about taking care of a kid."

"Doesn't matter. You're family. You'll figure it out." Holly's voice had taken on a firm edge. She softened it as she added, "And I'll be around to help."

He shook his head. It was crazy, what she was asking.

"Willow knows you, Jed. She needs someone she can trust, and apparently that's you."

"She trusts you more. Maybe you should take AJ and let me be the one who helps you."

"She's terrified the state will take her son away from her.

She needs family. She has none of her own, so it has to be AJ's family. With Chris gone, that's you. Her experiences in foster care weren't good. You can't let the same thing happen to your nephew. You can't."

"He's safe at the shelter for the moment."

"If she's not there, he won't be able to stay for long. The shelter isn't a day-care facility. The state will step in. And even when Willow can go back to the shelter, she won't be able to take care of him right away. Not with those burns. Not for a while."

Even when it doesn't make sense, do what He asks you to do. Only last night, Jed had prayed that his default would be to always say yes to God, even if it didn't make sense. Now look at him. He was finding every excuse to refuse. *Sorry, God.* He drew a breath to steady himself. "Okay. Okay, I'll do it. But how will anyone know I'm his uncle?"

"She had the nurse write this note." Holly lifted her right hand, a folded piece of paper pressed between her palm and thumb. "And she told me where to find AJ's birth certificate. Chris had it updated to name him as AJ's father, and it won't be hard to prove your relationship to Chris."

This wasn't how he'd envisioned this day when he left his apartment, wanting to see and talk to Holly. He'd thought he might kiss her, might tell her how much she meant to him, might learn if she felt the same way about him, perhaps begin learning how they might make a relationship work. Suddenly, instead of laying claim to a girlfriend, he'd landed a nephew. A two-year-old nephew in need of a temporary guardian.

Holly glanced over at Jed as he drove them to the children's store. Tension was etched on his face. He'd agreed to Willow's request to take care of AJ, but it was obvious he wasn't looking forward to the experience. She suspected he hadn't spent much time around kids. Especially not children as young as AJ. How could he, a single guy working seventy- and eighty-hour weeks?

After parking the car in the lot, Jed sat still, staring out the window, his expression grim. "Chris has screwed up a lot, but I never thought he'd ignore a text about Willow getting hurt. He has to know she's worried about AJ even if he doesn't care about her." He glanced over at Holly. "He said he wants to be in his kid's life, but then he goes AWOL when he's needed. What kind of man does that?"

"You don't know why he hasn't called you back. Maybe there's a good reason."

"And maybe I'll win the lottery without buying a ticket." He opened his car door, then looked at her again. "Sorry. Didn't mean to take it out on you."

"You didn't."

"If I don't hear from Chris in a few hours, I'll have to call my parents. They'll need to know about AJ if Chris doesn't step up." He took a breath. "I'm a lot better at running a business than I am with this kind of thing. I'm mad, and I'm fed up."

This was a side of Jed she hadn't seen before. Not that he'd done anything wrong. He had a right to be angry with his brother, given the situation. Still, it made her wonder what else she might not know about him. How many hidden facets might there be to this man? Might his charming smile and easy laughter hide other traits less appealing? The questions frightened her. She didn't want to be wrong about his true character. But what if she was? She'd been fooled before.

"Let's get this shopping over with," he said and got out of the car.

She followed suit, her troubled thoughts going with her.

Half an hour later, they loaded a new car seat and portable bed into his car, then drove to the shelter. Jed waited in the common room while Holly answered questions from the women who were not working or in classes at that time on a weekday. All were anxious to know if Willow would be all right. Afterward, the director took Holly to Willow's room, where she found the birth certificate and showed it to the director, then collected everything she thought AJ might need while he was with his uncle.

"Will you give this room to someone else?" she asked as she filled a suitcase with the collected items.

"No. It'll be waiting for Willow when she gets out of the hospital. She'll be able to do the remainder of her recovery here. We aren't tossing her out on the street."

Holly turned toward the woman. "Of course you aren't."

"I'm thankful she has family who can step in to take care of AJ until she's able. Very thankful."

Holly's throat tightened. All she could do was nod in reply.

She returned to the common area and discovered that someone had brought AJ there. Jed was sitting on the edge of a chair, not quite turned fully away from her. The little boy stood in front of him, staring upward while wearing a serious expression. Almost as if he understood that Jed had become someone important in his life.

"Heck of a thing, isn't it, AJ?" Jed said.

I can't be wrong. Look at him. He couldn't fool me that much.

She must have made a sound, because Jed looked over his shoulder.

She forced a smile. "I've got everything."

"Then we're ready to go?"

"Yes."

"Okay, then." He stood. "What do you think, AJ? You ready too?"

AJ remained silent and wide-eyed.

"All right." Jed scooped the boy up into his arms. "We're off." He turned to face Holly.

O God, don't let me be wrong about him.

They left the shelter in silence.

That night, after more than a few rough hours, Jed stared down at the sleeping child. Things hadn't been too bad until AJ started to miss his mom. Then the tears had begun and hadn't stopped until the little guy wore himself out. Holly had been with Jed part of that time, but she'd been called into the restaurant, and he'd had to muddle through on his own.

"Okay, God. I said yes to You. Now what?"

His phone buzzed. As he left the bedroom, he slipped the phone out of his pocket, hoping he would see his brother's face on the screen. Instead, it was his dad's. Was he ready to have this conversation? If not, he could simply not answer. But that didn't seem right.

"Hey, Dad."

"Hope I didn't wake you."

"No. I'm up. But I've had a crazy kind of day."

"Oh?"

While pacing the living room, Jed relayed all that he'd learned and all that had happened over the past couple of days. His dad listened without interruption.

"The kid's sleeping now," Jed finished. "I hope he'll stay that way through the night. I'm feeling lost. I don't know what I'm doing."

"Make sure small things and poisonous things are put up high. Other than that, you'll figure it out as you go along. He's not an infant. He'll communicate more than you realize."

"Thanks." He said the word without meaning it.

"You know, your mom had her suspicions that a girl was somehow involved in Chris taking off the way he did. She mentioned it again a few days ago. But neither one of us had an inkling we had a two-year-old grandchild. It's a lot to take in. Have you told your mom?"

"Not yet."

"Would you like me to tell her?"

He considered the question, then answered, "Maybe you'd better."

"She'll want to get in the car and drive to Boise as soon as she learns about AJ."

"I'm not sure she should do that, Dad. Willow might freak out. She doesn't want to hide AJ from family, but her history makes her a bit wary. That's my read on it."

"Okay, son. I'll trust your judgment on this and ask your mom to do the same."

"Thanks."

"You sound tired. I'll let you go. Keep me informed."

"I will. 'Night, Dad."

"Good night."

As he slid the phone into his pocket, he returned to the bedroom doorway and stared at his nephew's sleeping form. *Take care of him, God. He hasn't had the best start. Turn Chris around. Make him a good dad to this boy. I don't know how to fix any of it, but You do. I'll trust You for the answers. One day at a time.*

Wednesday, December 31, 1969

On New Year's Eve, two hours before midnight, the house was quiet except for the creaks and groans caused by the cold wind blowing in from the northwest. Helen was in bed, sound asleep, and Grant and Charlotte were at a friend's party, ready to welcome in the new year. Andrew remained in the kitchen, sipping a cup of decaf coffee, his Bible open on the table before him, a notepad and pen nearby. It felt familiar, this night, this room, this quiet house. Even when the children were young and at home, Andrew had usually been alone in the kitchen as the calendar turned from December to January. He'd read his Bible here. He'd prayed here. He'd sat at this table and written to his sons when they were serving in the armed forces.

He wouldn't be sorry to say farewell to 1969. So many troubling things had happened. Not only Helen's health issues. Not only his own physical troubles. Troubles far beyond the two of them. There'd been that accident involving Senator Edward Kennedy that had killed a young woman in a place called Chappaquiddick. There'd been those ghastly murders in California at the home of that young actress, Sharon Tate. Hurricane Camille and the flooding that followed had killed more than four hundred people across several southern states. And only last month had come the news of the My Lai massacre in Vietnam, a horror that had occurred more than a year earlier.

"God, save us from ourselves," Andrew whispered as he rose from his chair and went to the rack near the door. There he donned coat, hat, and gloves and stepped outside into the frigid night air. Leaning into the wind, he made his way to the barn. One of the horses nickered as Andrew entered. Another horse bobbed its head, as if to say, "Good to see you. Did you bring a midnight snack?"

Andrew moved to the first stall and rubbed Blue Boy's head. The dappled-gray gelding was aging, like Andrew himself, but he was able to carry grandkids when they came to the farm for a visit. Those visits happened too infrequently to suit Andrew. No matter how many years passed, he still wasn't used to how quiet the farm had become without a passel of children around.

"Gets a little boring, doesn't it?" He patted Blue Boy's neck again.

Helen had asked him why he kept the horses, now that his bad back made it impossible to ride. The beef steer and the chickens were sensible, she'd told him. They provided food. But what good were the horses? Andrew had answered that they were good for the soul, if nothing else.

He moved to the next stall and stared into the eyes of the mare. Her name was Tempest. A light chestnut with flaxen mane and tail, she would turn thirteen in the spring. He stroked the narrow white blaze on her forehead, stopping when he reached the softness of her muzzle.

Of their three remaining horses, Tempest was his favorite because her lineage could be traced back to the beginning of this farm. Belle had been his father-in-law's favorite mare back in the twenties, and Andrew had been present for the birth of Belle's first foal, Jewel. Later he'd been present for the birth of Jewel's foal, Sunrise; for the birth of Sunrise's foal, Bunny; and for the birth of Bunny's foal, Tempest. Tempest's only foal had been a colt. Andrew had named him Kennedy, in honor of the president who'd been shot two months before the colt's birth. Kennedy, a darker chestnut than his dam, stood in the stall on the opposite side of the barn. Andrew crossed to the gelding and spoke softly as he doled out pats on the neck.

"You're the last of the line, boy. Guess that makes you special too."

He thought of his own family. For now, there was no end in sight of the Henning line. But other things would undoubtedly come to an end, including life here on the farm. Grant would have ideas of his own. Would he keep these horses and the chickens? Would he continue raising alfalfa, or would he want a different crop? What about the garden? Was Charlotte a gardener, or would she turn the large plot back into lawn?

"I don't like change. I hadn't realized how much I dislike it until this year."

Kennedy gave him a shove with his muzzle.

"Yeah. I know." He chuckled. "Change is the only constant."

He gave the horse one last pat, then headed back to the house to see in another new year.

Chapter 24

Holly sat at her kitchen table, laptop open before her, papers strewn across the table. She closed her eyes as she took another sip of coffee from her mug. Tension coiled in her stomach.

"What am I going to do?"

She'd been called to the restaurant the previous afternoon because one of the servers had abruptly quit, and she'd been needed to fill in. But that had been a minor problem compared to what she'd found waiting in her office. A letter informing her that there were past-due taxes on the building, and the penalties were steep. Nathan—before the breakup—had supposedly taken care of the taxes and insurance and so many other financial matters. She'd trusted he'd done as he'd said. But apparently he'd let more slide than their relationship.

"I've been such a fool."

Her gaze shifted to the beautiful new range. If she'd known about the taxes, she never would have used the rent money from Jed to buy it. As wonderful as it was, it wasn't a necessity. She could have made do without it. It wasn't as if she had a lot of spare time for baking anyway. It wasn't as if there was any hope left of starting a home-based business. That dream was dead. She'd lost it when she thought she could trust her heart.

From the basement, she heard AJ squeal, a sound of delight rather than distress. She was glad of that, for Jed's sake. But she couldn't do anything to help him. She couldn't even help herself. Better to leave him to his own devices. Better to put distance between them now, before it was too late. Even if he was everything she'd wanted him to be, even if she wasn't wrong about him, it was all too late. His stay in Boise was temporary. He'd met with his brother. Something would be worked out. Jed would go back to Washington. Maybe so would Chris. Perhaps even Willow and AJ.

And none of it's my concern. I can't let it be my concern.

With a sigh, she rose from her chair and walked toward the bedroom. Time to shower and dress and leave for the restaurant. None of her troubles would be solved by wishing them away.

Holly cried on the way home that night. She'd had to keep up a brave front during her hours at the restaurant, but once in her car, she'd given in to her tattered emotions. That afternoon she'd had a long talk with her CPA, and his first impression about her financial situation hadn't given her a lot of hope.

It would be bad enough if she had to close the restaurant. She would feel like a complete failure if she lost the inheritance from her aunt and uncle, even if reopening Sweet Caroline's hadn't been her idea, even if managing it felt like a daily struggle. But worst of all were the people who would be hurt if Sweet Caroline's closed down again. Her employees. The women from the shelter who were learning to cook. Even the customers who'd become regulars. All would be affected because she'd made serious mistakes, because she'd trusted someone she shouldn't have trusted, because she hadn't checked and double-checked and triple-checked every detail.

After pulling the car into the garage, Holly turned off the engine. Then she sat there, unmoving, waiting for enough energy to open the door. It didn't happen for a long while.

She'd always been an independent kind of girl. Even in her relationships with others, she'd never been afraid to make her own way or to have a mind of her own. She had her faith, too, trusting in God's guidance. But when it came to Sweet Caroline's, had she listened to His voice, or had she relied on her own wants and desires? Why had He let it come to this? To the point where she could lose it all? If it all came crumbling down, if she lost her home, too, how would she support herself? She couldn't launch a catering business after this. No one would give her a loan. And even if they would, if she lost her home, too, she wouldn't have a kitchen to cook in. She had no reserves. It felt as if the dream was dying a second death.

She took a deep breath and released it slowly. At least she'd received some good news about Willow. Her young friend was expected to leave the hospital next week. The use of her arms would be limited for a while to come, and her wounds would need tender care, but at least she could heal in a more homelike environment. At Lighthouse the other women would tend to her and love on her. Maybe AJ could visit her there if it wouldn't upset him too much to leave again.

Another deep breath, and Holly was ready to get out of the car and go inside.

When she closed the side door of the garage, she appreciated how easily it moved since Jed had repaired it. Reminded of him, she wondered how his day had been. Was AJ happy, staying with the uncle he barely knew? Did Jed look anything like Chris, making the child feel some measure of comfort?

I can't think about him. I can't. Let it go. Let him go.

Only two days had passed since she'd admitted to herself that, like it or not, she was falling for Jed, but it seemed a lifetime ago. So much had happened in those two days. She hardly felt like the same woman who'd stared at her reflection in the dressing room mirror and reminded herself that she wanted to see life as a cup half full. But her life wasn't half full. It was empty . . . because she'd trusted where she shouldn't trust, because she saw what she wanted to see, not what was true.

She huffed out a breath of air as she moved on.

Inside, Pumpkin welcomed her home with a loud meow. After setting aside her purse, Holly picked up the cat and buried her face in the feline's long hair.

"Sweetheart, what am I going to do?"

Pumpkin answered with a purr.

"You never lie to me, do you? You're just who you say you are."

She carried the cat with her into the living room, stopping long enough to turn on the lamp before settling onto the sofa.

"I'm at the end. I don't know what to do. God, I need Your help. There's no hope without You."

The buzz of his mobile phone penetrated Jed's sleep. He sat up, surprised to find himself on the sofa. He didn't remember lying down, but he must have at some point while watching television. It was still on, the volume turned low. He reached for his phone, but it stopped vibrating before he picked it up. A missed call notice was on the screen, the Idaho number unknown to him and no caller ID. Probably a spam call. He set the phone on the coffee table again.

Stifling a yawn, he checked the time. Ten o'clock, but it could have been midnight, judging by how tired he was. He wondered if Holly was home from the restaurant. She usually was before now. But if so, he'd slept through any sounds she might have made.

He got up and went to the bedroom doorway, looking in on his nephew. Light from the kitchen revealed AJ sleeping on his belly, his knees tucked beneath him. Cute kid, especially now that he was asleep. It had been a long day for the both of them, but somehow they'd made it through.

Jed turned toward the bathroom. A few minutes later, after brushing his teeth and donning pajama bottoms, he returned to the living room to turn off the lights and television. He was reaching for the control when his phone began to vibrate. He picked it up. It was the same number as before.

"Hello?"

"Jed . . . me."

"Chris." He felt a spark of anger. "Where the heck are you?"

His brother's brief response broke up, crackling sounds blurring his words.

"I've left you messages. About Willow."

"This job . . . would. Will . . . couple days."

Frustrated, his grip tightened on the phone. "Chris, can you hear me? It's important you know what's happened."

Only crackling sounds came through the speaker. Then silence.

"Chris?" Sinking onto the sofa, Jed looked at the phone. Nothing. Its screen had gone dark.

Did he hang up on me?

His temper started to rise a second time, but he checked it. Something didn't add up. Obviously his brother was having phone troubles, no matter where he was or why he was there. Did that mean he didn't know what had happened to Willow? Did Chris not know she was in the hospital and AJ was staying with Jed? And if he didn't know, did Jed have cause to be angry?

What he wouldn't give to be able to talk about this with Holly. Being with her put him at ease for some reason. Even yesterday, when he'd felt so uncertain about taking charge of his young nephew, he'd felt steadier when she was with him. Being without her felt . . . wrong.

Monday, January 12, 1970

A snowstorm left behind a world of white. Trees bowed beneath the weight of dense snow, and the fence across the road looked like nothing more than bumps beneath an ivory carpet. Andrew stared out the window above the kitchen sink at the slate-gray sky. The weatherman had promised them a second round of snow before the day was done.

"It's really slick, Grandpa," Grant had told him before he and Charlotte left for their jobs in Boise. "Don't go out in it. There's no need to. All the chores are done, and the last thing you need is to slip and fall."

A retort had risen to Andrew's lips, but he'd swallowed it back. His grandson hadn't meant to sound as if he were talking to a child. Still, that's how it felt to Andrew, and several months' worth of such comments from children, grandchildren, and friends had begun to wear on him. His back was the problem, not his mind. He still had a measure of common sense. It seemed that the popular phrase "Don't trust anyone over thirty" had morphed from distrust into disregard. In his day they'd respected people of mature years. In his day they'd—

He brought his thoughts up short, knowing he was making a mountain out of a molehill. Grant showed him nothing but respect and love. It was the inactivity that had made Andrew supersensitive.

With a sigh, he turned away from the snowy landscape beyond the window. If nothing else, it was a good sort of day to sit in his chair and read. He was halfway through *The Silver Chalice* by Thomas B. Costain and was enjoying it so much that he wondered why it had taken him this long to get around to reading it.

When he entered the living room, he saw Helen in her chair, her Bible held against her chest, her eyes closed. Love welled in his chest, making him forget the frustration of moments before. A love for this woman who'd shared the ups and downs of life with him. They'd weathered hard times together. They'd rejoiced together in happier moments. Many happier moments. They finished each other's sentences and each other's thoughts. They laughed at the same jokes. He'd been hardly more than a boy when he'd fallen in love with Helen Greyson, and through the years, the feeling had deepened and matured. It was the same and yet more. So much more. The dross had been burned away in the refiner's fire, and what remained was pure and of great value.

He settled into his easy chair and took the novel into his lap, but he didn't open it. His thoughts remained on his wife. Their trip to Oregon in November—cold, windy, and rainy—had been a wonderful time for the two of them. It had refreshed and uplifted them even more than he'd hoped it would. He would love to be able to take her some place new in the spring. An even better trip than blustery Oregon. A real vacation. Someplace warm. Someplace they'd never been before. Not hard to do since neither of them had traveled much. Helen's health had been good, despite the doctor's dire diagnosis. Unlike Andrew with his nagging back, she'd seemed her old self for many weeks.

California, he thought. That might be the place to take her. San Francisco would be fun. He'd gone to that city with Louisa during the war, but it must be a very different place over twenty-five years later. What about Los Angeles? Were they too old to enjoy Disneyland? They both liked to watch *Walt Disney Presents* on Sunday evenings. Maybe they would enjoy a visit to the happiest place on earth. Would Helen want to go on a roller coaster through the Matterhorn? He could almost hear her screaming, and he chuckled to himself.

"What do you find so amusing?" Helen watched him, a small smile curving her mouth.

"Nothing in particular."

"I'll bet." She set her Bible on the coffee table. "Is it still snowing?"

"Not right now, but the weatherman says it'll start up again later today."

"I wish Grant and Charlotte didn't have to drive in this weather."

"I had them take the Jeep this morning. Better traction in the snow than his truck."

Helen rose from the chair. "What do you want for lunch? Leftovers okay?"

"Sounds good. Need any help in the kitchen?"

"Heavens, no. Doesn't take anything to warm up a stew. You sit there and enjoy your book."

Andrew opened the novel and began to read. Very soon he'd forgotten images of Disneyland and was engrossed in the tale of Basil, a young silversmith, in the time following the death and resurrection of Jesus. Danger surrounded the character, and Andrew's breath caught in his chest as he turned the pages.

Chapter 25

Holly didn't go to the restaurant on Saturday morning. She needed to think and pray. Then she needed to call her dad for some advice, a task she dreaded. He'd never been keen on her marrying—almost marrying—Nathan, and he'd been even less keen when she'd allowed herself to be talked into reopening Sweet Caroline's. He'd warned her that too much debt came with doing so. But she'd listened to Nathan instead of her dad. She could only imagine what he would say to her now when she admitted the dire straits she was in.

Thinking about Nathan Estes—which the situation at the restaurant had caused her to do more of than usual—hadn't helped her mood. She'd fallen for Nathan quickly, had succumbed to his charms with complete abandon, believing their love would last a lifetime. She'd believed him to be all that he appeared on the surface. A good man. A Christian man. A hardworking man. An honest man. A man who would keep his promises. Learning she was wrong—horribly, terribly, utterly wrong—had been a cruel lesson. Cruel . . . and a lesson she shouldn't let herself forget, even if her little sister did think opening her heart was a good idea.

She'd known Jed how long? A little more than a month.

And in that brief time, she'd allowed him to become her friend and then to become something more. She'd laughed with him, opened up to him, kissed him. She believed him to be a good man, a Christian man, a hardworking man, an honest man, a man who kept his promises. But how could she know for certain? Based on what? Her own poor track record? How could she ever be sure about people? Everyone put their best foot forward when meeting others. No one went around announcing that they were unreliable or only a lukewarm Christian or lazy or a liar.

"I trust too easily." Clad in a loose T-shirt and a pair of cutoff sweatpants, her hair in a messy bun, yesterday's mascara smudged under her eyes, she walked circles around her kitchen, a cup of coffee in hand. "I'm a fool. I let my emotions blind me to the truth. I didn't know Nathan, even after more than a year. How can I think I know Jed after a month? I have enough troubles as it is. I don't need more."

Sitting on a nearby stool, Pumpkin flicked her tail as if in agreement.

A knock sounded at Holly's back door. It had to be Jed. Who else would it be at this time on a Saturday? She went to answer it, too tired and worried to care about her appearance. Judging by the way his eyes widened when he saw her, she looked even worse than she'd thought.

"Morning." He held AJ with one arm, the little boy riding on his hip.

"Morning."

"We're heading out to the farm. Care to go with us?"

She shook her head.

"Gotta work?"

"No. Not today. But there are some—"

"Then come with me. With us. We won't stay the whole day. In fact, you can decide when it's time to leave. Half an hour. Five hours. Totally up to you. Whatever you want."

His words tugged at her heart. She wanted to go with him in the worst way. She wanted to be in his company. She would love for him to make her laugh, hold her hand, perhaps kiss her again. She would love for him to make her forget about the financial anvil hanging over her head and the stupid mistakes she'd made.

But weren't those the very reasons why she shouldn't go? She couldn't trust her judgment. She couldn't trust her feelings. The heart was deceitful, as she'd learned the hard way. And her heart was in grave danger when it came to Jed Henning.

"I can't go with you, Jed. I'm sorry. You and AJ have a good time." She narrowed the opening.

"Hey, is something wrong?"

She shook her head.

"Have *I* done something wrong?"

Tears burned in the back of her throat. "No. It's just . . . I can't go with you. It's too . . . I'm not . . ." She swallowed. "I've got to go. Sorry." She closed the door.

She felt the closing of her heart too. She felt it in her chest. Like a thud. Or a punch. Or a slam.

Ashley came to greet Jed as he unbuckled AJ from his car seat. Then she held out her arms. "I'll take him, if that's okay."

"Sure." He wasn't about to turn down an offer of help.

AJ went to Ashley without a fuss. Maybe he was sick of his uncle already. Maybe he was ready for someone who knew more about kids. Whatever the reason, he seemed happy to be in her arms.

Holding the toddler close, Ashley frowned at Jed. "Are you all right?"

"I'm not sure." He swept the area with his gaze. "Is Ben around?"

"You'll find him on the other side of the barn." Glancing down at the boy, she said, "Let's go play in the yard, shall we? I've got some toys for you." AJ seemed happy with the suggestion.

Jed watched them go, then swiveled on his heel. He found Ben in the small pen beyond the barn, along with a wide-eyed dun gelding. Jed didn't say anything when he arrived at the fence, content to watch as Ben attempted to settle the nervous animal. If only something could settle Jed.

All the way out to the farm, he'd replayed the moment when Holly had closed the door after refusing to come with him. Maybe it hadn't been a slammed door, precisely, but it felt like it. Had he done something to cause her to withdraw from him? Had he unintentionally offended or hurt her in some way? The past few days had been crazy. No doubt about that. But what had he done in that time to take them from a reciprocated kiss on a hike in the foothills to a door closed in his face? It didn't make sense to him. Worse, it scared him. Scared him that what had seemed a special connection between him and Holly might already be broken.

"Ashley got AJ?" Ben asked in a low voice.

It took a moment for Jed to realize the question had been directed at him. "Yeah."

"How does it feel to be an uncle in charge?" Ben held out a hand toward the horse, keeping his words soft and soothing.

"Scary at times. But it's getting better."

"How's his mom?"

"Doing better than expected, I guess. She called me this morning before I headed out here."

Ben drew in a slow, deep breath, still watching the gelding as he took a step backward, then another and another until his back touched the gate. Only then did he turn away from the horse and leave the pen.

"What's this guy's story?" Jed asked, nodding at the dun.

"Not sure. Whatever happened to him, he's skittish around people. Somebody did something bad to him. It'll take time before he's ready to trust again."

Jed continued to stare at the horse. Something about the way the animal had looked at Ben made him think of Holly when she'd opened the door that morning. Skittish. Afraid. Not ready to trust.

"You okay?" Ben asked, echoing Ashley's question from a short while before.

Jed shrugged.

"Is it Chris?"

"No." He looked at his cousin. "Although he called me last night."

"He did? Is he on his way back?"

"I don't know." He quickly told Ben about the problems with the call. "I don't know if he heard me any better than I heard him. He may not even know about Willow. If he'd told me or Willow who he was working for or what sort of employment he's taken, it might help us track him down. As it is . . ." He let his voice trail into silence.

"Sounds to me like he's in a remote area. Plenty of Idaho

doesn't have good phone coverage." Ben took a step closer to Jed. "But now tell me what's really bothering you."

"Holly."

Ben's eyebrows went up.

"I thought things were going well between us. Really well. Now, all of a sudden, she's pulled back. On the way out here, I was trying to figure out what I might have done or said to upset her or make her mad or hurt her. I can't think of a thing."

His cousin remained silent but gave a small nod.

"When I saw her this morning—I asked her to come to the farm with us—she almost looked . . . I don't know . . . afraid of me."

"Afraid?"

Jed glanced back at the dun gelding in the pen. "Kind of like that horse was looking at you a bit ago." He drew in a slow breath. "Not ready to trust," he added softly.

Sunday, February 1, 1970

On that first Sunday in February, there wasn't a bit of evidence left of the January storms that had dumped nearly a foot of snow on the farm. Warmer weather had blown into the valley, melting away the pristine white and leaving mud and barren tree branches behind. Poor Chester had been relegated to the porch until he could be bathed. Not a terrible punishment with the sun out and temperatures inching into the fifties.

After enjoying dinner with Grant, Charlotte, and Helen, Andrew went onto the porch to sit with his faithful companion. The brilliant blue of the sky almost blinded him without his dark glasses, but he was too full and too lazy to go fetch them. After about five or ten minutes, Grant joined him, taking a nearby chair.

"It'll be planting time before we know it," Andrew said without looking at the younger man.

"Speaking of that, Charlotte and I talked last night." Grant paused a moment. "I'm thinking about quitting my job and working the farm full-time."

Andrew blinked in surprise.

"I know I didn't plan to quit this soon, but Charlotte and I have saved up quite a bit since moving in with you. And we got some money for wedding gifts that we didn't spend. So we're ahead of the game there. We'll be able to give you the spring payment with no problem and still have money in reserve."

"I wasn't worried about your payment."

"I know you weren't." Grant drew a breath. "Grandpa, you took care of your family for forty years on this farm, right? Once you were farming, you never took an outside job. Isn't that right too? You fed and clothed your kids right through the Depression and the war years.

Somehow you managed to help my dad and my aunts and uncle go to college. If I'm smart about the crops I raise and how I manage the land, I think I can take care of all of us too."

Andrew leaned back in his chair. "Are you trying to convince me or yourself?"

"Neither." He grinned. "Both."

Andrew laughed softly.

"It's what I want, Grandpa. It's what I think I'm supposed to do. I want to spend my days here, making it better. We're all getting along great, you and me and Grandma and Charlotte. Don't you think?"

"Yes, I'd say we are." There'd been no dustups between the women, no disagreements between him and Grant. He hoped it would stay that way, although human relations could be tricky when people lived in close quarters. But he kept those thoughts to himself.

"And with Charlotte working, she and I'll still have some regular income."

"What about when kids come along?"

Grant shrugged. "We're not in a hurry to start a family. Maybe we'll be ready for a baby in a couple of years or so. But not before then."

Andrew's thoughts drifted back in time. Helen had gotten pregnant a couple of months after their wedding. They'd been so excited, despite the economic hard times. Love had created that baby, and their joy had known no bounds. And when that baby was stillborn, arriving two months early, the loss had nearly destroyed their marriage. Only God had been able to put it back together again. Only God had been able to bring beauty from ashes.

"Grant!" Charlotte's cry came from somewhere inside the house. "Grandpa! Come quick!"

Heart slamming against the wall of his chest, Andrew was on his feet in a flash, oblivious to pain. Grant led the way inside, where they discovered Helen on the floor in the living room, Charlotte kneeling beside her.

"Helen." Somehow Andrew knelt too. "Helen." She didn't answer. He realized, even as he heard Grant calling for an ambulance, that she would never answer him again. Even so, he whispered, "Don't leave me, my girl. Don't go. Not yet."

Her expression was peaceful, eyes closed, as if she'd nodded off for a nap, as if she'd wanted a rest but hadn't wanted to walk to the bedroom.

What a fool I've been. What a stupid, old fool.

He'd thought himself prepared for this moment. He'd had months to prepare for it. He hadn't wanted her to suffer a lengthy, drawn-out death full of pain. He hadn't wanted her illness to affect her memory or leave her isolated and afraid. He'd thought if God took her quickly, suddenly, his own pain would be lessened.

How wrong could a man be?

He took hold of her still-warm hand. The skin was delicate, like parchment. He'd rarely seen her fingers this still. He was used to watching them stir something in the kitchen or knit or mend something as she sat in the living room. Busy hands. Serving hands. Loving hands. He touched the simple ring she'd worn for four decades. He'd always meant to buy her something grander.

Tears dropped from his eyes, splatting onto his wrist. He heard a groan. A moment later he realized the sound had been torn from his own chest.

Strike me down, Lord. Take me with her.

He'd known pain. He'd known loss. But this . . . Somehow he hadn't imagined it could feel like this.

O God, let me die too.

Chapter 26

When Ashley offered to keep AJ for the rest of the day, Jed was quick to accept. He took the car seat out of his rental car, confirmed that she had everything needed to get by until she and Ben brought the boy to Boise after dinner, and then he was off. It was hard not to speed along the country roads. Everything in him wanted to get back to the house, back to Holly, as fast as possible. It was as if, with every minute that passed, he could feel her pulling farther away from him. He needed to look her in the eyes and convince her she could trust him. And if she wasn't ready to trust him, tell her that he was willing to wait until she could.

Jed had arrived in Boise at the end of March with a heavy weight on his shoulders. He'd been worried about Laffriot and angry with his brother. Now, all of that paled beside his feelings for Holly. He wanted to be more than her friend—and he definitely wanted to be more than a tenant in the basement apartment. A week earlier they'd been on the right trajectory, as far as he was concerned. He'd thought she felt the same.

His phone rang as he began to merge with traffic onto the

freeway. Since it was attached to the Bluetooth in the car, he was able to answer it, not even trying to see the caller ID. "Hello?"

"Jed, it's me."

"Chris?" His gaze latched onto the off-ramp about a mile up ahead. "Where are you?" He flipped on his turn signal.

"We just pulled into a tiny town called Challis. Way up in the mountains. I've been on a job north of here."

"Did you get my messages?"

"No. I'm calling from a pay phone. My phone got run over by a truck. What's going on? I know you were trying to tell me something last night when I called, but I couldn't tell what. The connection was bad."

Jed slowed as he drove off the freeway. "Hang on a second. I'm driving and need to concentrate." He turned onto a major thoroughfare and moments later into a motel parking lot. "You still there?"

"I'm here."

"It's about Willow. And AJ."

There was a pause before Chris said, "So she told you, huh?"

"Yeah."

"I suppose you're gonna let me know how I've screwed up again."

Jed closed his eyes, sorry that was the first thing Chris expected from him. "No. I need to tell you that Willow's in the hospital."

"Hospital?" Chris shouted the word into the phone, his concern evident. "What happened?"

Quickly, Jed explained about the accident. He also told Chris that he had AJ and why.

"Hold on a second," Chris said.

Jed could tell his brother was talking to someone else, although he couldn't hear what was said.

"I just talked to the guy driving the truck. He says we oughta be back to Boise by four. Five at the latest. What hospital's she in?"

"St. Al's. Don't know the room number."

"And AJ's okay?"

"He's good. We're getting to know each other."

"Thanks for stepping in to help."

Jed's chest tightened. "We're family, bro. I love him because I love you." He couldn't remember the last time he'd told his brother he loved him. But he meant it. More than expected. "Call me after you've seen Willow."

"I will." There was a catch in Chris's voice, as if he was equally surprised by Jed's words. "Bye."

"Bye."

As soon as the call ended, Jed started the car. Talking about love, remembering the importance of family, had made him more ready than ever to see Holly.

The phone call with her dad wasn't nearly as bad as Holly had feared it would be. He'd listened without comment or interruption, and when she was done, he hadn't chastised her for any of her decisions, not even the bad ones. Instead, he'd shared words of encouragement. By the end of the call, while her situation hadn't changed, her emotions had calmed. And that was a victory in Holly's mind.

Going into the restaurant, poring over spreadsheets, staring at the accounting program on the computer, none of it would alter anything today. Monday she would have to start taking steps and making new, hopefully better, decisions. Difficult ones but better. But for the rest of today, she was going to do something that made her happy.

Baking made her happy. Baking had always made her happy. And so that was what she planned to do now.

When Holly had bought this house, the workspace in the kitchen had been the deciding factor. While the room wasn't huge, it was perfectly arranged. She'd known it would be perfect for the cottage industry she'd wanted to launch. Cakes, cookies, and cupcakes. Brownies and muffins. Fruit pies, pastries, biscotti. Even dog biscuits. She could have started her home baking business with any of them or all of them—if she hadn't been tied to the restaurant. To a restaurant she would probably have to close. With employees she would probably have to let go.

Today was a day to make cupcakes, she decided, because they would allow her to experiment with various frostings and decorations. Cupcakes would make her smile again, if only for a little while.

She grabbed an apron from the hook on the back of the utility room door. A birthday gift from her sisters, the apron made her happy too. Fluorescent colors seemed to explode across the fabric. Trixie claimed it could blind a person if stared at too long.

The next thing she needed was the perfect playlist. That was easy. "Alexa, play my 1960s dance music."

To the words and melody of "Feeling Good," she slow danced around the kitchen, getting the ingredients and utensils she would need from cupboards, drawers, pantry, and refrigerator. The Monkees serenaded her as she measured flour and sugar and vanilla, convincing her that she was a believer. By the time the Drifters made her imagine herself under the boardwalk, she had the first twelve cupcakes ready to slide onto the center rack of the oven. And almost as if preplanned, "How Sweet It Is" began to play as she spread frosting on the finished product.

"'How sweet it is to be loved by you,'" she joined in. But as she sang, her thoughts turned in a heartbeat from sugary confections to Jed, and her happiness evaporated. Tears welled in her eyes. Oh, why hadn't she been more careful with her heart? It would have been sweet to be loved by him, but—

"Holly!" Jed's voice came to her through an open kitchen window. "Holly, I need to talk to you." His knock sounded on the front door, making her jump.

Wiping her eyes with a dish towel, she went to answer it. He stood on the stoop, alone. "Where's AJ? What's wrong?"

"AJ's fine. He's with Ashley and Ben. And I talked to Chris. He's on his way back to Boise. He's anxious to get to Willow. You don't have to worry about those three. I have a feeling they're going to be all right." He paused, a small frown crinkling his forehead. "But what about us, Holly?"

"Us?"

He took a step toward her. "A couple weeks ago, I told you I wanted to see if we might become something more than friends. I think we were doing that. Becoming more than friends. I know it's true for me. Don't pull away now. Don't end the good that might happen just because you're afraid to trust me."

"I never said—"

"No, you haven't said it. But I'm right, aren't I? You don't trust me."

Her heart hammered in her chest. She felt in danger of tears again.

"Holly?"

"No, you aren't right. It isn't you I don't trust." She drew in a quick breath. "It's me. I don't trust myself." She turned, leaving the door open, and returned to the kitchen.

Friday, February 6, 1970

God wrapped Andrew in His love on the day of Helen's funeral. A cocoon of peace that surpassed all understanding. It shielded him from the effects of too many expressions of sympathy. It protected him as people shared their personal stories about Helen, reminding him of all that he'd lost. It gave him the ability to move through that sad and trying day, from the memorial in the church, to the graveside service, to the reception at the grange hall, and finally back home again.

Throughout the day there had been someone always by his side, but it hadn't been the person he most wanted to be there. He wouldn't have that privilege again until he stepped into paradise for himself.

In the five days since Helen's passing, Andrew had learned a new lesson: It was possible to grieve deeply and still trust in the goodness of God. It was possible to weep unstoppable tears and still know that God loved him. He hadn't understood that before. He understood it now.

"Grief takes its own time," someone had said to him at the cemetery. "Don't try to rush it. It takes as long as it takes."

He knew that platitude—and all of the others he'd heard throughout the day—had been kindly meant. He knew the words had been spoken out of love and concern. He even knew that he'd said similar words upon similar occasions in his lifetime. He wished now that he could take some of the words back. He wished he'd known a better way to comfort and encourage.

Perhaps there wasn't a better way.

When the last of his family had left the farm—returning to their own homes, carrying their own grief—Andrew bid Grant and Charlotte an early goodnight and went to his room. The room that had been theirs, his and Helen's, for a lifetime. The room that should still be theirs. Evidence of his wife was everywhere. The brocade curtains she'd made a few summers ago. A shawl draped over the back of a chair. Her spare glasses on the nightstand. A large, framed drawing of a calf that she'd talked him into buying at the fair, calling it an early anniversary gift to them both; it had hung above their bed for twenty-some years.

At her dressing table, he picked up the silver-handled hairbrush. The set—brush, comb, and mirror, along with a silver tray—had been a high school graduation present from her parents. Years ago the bristles had captured long dark hairs. Now, shorter gray hairs were woven through them. He held the brush close to his nose, wanting to catch a whiff of the floral-scented shampoo she'd favored. It wasn't there. Less than a week had passed, but the fragrance was gone. He felt robbed—and unbearably alone.

"Oh, my girl. My darling girl."

He sank onto the padded stool, picturing Helen as she'd sat on it through the years, looking at her reflection in the mirror. Big with pregnancy. Getting gussied up for one of their rare nights out. Bemoaning the changes in her appearance as she'd grown older.

"How will I manage without you?"

He closed his eyes, remembering her in his arms as they slow danced in the living room while Nat King Cole crooned "Unforgettable" on the radio. It had been one of Helen's favorite songs. Whenever she'd heard it, she'd wanted him to dance with her, despite his two left feet.

"Who'll dance with me now?"

Tears welled, blurring his vision, making the room swim before him. He wanted to rail against the disease that had robbed him of his other half. God had joined him to Helen. God had made the two into one, and now his other half had been torn away, taking part of his heart with it. How was it possible to go on living in this half state? Shouldn't he fall down dead too?

"Why art thou cast down, O my soul? and why art thou disquieted in me? Hope thou in God."

Despite the tears streaking his cheeks, Andrew felt his spirit grow calm.

"'Hope thou in God,'" he whispered.

That was how he would go on living. He would hope in God. One day at a time. One hour at a time. Perhaps one minute at a time. When the pain grew too much to imagine a tomorrow without Helen, then he would simply do the next thing that needed to be done today. God's grace came not a moment too soon or too late. It came in the moment it was needed. That was a truth he'd learned in the past, but he would have to recall it again and again.

"Why art thou cast down, O my soul? and why art thou disquieted in me? Hope thou in God."

He released a breath as he pushed himself up from the stool, able to rise, despite his broken heart, because he still hoped in God.

Chapter 27

Still on the stoop, Jed said a quick silent prayer for guidance, then followed Holly inside, stopping in the archway between living room and kitchen. Signs of baking were everywhere, and dance music played from a speaker. More of her favorite oldies, judging by the current tune.

"Alexa, off," Holly said, and silence filled the room.

Jed moved to the opposite side of the island. "Now let's talk about me. I've decided I'm not going back to Tacoma."

That made her eyes widen.

"First reason is because you're here, so here is where I want to be. We can't figure out if there's going to be an us if we're in two separate places. Relationships require proximity and time."

"What about Laffriot?"

"I haven't decided. I'll have to discuss things with my dad. Whatever we decide, I'll still be here." He leaned toward her, hands on the counter. "One thing I won't do is go back to working twelve- and fourteen-hour days, week in and week out. I've discovered there's more to life than work. There's more to life than building a business and chasing financial success. You've taught me that."

"*I* have?" She looked fragile and uncertain. Lost, maybe.

He longed to take her in his arms and comfort her. "Yes, you. You work hard, but you also make time for God and you make time to love others. You make time for Willow and all the other gals from the shelter. You care about people at church. You give of yourself, even when it isn't easy or convenient."

Tears welled in her eyes. "I may have a lot more time for all of that in the future."

"What do you mean?"

She shook her head even as she took a step back from the counter, as if needing space between them.

"Come on, Holly. Take a chance. I'm here. I'm not going anywhere. I'm sticking around. That's my commitment to you. That I'll give you the time you need to figure this out."

He could read the internal struggle in her eyes. For a while, he thought he would come out on the losing end.

Unexpectedly, she reached for a cupcake and held it out to him. "Try one?"

"Sure." He took it. Even if he hated cupcakes—which he didn't—he would have accepted it just to please her.

"Jed, I may lose the restaurant. I may lose the house. Maybe I'll end up bankrupt."

He stopped peeling the paper cup from the cake.

"I made some poor decisions a year ago, and they're coming back to haunt me now."

He set the cupcake aside. "Tell me."

There followed a lengthy silence, then finally, "See the cup half full, not half empty." Her eyes were downcast, her voice barely audible.

It seemed a strange thing to say, but he schooled his face not to reveal that thought, should she look up. When Holly moved to the table and sat down, he followed, taking the chair opposite her. She drew a slow, deep breath, and then began.

In a halting voice, Holly told him everything, told him every stupid choice she'd made. She told him how overwhelmed she was by the debt and the responsibility. She didn't try to paint herself in a favorable light. How could she? She hadn't been forced to take out loans or to open the restaurant. She'd chosen. Perhaps she'd been influenced by Nathan, but it had still been her choice. The results were her own fault. She talked with her gaze locked on her folded hands, not wanting to see the moment he realized what a fool she'd been—even though she'd told him that in advance. When she finished the lengthy tale, she fell silent, hardly breathing, and waited.

"You know what you haven't said." Jed waited a moment, forcing her to make eye contact. "You haven't said what you really want."

"I want to be out of debt. I don't want to let other people down. I don't want to fail."

"No. What do *you* want, Holly?" He leaned closer. "I'm a good businessman. I can help you get through this crisis. I know I can. Together we can figure out the tax situation and how to get the restaurant back on a firm financial foundation. And we can rescue your personal finances too."

"I wasn't asking you to—"

"But what do you want *after* all of that's done? We'll sort through all the financial problems. But then what? What does Holly want? What's your dream?"

His questions made tears well in her eyes, and no amount of blinking or swallowing could stop them from falling. She heard the genuine caring in his voice. He wanted her to have her dream, whatever it was. Almost from the day he'd moved into the basement apartment, he'd been chipping away at the wall around her heart. But this—his desire to see her pursue a dream—caused it to crumble.

"Jed, I can't ask you to—"

He reached across the table and took hold of her hand. "I know you aren't asking for my help. I'm offering. Because I'm in love with you. Maybe it's crazy. Maybe we haven't known each other all that long. But that's how I feel. That's how it is with love. You fall in love gradually, and then suddenly. Well, I'm at the 'suddenly' part, and all I want is a chance to show you what that means. All I want is the chance to prove I'm the guy who'll be at your side. Always."

His words made her heart somersault.

"I won't let you down, Holly. Not ever."

Oddly enough, she believed him.

How Sweet It Is

Saturday, May 30, 1970

Andrew walked across the small cemetery toward the resting places of his wife and their middle son. It was the twenty-fourth time he'd made this walk on a Memorial Day, but the first Memorial Day that he'd made the walk alone. The place was quiet this morning, although he saw American flags and flowers decorating a number of graves, so he knew others had been there before him.

Reaching his destination, he opened the folding stool he'd brought with him and sat upon it. A light breeze rustled the leaves in a nearby tree.

"I'm here again, Helen. Another Decoration Day."

He knew, of course, that his wife wasn't in the grave. Her earthly remains were there, but not Helen. She'd been set free four months ago. But still, it was comfortable to talk as if she was there, as if she could hear him from heaven.

"You won't believe it, but I bought myself some art supplies. I'm trying my hand at painting. I even signed up for a class this summer at the high school." He chuckled. "Not sure there's any hope for me. Not sure I've got that artistic soul you spoke of, but I'll give it a whirl. For you."

He remembered the day she'd told him to get a hobby. He'd thought her suggestion a little crazy. He wished now that he'd bought the art supplies while she'd been with him. He could imagine how she would have enjoyed his early efforts. She might even have teased him. He missed her teasing.

"Oh, my girl. I wish you were here. Some days I think I'm doing well. Others are harder. Sometimes I feel stuck. Like I'm in a waiting room. Like I can't go forward and I can't go back. Do I even have a purpose anymore? That's what I've wondered. Grant is ably running the farm, and Charlotte is such a help to him. Reminds me of us when we were young."

He looked up at the blue sky, puffs of clouds interspersed here and there, moving slowly from west to east. Memories drifted through his mind in the same way. After a while, he drew a deep breath and looked down, this time reaching for the Bible he'd brought with him.

"Listen to this, Helen." He opened it, thumbing the pages until he found the one he wanted. "'The steps of a good man are ordered by the LORD: and he delighteth in his way. Though he fall, he shall not be utterly cast down: for the LORD upholdeth him with his hand.' That's from Psalm 37. And I realized something when I read it this morning. God directs our steps, but He also directs our stops. There's a purpose in His delays. I've learned that walking is easier than waiting. Waiting takes patience, and I haven't always had an abundance of that. I grow frustrated with inaction."

The breeze picked up, and for a moment he would have sworn he heard her laughter.

Smiling sadly, he closed the Bible. "I told the Lord that I trusted Him to guide my steps and to help me when I'm stopped and feel stuck. Like now. I asked Him to help me serve Him where I am today, even in my old age, even with my infirmities, and not to be impatient about where I want to be tomorrow."

There'd been many times during the past few months when Andrew had wished God would take him home to heaven. Asked Him to. Begged Him to. Without Helen at his side, it seemed that some of the light had gone out of the world, despite all his many blessings. But this morning, as he'd read God's Word, he'd felt the Lord quickening his spirit. He'd seemed to hear God reminding him that as long as Andrew drew breath, the Lord had a purpose for him.

Life was sweet. A gift. One not to be squandered or wished away.

There had been pain in his life. There had been unhappiness. There would be more pain in his future. He would go on missing Helen. He would still feel that a part of him had been ripped away. But always, always, there would be a purpose. He would learn to rest in that knowledge, for as many breaths as the good Lord chose to give him. And when it was his time to step into his forever home, he prayed that what he would leave behind would be, first and foremost, a legacy of faith.

Chapter 28

Four months later . . .

Holly stood near the cake table in the church's fellowship hall, watching as wedding guests spilled into the room soon after the bride and groom, along with the maid of honor and best man, had taken their places for the reception line. It was a small affair, as weddings went, but an eagerly awaited and happy one. Holly had observed the exchange of vows between Chris and Willow and had seen them kiss moments before she'd hurried to the hall to be certain all was in place.

Trixie, her volunteer assistant, stepped through the kitchen doorway and stopped at Holly's side. "The cake is beautiful, sis. Almost as beautiful as the one you made for my wedding."

"Thanks." She smiled at the compliment, but her gaze had shifted to the best man. Jed looked incredibly handsome in his dark suit and sky-blue shirt.

"Down!" a familiar voice demanded.

She turned her head in time to see AJ wriggle free of his grandmother's grasp and dash through the guests to his parents. Chris picked up the boy and balanced him on his hip while he continued to shake hands and smile while accepting congratulations.

"Will they be happy, do you think?" Trixie asked.

Holly's throat grew tight with emotion, making it hard to answer. She blinked back tears as she nodded.

Yes, if they trust God in every circumstance. Yes, if they trust each other, even in the really hard times. Yes, if they put each other first when what they want to be is selfish. Yes, if they stick like glue.

Once more her gaze went to Jed. He'd stuck to her like glue, even in the moments she'd tried to push him away. She found him looking at her now, a smile on his lips. No more guests were in the line. He said something to his brother, then strode across the hall toward Holly.

"I'll check on something in the kitchen," Trixie said before leaving Holly's side.

Jed stopped a couple of feet away from her. "Well, they did it."

"They did it."

He motioned with his head but didn't look at Chris. "I'm proud of him. He's worked hard to prove himself."

"God's worked hard in him."

"And in me." He leaned forward, bringing his forehead close to hers, their gazes locked.

She saw the love in his eyes, and joy swirled inside of her.

His smile widening, he stepped to her side, turned, and put an arm around her shoulders. "The whole family is here. Every Andrew Henning descendant still living made it to the wedding. Bless them."

"And all of Willow's family is here too." Holly looked at the small group of women who'd been with Willow at Lighthouse in the spring and throughout the summer. They stood together, talking and laughing, rejoicing for and with their friend.

Jed nudged her with his elbow. "Mom and Dad seem to be getting along."

She saw his parents, standing together, talking. Whether or not they would reconcile was still in question, but at least Gloria Henning didn't seem completely opposed to the idea, as she once had.

"With Laffriot's offices relocated to Boise," Jed continued, "and both Chris and me here, I think Mom will move back to Idaho too."

"I don't want to burst your bubble, Jed Henning, but if your mom moves to Idaho, it will have more to do with a little guy named AJ than with you or your brother. You two would be a bonus, but that's all."

He laughed in agreement.

"What about your dad? Will he follow her?"

"The odds are good. He can relocate his business wherever he wants."

Over the summer, Holly had come to know and love Jed's parents, as well as his brother and extended family. She loved them almost as much as she loved Jed himself. And as he'd helped her work through her financial problems and eventually the sale of Sweet Caroline's to Zachary Holmes, she'd discovered countless more reasons for the love she felt for him. Jed was steadfast and devoted. He wasn't afraid to say when he was wrong or reluctant to ask for forgiveness. When he saw a need for change, he made the change happen, whether in business or in himself. His quirky sense of humor surprised her, and his tenderness made her putty in his hands. Trusting him now came as easily to her as dreaming up confections for her new bakery, Sweet Somethings Cake Studio.

Jed leaned his head close to hers again. "Looking at all this reminds me of something Grandpa Andrew marked in his Bible.

'The steps of a man are established by the Lord, and He delights in his way. When he falls, he will not be hurled headlong, because the Lord is the One who holds his hand.' If Chris hadn't taken off and come to Boise, if I hadn't followed him here, none of this would have happened. At least not this way." His arm drew her closer to his side. "I only wanted to find my brother and knock some sense into him, but God knew the real reason I needed to be here. He established my steps and brought me straight to you."

"Don't do that. You'll make me cry." But her protest was too late to stop the tears.

"God knew that, too, my love," he said softly, a hint of laughter in his voice.

"How sweet it is to be loved by you." The music and lyrics of the old song played in her heart, happiness flowing through her, and she leaned into Jed, able to trust in tomorrow because she knew the One who had established their steps.

A Note from the Author

Dear Friend,

It was a bittersweet moment when I wrote the last line of *How Sweet It Is* because that was also the last line in the Legacy of Faith series. Saying farewell to Andrew Henning, his wife, his children, and his descendants was even more difficult than I'd imagined it would be. I've come to love them all so much, and their stories will linger with me for a long time to come.

The Henning farm was inspired by the forty acres owned by my maternal grandparents and later my aunt and uncle. Andrew's Bible was inspired by the one given to my grandmother by my grandfather during WWII. And the idea for the legacy of faith series was inspired by all of the notes, dates, and underlining I've done in my personal Bible (the one I've used for nearly twenty-five years). I hope and pray that those notes, those lessons learned, will mean something to my own descendants after I'm gone, the same way Andrew's notes meant something to Jessica (*Who I Am with You*), Ben (*Cross My Heart*), and Jed (*How Sweet It Is*).

Following a single character and his family through the

Great Depression, World War II, and into the tumultuous sixties over the course of three books was a new experience for me as a writer. An experience that I dearly loved. I hope you felt the same way about it.

By the time you read this note in the back of *How Sweet It Is,* I will have been hard at work for months on another book or even two. If you want to stay up-to-date on what's new and what's coming, I hope you'll sign up for my e-newsletter on my website (robinleehatcher.com). From my website, you can also find me on social media, where I love to interact with readers.

Until next time,
many blessings to you,
Robin Lee Hatcher

Acknowledgments

First and foremost, my thanks goes to my Savior who has walked me through so many of life's challenges, teaching me along the way, so that I have something worthwhile to write about.

Thanks to the amazing fiction team at HarperCollins Christian Publishing. You are the best.

Thanks to my editors, Jocelyn Bailey and Leslie Peterson. I would be completely lost without you. It's such a privilege to work with you.

Thanks to my sisters in Christ and of the heart who gather together each summer to plot, pray, and play. Your love and prayers have carried me again and again over the years. You're terrific brainstormers, but even more, your legacies of faith have guided and encouraged me.

Finally, thanks to my readers. I read every email you send, every post you leave on social media. Your kind encouragements make a difference every single day. Thank you for being a part of my life through my fiction.

Discussion Questions

1. Which character in *How Sweet It Is* did you most relate to and why?
2. Jed blamed his brother (and in some part, his father) for the troubles Laffriot was facing. Was he able to see his own part in those troubles? Are you able to see all sides of a difficult situation when it comes your way?
3. Holly was struggling financially because of a business she didn't want to own. She was also struggling emotionally because trust had been broken. Which of these struggles was actually the most difficult for her to overcome? Are internal struggles harder for you or are external ones?
4. Despite her emotional struggles, Holly continued to give of herself to others. Are you involved with the community around you, whether through your church or through other charitable organizations? Are you able to give of your time even when you can't give financially?

5. Jed let work become his whole life while other matters of importance slipped away (his Christian walk, his relationships with family and friends). Have you ever done something similar? How did you bring your life back into balance?
6. As Andrew grew older, he began to question his purpose in life. Have you experienced something similar? How were you able to find your purpose again? Or how can you help someone else if they are struggling with it?
7. Andrew experiences the loss of his lifelong spouse in this book. What did you think of the way he dealt with her death, both as her death approached and afterward? Did you learn anything from his experience?
8. Andrew's Bible became a source of comfort and instruction for Jed (and Jed's cousins in the previous books). Do you write in your Bible? What will your descendants find therein to encourage them, even after you're gone?

DISCOVER MORE FROM ROBIN LEE HATCHER!

AVAILABLE IN PRINT,
E-BOOK, AND AUDIO

About the Author

Robin Lee Hatcher is the author of over eighty novels and novellas with over five million copies of her books in print. She is known for her heartwarming and emotionally charged stories of faith, courage, and love. Her numerous accolades include the RITA Award, the Carol Award, the Christy Award, the HOLT Medallion, the National Reader's Choice Award, and the Faith, Hope & Love Reader's Choice Award. Robin is also the recipient of prestigious Lifetime Achievement Awards from both American Christian Fiction Writers and Romance Writers of America. When not writing, she enjoys being with her family, spending time in the beautiful Idaho outdoors, Bible art journaling, reading books that make her cry, watching romantic movies, and decorative planning. Robin makes her home on the outskirts of Boise, sharing it with a demanding papillon dog and a persnickety tuxedo cat.